Praise for The Talented Fairy Tales

"The twists and turns come fast and furious in this rapid paced novel... Filled with intrigue and skilled fighting, this fantasy is sure to have hearts pumping and blood racing. The next in this series can't come soon enough!" – *InD'tale Magazine review of Beauty and the Blade*

"Peaky Blinders meets Bridgerton in this lush reimagining of *Beauty and the Beast* with an endearing cast of characters, subtle magic, and a deliciously agonizing slow burn romance. This book was absolutely everything I wanted it to be and more." – *Megan Van Dyke, author of Second Star to the Left*

"Beauty and the Blade by S.C. Grayson entertained me for hours with the perfect combination of fairy-tale and adventure stories." – *Readers' Favorite*

"A fantastic tale with a little magic, fighting, deception, true love, and adventure... this book is incredibly hard to put down with so many laughable lines, and the interactions between Scarlett and Benedict are priceless." – *InD'tale Magazine review of Little Red Shadow*

Little Red Shadow

S.C. GRAYSON

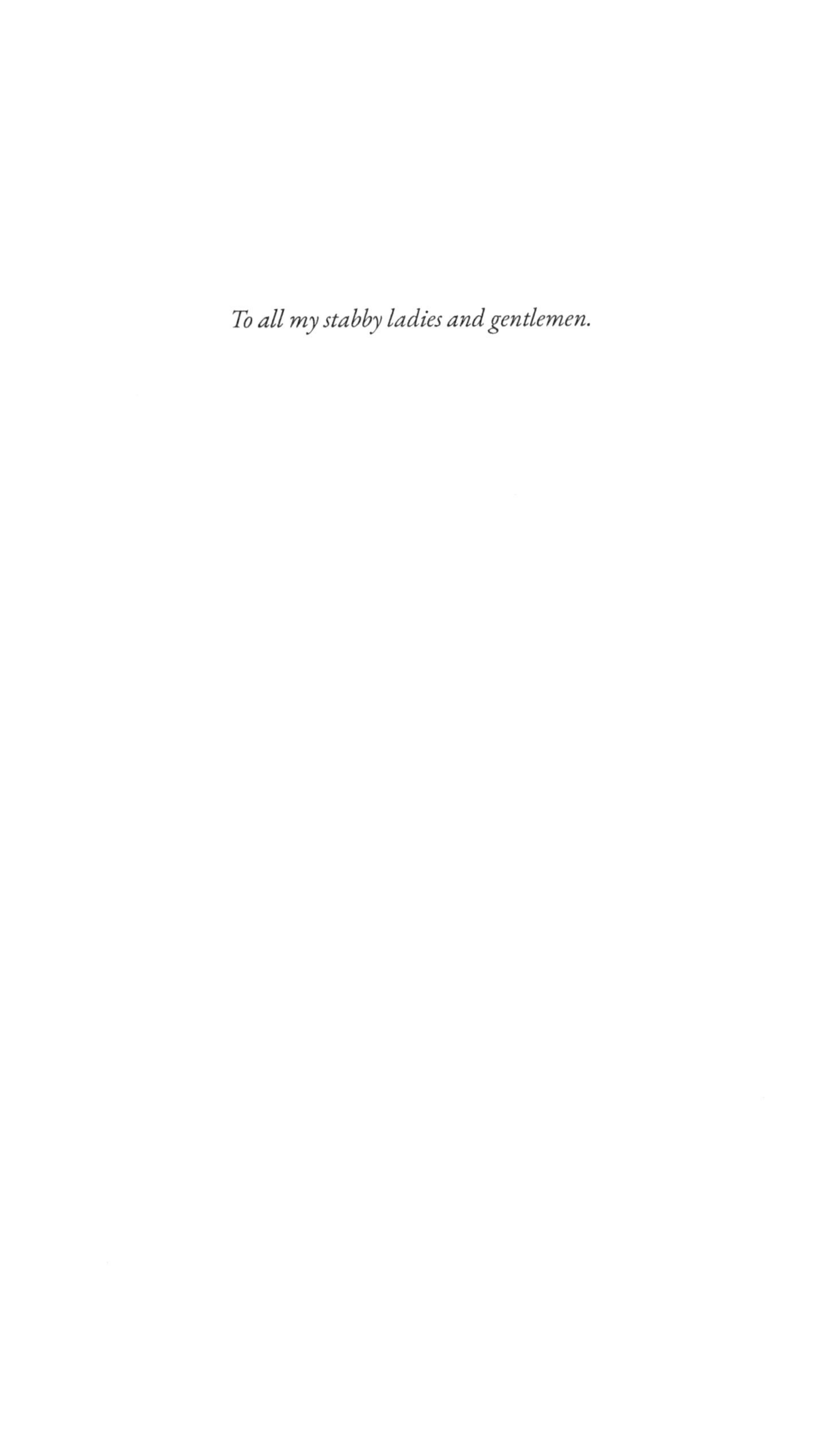

To all my stabby ladies and gentlemen.

Chapter One

The ball would have been lovely if Scarlett wasn't expecting to be killed at any moment. Or rather, she anticipated somebody attempting to kill her, but she had no intention of letting them succeed.

Scarlett wove through the crowds of society's finest, gowns and jewels glimmering gaudily under crystal chandeliers that had been hung in the garden of all places. She shoved down the instinct bubbling up in her chest, telling her to cling to the edges of the party where she could listen to conversations unnoticed. Instead, Scarlett held her chin high, causing her feathered headdress to flounce above the socialites' heads despite her small stature. The blue silk of her voluminous skirts cut a wide swath through the crowds.

Heads turned as she walked, gossip tittering behind gloved hands. Scarlett fought to keep her shoulders square, reminding herself they weren't really looking at her. When she passed by, all they saw was the prize of the social season, with a dowry to match.

A bolt of energy shot up Scarlett's spine as she caught the assassin's attention, the back of her neck prickling as his gaze fell on her. A nervous shift and a hand sliding into a coat as if to grasp a weapon, and she knew she had found her mark. It took all of Scarlett's self-discipline to maintain her composure as she let her eyes drift up to the lower half of the man's face, not quite reaching his eyes. She offered what she hoped was a coy smile befitting a lady of her standing. If she hadn't known he was the would-be killer before, the tight twist of his mouth that passed for a smirk would have given him away.

Scarlett didn't linger, instead continuing to pick her way through the crowd. She loosened the reins on her instincts, letting them guide her to the edges of the revelry, where the light from the chandeliers was thin and the shadows could partially obscure her. A prickle on the back of her neck told her the man still followed, but at least now other partygoers were less likely to see her disappear with a man who turned up dead later. Scarlett ignored the sharp ache stabbing the base of her skull at that thought, instead slipping into the privacy of the hedge maze.

The dense shrubbery muted the sounds of the revelry, lending a distant feeling that helped her focus on the task at hand. Having space for something as frivolous as a hedge maze in the tight quarters of London struck Scarlett as ostentatious, even if it was lovely, but she was glad for the cover. She rounded a few corners, carefully listening for the sounds of couples stealing an illicit moment, breathing a sigh of relief when she heard none. Instead, boots tromped at the entrance to the maze, and she frowned at the would-be assassin's lack of stealth. Still, it would make her job easy.

Darkness curled around Scarlett as she stepped back into the shrubbery, urged on by her Talent, melding her midnight blue dress with her surroundings. Here in the shadows, she felt the most at ease she had all night, even as she slipped a knife from her lacy sleeve.

The tromping footsteps came closer, and her mark rounded the corner. He passed by her hiding spot, not looking in her direction, a small pistol raised in his hand. Scarlett coiled in on herself, ready to pounce, when the moonlight shimmered on the ornate barrel of the gun, illumi-nating the man's shaking hand.

Scarlett hesitated, taking a small step instead of leaping forward, knife first, as she had intended. That movement was enough to alert the man to her presence, and he spun to face her, gun inches from her face. They stood frozen like that for the barest of moments, although time seemed to stretch, looking into his wide dark eyes. Then Scarlett grabbed his wrist and twisted, digging her fingernails into the soft flesh between tendons. The pistol dropped from his grasp as he let out a breathy curse, and Scarlett snatched it from the air with her other hand before it could hit the ground.

The man's hands flew up in surrender as Scarlett leveled both weapons at him and got her first good look at his face. His full lips were parted in shock, but his eyes held something softer—something that looked strangely like relief, which was odd considering Scarlett could end his life at any moment. His nose lacked any of the tale-tale crookedness of repeated breaking, and the way he held his shoulders in his navy velvet waistcoat spoke of a comfort with fine clothing. This was no street brawler or undercover gang member before her. As she contemplated him, his dark brows drew together as he regarded her in return.

"You're not Georgette Ward." His voice was surprisingly steady.

Scarlett didn't attempt to deny it.

"You're not an assassin," she fired back, chancing a glance at the pistol in her hand. The flowery engravings along the barrel and the finely polished surface marked it as a dueling pistol, and not something to be hastily tucked into waistbands of lower city thugs.

"What gave me away?" he sighed, cocking his head as if he were be-moaning losing at a hand of cards and not attempted murder. If Scarlett had any doubts about her snap decision against slitting his throat, they were fading fast.

"Why do you want to kill Georgette Ward?" Scarlett demanded instead of answering his question.

"I have nothing against her, even if she is a little angelic for my taste," the man hedged, taking a shuffling step back. Scarlett matched his movement, not willing to let him forget about the gun pointed at his face.

"If you have no quarrel with her, then why follow me in here, thinking I'm Miss Ward, with a gun drawn?" Scarlett's tone was icy, even as she was tempted to believe the man before her. The anger that boiled under her skin at the thought of a threat to Georgette's life cooled in the face of his manner. He didn't strike her as a killer, and Scarlett was far too familiar with the lifeless look of an assassin's gaze.

"I personally wish her no ill, but somebody else wants her dead, and they've made it my business," he said.

"The Wolves." It wasn't a question. The clawed pawprint on the bottom of the threatening letter Georgette had received made that part clear enough. It was why a ruthless street gang was after a socialite who had never even set foot in their territory that Scarlett couldn't puzzle out. The scribbled mess slipped through Georgette's open window as she slept hadn't even demanded money or favors.

"I'm not a Wolf," the man insisted, "I've just had some unpleasant run-ins with them. I'll even let you inspect my body to see I carry no gang tattoo, if you ask nicely."

The roguish wink he offered would have been enough to make Scarlett roll her eyes if his exaggerated manner hadn't made it clear he didn't ever take himself too seriously, even when flirting with a would-be murderer.

Clearly not somebody well acquainted with the harsh realities of gang life.

"If you're not a Wolf, then who are you?"

"I could ask the same thing, considering you're clearly not Miss Ward. But since I am polite, I'll have you know that I am Lord Benedict Pearce. Pleasure to make your acquaintance." He offered one of his hands to shake, but Scarlett's grip was full of weapons. Still, she let the gun and the knife drop to her sides. She was far less comfortable threatening the younger son of a duke than she was another piece of lower city scum. Now that she thought of it, alone with the son of a duke holding multiple weapons was not a position she wanted to be caught in.

"And you are?" he pressed.

"A friend of Georgette's," was all Scarlett offered. "And if you or any of your Wolf friends come after her again, I won't hesitate to start relieving you of body parts."

With that, Scarlett stepped back into the darkened passage in which she had hidden before. A flick of the wrist was all it took for shadows to leap into action, thickening until she was all but invisible.

Looking startled, Lord Pearce started after her, only to find the narrow row of hedges deserted except for darkness. He jogged down the pathway he thought she had escaped through, and Scarlett pressed against the leafy wall to let him pass, before doubling back to escape the maze.

As Lord Pearce passed, Scarlett thought she heard him mutter something under his breath sounding vaguely like "not friends with Wolves." Scarlett kept her shadows gathered around her as she ducked back into the garden, just enough to make her appear like a dark flicker to anybody that might look in her direction. She shoved her knife and the stolen pistol into her bodice as she picked across the lawn. Instead of heading back to the party in the main part of the garden, she darted to the back fence before launching herself upward to climb over it—a task that would have been much more difficult if she hadn't insisted on wearing her pants under the skirts. Still, she heard a rip as a loose piece of lace caught on a wrought iron pole, and she made a mental note to apologize to Georgette for damaging her dress.

It was only a handful of moments before Scarlett pushed through the doorway to a cellar a few blocks away and let out a sigh of relief as she threw the bolt behind her. As soon as she knew she was alone, she tore the elaborate wig off her head, dropping the mass of chestnut curls unceremoniously on a crate beside her. Shaking out her own mousey brown hair, ends just tickling her ears, restored a sense of normalcy to an evening full of surprises. Scarlett was no longer comfortable with the weight of headdresses and sculpted hairstyles, making the weight of her disguise a constant reminder of a life she had left behind.

She moved on to unlacing the dress, pushing the stiff fabric down her hips and pulling on the loose gray shirt she had stashed here earlier. Fabric that had once been white and crisp now draped against her skin, soft with years of daily wear. She glanced at the dueling pistol laying atop the heap of skirts, gleaming gently in the line of moonlight shining in through a gap in the doorframe. Scarlett considered for a moment before snatching it up and shoving it in her belt. It could fetch enough money to pay her rent at Granny's for a year.

Transformation complete, she shoved the discarded disguise into an empty barrel, making note of where it was so she could tell one of the Wards' manservants where to fetch it later. The weight of makeup still itched at her eyes and cheeks, and Scarlett scrubbed at it idly with her sleeve as she exited back onto the street, more in her element than she had been in hours.

The sound of a carriage clattering across the cobblestones approached. Scarlett darted through the dark patches between the flickering street-lamps so they wouldn't see her pass, making her way down the street as little more than a wraith.

~

"You know we have a front door," Georgette pointed out as Scarlett tumbled through the bedroom window, as she did every week when Scarlett made a late-night visit. It passed as a greeting between the two of them now, and Scarlett simply shrugged, as she always did.

"I'm assuming if you're here and whole, that the ball went as planned?" Georgette stood from her dressing table and pulled her silk robe more tightly around her, inspecting Scarlett with a worried gaze. Scarlett held out her arms, displaying her lack of injuries, and Georgette's round face relaxed.

"My mother and father still aren't home. I assume they're still at the ball trying to act as normal as possible to not give you away, although they will have to come up with some excuse as to why they came with a daughter and are leaving without one," Georgette fussed, pulling Scarlett farther into the warm bedroom, away from the chill drifting in from the still-open window.

"They'll just say you felt faint and went home to lie down," Scarlett assured Georgette. "It won't be hard to believe with how delicate you look and how tight you wear your corsets."

Georgette huffed in feigned exasperation. "I'm not as much of a princess and you and my parents seem to think I am, you know."

Georgette's appearance undercut her statement, with chestnut curls framing a face so pale and so fine-featured, it would be perfectly suited to a porcelain doll if not for her tendency to grin so wide you could count her teeth, or to scrunch up her nose when she was amused. The only reason Scarlett was able to successfully impersonate her was their similar heights and the fact Georgette hadn't been out in society for long enough for everybody to recognize her easily. She had only attended a few parties before the mysterious death threat confined her to her house. Still, it had taken a lot of powder to cover Scarlett's freckles enough for the disguise to be passable.

At the reminder, Scarlett rubbed at her itchy face with a sleeve, probably only making her face dirtier.

"Come here and I'll get that makeup off, now that you've already smeared it all over yourself. You can tell me what happened while I work, and I'll feel better if my hands are busy."

Scarlett did as she asked and sat down on the stool at the dressing table while Georgette dampened a cloth in the bowl on her washstand.

"Was there really an assassin?" Georgette murmured in a tremulous voice as she dabbed at the kohl around Scarlett's eyes.

"I wouldn't call it an assassin, but they did send somebody with orders to frighten you." Scarlett couldn't quite say he had been ordered to kill her, even though the threat to Georgette's life had been clear in the letter. Her life was just so soft and gentle, Scarlett couldn't bring herself to mar that any more than her presence already did.

"So, the Wolves did manage to infiltrate the ball." Georgette's voice was hardly more than a whisper.

"Not quite. They seem to have a man on the inside who they're having do their dirty work. Probably blackmailing him or having him rough you up as repayment for some corrupt business deal," Scarlett reflected, thinking about how adamant Lord Pearce had been the Wolves were no friends of his. Still, he had pointed a gun at her.

"If he's not a Wolf, maybe he will tell you why they're after me. And if he's not actually a gangster, he could just be a good man caught in a bad situation," Georgette insisted.

Scarlett smiled at her optimism, even as she bit her tongue to keep herself from pointing out that "good people" were the reason she was a lower city gang member herself.

"I'm not sure how much they've told him, but I'll see what I can do."

Georgette beamed as if the whole issue had been resolved and those who wanted her dead weren't still at large. The sight of it made Scarlett's chest warm even as it ached. It was that optimism that kept her coming back to visit her oldest friend every week, even when she had sworn off high society. Georgette was the one bright spot keeping her from slinking into the shadows of the slums and embracing the future as a lower-city gangster she knew to be inevitable. Scarlett was aware it couldn't last though, as the amount of blood on her hands grew. Sometimes she thought she should climb out Georgette's window and never come back, but she wouldn't do it now, with her life in peril. If some of the scars on her conscience could come from protecting Georgette, then she would consider them more well-earned than the rest.

"Do you want me to ring for some tea while we wait for my parents to return?" Georgette offered as she wiped the last of the red paint from Scarlett's lips.

"I need to get home," Scarlett declined as she examined herself in the mirror to find the unassuming lower city girl returned. "I'll leave a note for your father about how it went and let him know I'm still working on uncovering the Wolves' motives."

"Of course." Georgette didn't seem the least bit surprised by Scarlett's refusal of tea. "With how hard you work, I'm sure you have to get up early. At least take this for your breakfast." She held out a packet of brown paper to Scarlett. "I had Cook make them up since I know they're your favorite."

Scarlett took the package even as she insisted, "You shouldn't have."

"I know, but I do anyway." Georgette smiled. This was one of their rituals too.

With that, Scarlett shoved the package in her shirt for safe keeping, finding it still warm against her skin and catching a whiff of the buttery scent of kippers. Her mouth watered, but she had places to be, so she would eat as she went.

With a final wave, Scarlett clambered back out the window, shimmying down a drainpipe before dropping the last few feet to the lawn. The guard on the ground jumped and whipped around but lowered his cudgel upon seeing Scarlett. Even if they were there to keep out thieves and would-be murderers, Scarlett creeping through the Wards' garden was a common sight. They knew she was a tame gangster.

Scarlett gave a mock salute to the familiar guard before ducking out through a gap in the hedges and turning her steps towards the lower city. After all, the night was young and the Talented of the lower city never slept.

~

The Roost was only a fifteen-minute walk from the Wards' mansion, but it might as well have been a world away. As Scarlett wolfed down her kippers, the neat brick homes with manicured hedges became more and more cramped, eventually giving way to wooden slat houses that looked as if they stayed upright only by virtue of leaning on each other. The horse-drawn carriages of socialites coming home from evening festivities were replaced by carts pulled by worn-down donkeys and thugs throwing dice on street corners. Even the air was different here, hazy with the smoke from the nearby factory district, cut with a sharp breeze from the docks.

Scarlett slipped into the Roost to be instantly accosted with the racket of gambling and fighting, while the light afforded by the oil lamps hanging from the ceiling was only slightly more than that in the street. Scarlett didn't mind the dark though, slipping into it like a well-worn coat that made her practically invisible, barely worth a second glance.

Of course, some people still spotted her.

"You're late," barked Jason from behind the bar, folding his arms in a way that made his biceps bulge, distorting the vulture inked on his upper arm—not that it was a very well-done tattoo to begin with.

"I had some family business I had to deal with," Scarlett defended, sliding up to the counter but not taking a seat on the empty bar stool.

"Ain't no family here besides the Raptors." He snorted, retrieving a sheaf of papers from underneath the bar and sliding it across to her. "Amos didn't want to wait for you. Left this here and told you that you better get it done by morning, no matter how much 'family business' you have."

Scarlett paid him no mind, flipping through the envelopes, seeing mostly names she didn't recognize, although a few names that rang a bell from the middle and even upper city.

"Just more messages tonight? Amos hasn't asked me to lift any jewels in a while," Scarlett mused.

"Lot of people haven't been paying up at the gambling tables recently." Jason commented with a shrug, grabbing a dusty glass to polish with an even dirtier rag. "These little messages normally do the trick. Nothing like waking up with a letter on the pillow next to them to scare a mark into coughing up."

Scarlett shoved the envelopes into her shirt, not one to turn down a reprieve from theft. After all, delivering threats to those who owed money without being seen was far less likely to turn violent than a burglary. Still, the letters sealed with the curled talon of the Raptors looked uncomfortably like the threat found at Georgette's window a few days earlier. Stealing and passing messages for the Raptors was what kept her safe in the lower city, and her Talent with the shadows made her perfect for the job.

"Mind if I take the back way?" Scarlett inclined her head towards the stairs leading up to the rooms where most of the Raptors lived. There was a window overlooking a roof there, useful for starting her night creeping above the city unseen.

"Course." Jason shrugged. "Although I don't know why you insist on renting at Granny's when you could just stay here. You've got the tattoo already."

Scarlett shrugged off his comment, even as it made her skin crawl, and started weaving her way through rowdy drinkers to the back steps. Moving into the Roost was another step in her inevitable descent into her lower city life, and Jason was right. Maybe once she could be sure Georgette was safe, she would stop digging in her heels.

~

The sun peeked over the pointed towers of the palace at the top of the hill by the time Scarlett slunk back to Granny's. She wasn't surprised to see Granny sweeping the floors when she slipped through the doorway, although the rambunctious urchins who tussled in the safehouse during the day were absent. She didn't know if Granny stayed up exceptionally late or woke up early, but Scarlett never seemed to catch her sleeping.

"Rent's due at the end of the week," the wizened woman barked, beady eyes flicking up briefly as Scarlett entered, before returning to her work. Her skin looked as rough as the wooden slats she swept, frown permanently etched on her face like a knot in a plank. Scarlett wasn't deterred by her sharp manner, finding it comforting in its familiarity.

"I'll have it to you this afternoon," Scarlett promised as she passed, heading for the steps in the back.

Granny just offered a grunt in response as Scarlett began trudging up the stairs, legs heavy from a long night of climbing up trellises and crouching on rooftops. As she unlocked her door, she hissed at the pulse in her fingertips where her nails had broken off as she clawed up a windowsill.

As she pushed into her room, barely big enough for a narrow bed and her trunk, Scarlett was tempted to collapse on her mattress face first and pass out just like that. Only habit carried her through her ritual.

She kicked open the chest at the foot of her bed, digging under her change of clothes to find the leather pouch hidden beneath. She fished it out, noting how light it had become in the past years, before dumping the contents on the threadbare mattress.

It didn't even take a minute to count the coins within. Enough for one last month at Granny's. A room in the Roost and a life running jobs for the Raptors now breathed down her neck. The money once intended for her dowry had allowed Scarlett to delay the inevitable, give her a choice for a time—but it was just an illusion. The Osprey tattooed on her shoulder blade gave her away as a member of the lower city gangs anyways.

Still, she was eternally grateful to Granny for letting her rent this room for as long as she had. It was a morning much like this when she had stumbled across Granny's threshold after wandering the streets for a night. Seeing the mud under her fingernails and the tear tracks on her face, a well-meaning urchin had pointed Scarlett towards Granny's, saying it was the safest place for runaway factory workers. She hadn't corrected him but staggered gratefully towards the promise of warmth and a place to sit down.

Granny had been about to snap at her to make herself useful the second she opened the door but stopped when she saw her. Scarlett's fine dress and pale skin had given her away as different from the normal urchins stopping in to scrub pots for a loaf of bread. Granny had taken pity on her, helping her blend with the other youth on the streets of London, even offering a few pointers on how to pick pockets. Allowing her to mix with the others until she found a gang that would make use of her Talent in exchange for protection from the Inquiries and even worse fates. Everybody in the lower city called her Granny almost ironically in reference to her harsh manners, unsure if she even had a name beyond that, but Scarlett knew the name fit.

Gathering up the handful of coins, Scarlett shoved them back into the pouch. Thoughtfully, she pulled the dueling pistol she still carried from her waistband, turning it over to examine it. She could still sell it. Maybe make enough to stay here for another year, although it wouldn't change much in the long run. Something about the thought of parting with it set her teeth on edge as well. Probably because it was the one clue she held to tracking down Georgette's would-be assassin.

Too tired to consider further, Scarlett hid the gun and the pouch back in the bottom of her trunk, catching a brief glint of the crimson fabric at the bottom——the one hidden treasure she allowed herself. Before she could think on that too long, she shed her clothes and finally collapsed onto the bed, letting sweet darkness overtake her mind.

<h1 style="text-align:center">Chapter Two</h1>

Scarlett dropped a handful of coins, the last of her dowry, on the counter as she left that afternoon. Granny snatched them up to count and pocket before the sharp-eyed children loitering about could filch any away. There were already several accomplished pickpockets among them, always happy to practice their skills. Scarlett kept the pistol well-hidden under her coat, where it was shoved into the back of her trousers.

Scarlett considered her path after pushing out the door into thready afternoon light, the sun obscured by smoke belching from the chimneys of nearby textile factories. She turned towards one of the shops where the Raptors pawned their stolen goods, and hesitated. Maybe Georgette was right about Lord Pearce being the key to uncovering the reason for the Wolves' threats. She didn't share the hope of him joining the cause from the goodness of his heart just because of his noble upbringing though. Perhaps the pistol could be used for leverage. There was always the possibility that he was wealthy enough to not be bothered by the loss of such a valuable weapon, but something this lovely might hold sentimental value.

Scarlett turned on her heel and trotted uphill towards the palace, around which the larger homes clustered. If the Pearces had not changed their London residence in the past few years, Scarlett remembered their street from her time living in the upper city.

Keeping her head down as she went, looking like a messenger boy or servant running an errand, she made her way into the wealthier neighborhoods with her hair tucked tightly into a cap. It wasn't the same invisibility afforded to her by her shadows at night, but the camouflage of anonymity was equally as familiar.

Reaching the ostentatious white stone house belonging to the Pearces, Scarlett paused to assess her strategy, bending down under the pretense of adjusting her bootlace. Before she could determine which window would best allow her to enter unseen, the clattering of carriage wheels forced her to leap out of the way.

A sleek black coach pulled up in front of the Pearce's house, and a man emerged through the house's front door. Scarlett quickly ducked her head, but not before catching sight of dimples and sparkling dark eyes. Lord Benedict Pearce.

Peeking up through lowered lashes, Scarlett saw him slide into the carriage before hearing a sharp wrap on the roof. The coach began trundling down the street. Scarlett only glanced at the house for a moment before trotting after. Thankfully the traffic at this time of afternoon was thick, forcing the large vehicle to maneuver slowly, while Scarlett could slip between pedestrians and carts. To her surprise, Lord Pearce's driver turned the horses towards the direction from which Scarlett had come. Around the point where the houses changed from stone to wood and there were no more window boxes to be seen, the carriage pulled to a stop.

Scarlett paused in the shadow of an open shop door, cap pulled low over her eyes, as Lord Pearce stepped down. He just offered his driver a jaunty wave before setting off on foot, continuing the way the carriage had been heading.

Trailing him down the street, casually weaving between the dense crush of people to remain unnoticed, Scarlett internally winced at Lord Pearce's manner. Even as he entered dodgier areas of the city, where hollow eyed urchins watched the silk trim on his top hat and his gold watchchain with open interest, he strolled as if he hadn't a care in the world. He turned towards Wolf territory, and Scarlett hesitated for only a moment. Trailing a mark in another gang's territory was dangerous, but it would only be a problem if Scarlett was seen.

Lord Pearce led her all the way to a large wooden building, the peeling paint on the door in the rough shape of a canine. As he opened the door to slip inside, the sound of dice being thrown and rowdy drinkers arguing, even at this time of day, drifted onto the street. Scarlett had never been here, but this must be the Wolves' Cave——just as the Roost was the center of the Raptor's operations.

As much as Lord Pearce had insisted he wasn't on good terms with the Wolves, all evidence now seemed to be to the contrary. If he was really working with them, the chances he knew of their motives—or their next move—were good.

Scarlett tugged on her sleeves, weighing her options, before pushing into the shop next door to the Cave. She pushed through the general store quickly, trailing the barest amount of shadows with her to avoid the shopkeeper's questioning, pleased she was distracted counting coins behind the counter. Finding the back door she sought, Scarlett pushed out into the alley and started climbing the wall of the Cave. If Lord Pearce was going to discuss a sensitive job with any of the Wolves lieutenants, they wouldn't chance doing it in the main gambling hall where they might be overheard. Scarlett would bet her dowry that Lord Pearce would be heading to one of the private offices on the top floors.

As her fingertips reached the third-floor windowsills, Scarlett paused to listen for sounds from within. Hearing none, she shimmied along the wall to the next windowsill, repeating the process. At the third windowsill, she paused as voices drifted to her ears.

"I'm surprised the headlines this morning weren't all about a murder at the Marquis's ball last night. Does that mean our little lordling didn't have the guts to do as he's told? Does he need a reminder of what's at stake?" The grating voice dipped low, rumbling in a way that set Scarlett's teeth on edge.

"No, I did as you asked, Gil." Lord Pearce's voice drifted through the window, conversational as it had been when Scarlett pointed a gun at his face in the garden. He was either uncommonly stupid or exceptionally brave. Scarlett hoped for his sake that it was the latter, because the longer she listened, the more the truth of his words regarding not being on friendly terms with the Wolves became apparent.

"Then she's dead?"

"Well, not technically, no."

"And what would you mean by 'not technically dead'?" The grating voice took on a growling tone.

"I guess I would mean that she's alive and well, but not for lack of trying. You see, there was some interference—"

A growl cut him off for a moment, and Benedict's words quickened.

"It would seem you warned Miss Ward of her eminent demise. I would have thought announcing your intentions would be bad form as an assassin."

For all his bluster, a slight tremor permeated Lord Pearce's words. He was not as unperturbed as his flippant façade would imply. Scarlett's arms began to tremble as she hung onto the windowsill to listen, but she stayed frozen, straining to hear every word.

"You see, threats don't make somebody do what you want unless you...threaten them."

There was some scuffling followed by a grunt and the distinctive metallic sound of a blade being drawn.

"Would you like me to demonstrate how exactly we go about threatening somebody?" The grating voice was low enough that Scarlett could barely hear it.

"I think that won't be nec—" Lord Pearce cut out with a strangled gurgle.

Scarlett moved before she could think, hauling herself through the window and rolling across the floor. Before the men in the room could register her entrance, she swept one leg out, knocking the gangster's base from under him and bearing him down to the floor.

As she pinned him to the ground, there was a moment of silence where both men gawked at Scarlett, and she stared in horror at what she had done. Up in smoke were her plans for secrecy—for uncovering the gang's secrets without being seen. Instead, she had quite literally thrown herself into a den of Wolves.

As the tension of surprise faded from the room, the thug beneath her opened his mouth. In a flash, Scarlett unsheathed her knife and pressed the tip to his Adam's apple, raising her eyebrows in a clear intimation of *see what happens.*

Instead of shouting for help, the man licked his lips before asking, "And who the hell might you be?"

Scarlett opened her mouth, but no sound came out.

"Come, come. That's no way to greet a lad who clearly wants to make sure our business remains civil, Gil," Lord Pearce said from where he was still pressed to the wall before where she knelt above the man on the ground. The breathlessness of his voice betrayed the lightness of his words.

Scarlett looked up at him, meeting his gaze as her mind raced.

"So, who might I thank for volunteering to mediate our...disagreement?" Benedict prompted.

"Scarlett," she admitted, her cover already blown to bits by her dramatic entrance.

Lord Pearce blinked in surprise at the feminine tone of her voice before his lips parted in recognition.

"Ah, this would be the interference I mentioned." He gestured to her. "It seems this little bird has a vested interest in Miss Ward staying alive. As you can see, she can be very persuasive when she wishes."

"What do you want with Georgette Ward?" The man beneath Scarlett growled.

"I need her alive," Scarlett said, grasping at straws. Searching for some explanation that would allow her and Lord Pearce to walk out alive.

"For what?" the man pressed.

"You know the Wards have an awful lot of money," Lord Pearce jumped in, saving Scarlett from her whirling thoughts.

"Killing Miss Ward won't change how much money her father has," the man growled.

"Ah yes, but then nobody would get the young lady's dowry." Lord Pearce raised his eyebrows meaningfully at Scarlett, staring at her with his dark eyes as if trying to speak directly into her mind.

"And you plan to steal her dowry?" The man seemed dubious.

What Lord Pearce was suggesting finally hit Scarlett so hard she nearly gasped, but suppressed the noise in favor of saying, "If somebody were to marry her before she met an unfortunate end, the dowry would belong to them."

"And I have the advantage of being a highly eligible bachelor." Lord Pearce threw in a roguish wink for effect, even though the thug couldn't see him from where he lay on the ground.

Scarlett looked back down at the man beneath her, practically able to see the gears turning in his bald head.

"And the Wolves would get a cut of the dowry?"

"Even split," Scarlett chimed in, easing the knife from his throat and removing her weight from his torso as a sign of good will. Still, her fingertips itched with the shadows lurking behind her if things didn't go as planned.

Gil rubbed his jaw with a meaty hand as he considered.

"Could work..."

Scarlett surreptitiously leaned in to hear what he mumbled under his breath. Apparently the Wolves kept him around for his bulging biceps and not his brains, as he had to think out loud, even when the person who had just been threatening him with a knife could overhear.

"Add insult to injury..."

"She does have the largest dowry of any of the young ladies to come out this season, does she not?" Lord Pearce asked Scarlett conversationally, as if he were a gossiping matchmaker at a garden party.

"The Wolves are in," Gil announced grudgingly. "But if your little plot puts our plans in jeopardy, we won't hesitate to kill you along with the girl."

"Pleasure doing business with you, as always." Lord Pearce bent to pick up his top hat where it had fallen on the floor in the earlier commotion. Before he could dust it off and place it on his head, Scarlett grabbed his arm and towed him backwards towards the window.

"We'll be in touch," Scarlett said before toppling over the sill, dragging Lord Pearce with her.

He screeched for the brief moment they were airborne, but Scarlett could barely hear it over the ringing in her ears as she pulled shadows to her so thickly that they created a pillow of darkness around them. The shadows' physical forms dissipated as soon they were deposited on the ground, dusty but unharmed, although Scarlett kept enough darkness pulled close to keep them partially obscured in the hazy light of the back alley. She squeezed her eyes shut for just a moment against the incessant ringing that always accompanied the use of her shadows in a tangible form. It was sure to result in a headache tomorrow morning as well, but she would deal with that later.

"What was—"

"Stop talking and move, or that whole stunt will have been for nothing." Scarlett cut Lord Pearce off, hauling him to his feet and dragging them through the back door of the shop. To her surprise, since Lord Pearce hadn't seemed to shut his mouth even in the face of death threats before, he remained silent as Scarlett led them back onto the street and on a twisting path through several back alleys. She even cut through a gambling den run by the Scorpions to be safe. Scarlett only stopped when she reached a familiar warehouse with metal rungs running up the side.

She clambered up them quickly, hearing a curse behind her as Lord Pearce tried to follow, clearly less well dressed for pell-mell escapes from gangsters. Still, they would be safe on the roof of this abandoned mill, hidden in the shadow of the silo on top. Scarlett had laid low on this particular roof after dicey jobs a handful of times before.

Lord Pearce reached the top of the ladder long moments after Scarlett, giving her a moment to survey the surrounding streets from their vantage point for any signs of pursuit. Luckily, the pedestrians all seemed to be milling about doing their usual business. They were back in Raptor territory anyways.

"You're Talented," Lord Pearce remarked as he clambered onto the roof, resting his hands on his knees as he caught his breath.

"It's not illegal anymore," Scarlett snapped, hackles rising as she narrowed her eyes at Lord Pearce.

His fine coat was covered in a thin layer of dust, and his dark hair fell forward over his face, yet it didn't make him look disheveled. Somehow, Scarlett thought he would manage to look debonair in a potato sack, and it irked her.

"I know, it just explains how you were able to escape me in the garden last night so easily," Lord Pearce said.

Scarlett relaxed infinitesimally but remained on the balls of her feet, ready to run at a moment's notice if need be. Even if Talents had been legal for almost a year now, the habit of hiding her abilities ran deep. After years of the Inquiries—of hearing angry crowds yell *cursed* and *witch* as people hung—a new way of living was slow to take hold.

"While the display of your Talent just now was impressive," Lord Pearce continued on, seemingly oblivious to Scarlett's tension, "I do have to wonder at its purpose. Diving out a window is a wonderfully dramatic way to make an exit, but I think Gil would have let us use the door once we came to an agreement."

"I didn't want to be recognized walking through the Cave and have news of me being there get back—get to the wrong ears. Not to mention, they would have had us followed, and you and I need to have a private chat. Starting with why on earth you thought it was a good idea wandering into a gang hideout unarmed after failing on a job for them?"

Scarlett huffed and folded her arms, wondering why she was bothering to scold a near stranger for almost getting themselves killed. Probably because her reluctance to let him die forced her to give her game away to the Wolves.

"I wasn't unarmed. I had this." Lord Pearce dug around in his coat before producing a thin metal instrument. The duke's crest of a blossoming tree gleamed in brass on the handle.

"That's a letter opener," Scarlett pointed out.

"So it is. But I bet it could still cause quite a bit of pain if you jabbed it in someone's delicate bits." He pantomimed exactly where he planned to stab his assailants in dramatic fashion.

A laugh bubbled up unbidden in Scarlett's throat. She bit her lips to stifle the sound, but not before it rang through the air for a brief moment. He offered her another dashing grin with an eyebrow raised. His nose was too long and bent to be traditionally handsome, but it fit perfectly with his crooked smile.

"Besides, you relieved me of my much more effective weapon last night, Miss... I'm sorry I don't think I caught your last name?"

"It's just Scarlett," she said, remembering the weight at the small of her back that was the dueling pistol.

"Well in that case, little bird, you may call me Benedict."

He sketched a polite bow as if Scarlett were a lady he was asking for a dance, even as she fished the pistol out of her waistband.

"I'm surprised you didn't sell it," he commented with raised brows upon seeing it.

"Me too," Scarlett admitted, offering the weapon to him handle first. Considering she had taken the liberty of unloading it earlier, it wouldn't do Benedict much more good than his letter opener at the moment. "That's two you owe me now."

"I think we're even on this most recent encounter actually," Benedict argued. "You may have tumbled in the window, weapons drawn like a ragamuffin savior, but my quick thinking got us the rest of the way out of that pinch."

"Well Benedict, your fast talking may have gotten us out of the Cave—"

"Thus proving that my mouth is more effective than any weapon I might have brought."

"—but it's only bought us time. The Wolves still want Georgette dead, and that is something I can't allow."

Benedict cocked his head to the side. "Who is Miss Ward to you? Did her father hire you to protect her?"

Something inside Scarlett bristled at his casual assumption that she was no more than a paid bodyguard to Georgette, even though that was how she intended to appear. She purposefully made herself seem as distant as possible from the refined and intelligent Georgette.

"Something like that," she grumbled. "Either way, I don't trust the Wolves not to go behind our back and kill Georgette despite our agreement. She's in danger until I find out why they want her dead and foil whatever it is they're planning."

"Until *we* figure it out," Benedict corrected.

"*We?* I thought we just established that you are not prepared to take on these gangs when you thought a letter opener was an adequate weapon." Scarlett put her hands on her hips.

"Yes, but I did just promise the Wolves I'd seduce a woman into marrying me before disposing of her and keeping the dowry. I've just taken a very skillful swan dive from the frying pan into the fire, so I'm afraid whatever you're planning will have to include me to some degree," argued Benedict.

"Nobody is seducing Georgette!" Scarlett threw up her hands in frustration. "I don't think her father will even let her leave the house until her life is no longer in danger."

"Then I guess I'll have to seduce you."

Scarlett opened her mouth to retort and then choked as the full force of his words hit her. She had lost track of this conversation.

"You posed as Georgette before. I can pretend to court her when it's really you, just in case the Wolves decide to go back on their deal. If they do come after us, you can help us escape with your—" Benedict wiggled his fingers in an imitation of Scarlett's shadows. "And we can use the time together to uncover the Wolves' motives."

Scarlett blinked as she regained her composure and digested his words. She hated to admit that it was a good plan, or the beginnings of one at least.

"I'll have to talk to the Wards," Scarlett hedged. "They'll need to be aware to help with our ruse. I can meet with them tonight and form a plan." Her mind already whirring with thoughts, Scarlett began to back away.

"Wait." Benedict took a step forward after her. "How will I contact you?"

"You won't, I'll find you."

"You better, little bird. Miss Ward's isn't the only life at stake here."

Scarlett pulled her shadows around her like a cloak and jumped from the rooftop, but not before catching a flash of urgency in Benedict's usually teasing gaze.

Chapter Three

Georgette shoved a rumpled piece of paper under her pillow as Scarlett opened the window. She did her the courtesy of pretending not to notice. Instead, Scarlett busied herself closing the window and drawing the curtains behind her to keep out the chill of the evening.

"Did you talk to the man from the ball? I'm getting tired of being cooped up in here," Georgette said as soon as Scarlett was fully in the room.

"I did, but I'm afraid it'll be a little bit longer," Scarlett admitted, shaking her head as Georgette motioned towards her window seat. Scarlett's pants were filthy from her earlier adventure, and she didn't have it in her to soil the delicately embroidered pillow.

"It sounds like you made some progress then?" Georgette's round eyes held as much hope as ever. Scarlett's lips twitched at her unyielding optimism.

Before she could answer, a sharp rap sounded at the door.

"Georgette dear, is that Scarlett?" Mr. Ward's voice filtered through the wood. "The guards told me she just arrived."

Bouncing from the bed, Georgette opened her bedroom door.

"She was just telling me about the headway she made," she explained as her father stepped into the room. The stern look he perpetually wore under his bushy mustache stayed in place even as he gave Scarlett a polite nod.

"You would know when she was here more easily if she just used the front door," Georgette shot over her shoulder to where Scarlett still stood by the window. "Tell her she can use the front door, Father."

The firm set of Mr. Ward's lips softened just a touch, the way it only did when he talked to his daughter.

"She knows how to use the door," he said over the top of Georgette's dark curly head. As their gazes met, Scarlett nodded at their unspoken agreement. Mr. Ward knew that a public friendship with Scarlett would hurt Georgette's reputation, the only thing the sole daughter of a wealthy family really had. Even if his heart held too much kindness to send Scarlett away, Mr. Ward preferred their friendship to exist in the shadows. Scarlett preferred to remain an invisible companion as well.

"What intelligence have you been able to gather on the Wolves' motives?" Mr. Ward pressed, moving further into the room and shutting the door behind him. Of course, he saw the advantages of having a pet gangster as a family friend as well.

Scarlett launched into the tale of her afternoon, internally cringing at the part where she leaped into a dangerous situation with no plan at all. She tried to play it off as more calculated, as her not wanting to lose her only lead, but couldn't quite convince herself. Even as she talked, she tried to exude the sense that she had the situation under control, that the danger was minimal, to avoid frightening Georgette. As she gauged her reactions though, the girl simply listened with wide eyes, betraying nothing.

"And you and this Lord Pearce are prepared to pose as a courting couple while you continue to investigate? I'll not have Georgette endanger herself for a ruse," Mr. Ward said at the end of Scarlett's story. Georgette only chewed on her lip and stayed silent.

Scarlett nodded, even though it was the part of the plot she dreaded the most. Something about playing at being a society lady picked at an old wound in her chest the way running the streets of the lower city never could. Benedict didn't seem like the type to make it painless either, although wrangling his antics might serve as a distraction.

"In that case, I'll have some preparations to make," Mr. Ward said. "Why don't you two ladies work on picking out some dresses for Scarlett for her outings." With a kiss pressed to the top of Georgette's head, he swept from the room.

"I'm sorry this means missing more of the social season," Scarlett apologized as Georgette opened her wardrobe with a thoughtful expression. "And if it appears you're being courted by the younger son of a duke, it will probably scare away any other callers. I know your father wanted to see you married during your first season."

"Truth be told, I don't mind. I wasn't impressed by any of the men I danced with at the opening ball. Besides, I doubt Lord Pearce will scare other suitors away. He's known for leaving a trail of heartbroken ladies in his wake," Georgette commented, her tone light as she pulled out a moss green dress dripping with lace. The pink spots high on her cheeks gave her away though.

"Oh really?" Scarlett asked, her tone teasing.

"This would be perfect for a stroll in the park." Georgette held the dress up to admire, seemingly trying to change the subject. "Very public too, for any Wolves who might be watching."

"Are you sure your lack of disappointment about missing the season doesn't have anything to do with a certain art dealer's son?" Scarlett pressed, unable to help the smile playing at her lips.

"I haven't the slightest idea what you mean," Georgette said, although the appearance of dimples on her cheeks betrayed her amusement.

Scarlett, who had been edging towards the bed, quickly snagged the paper Georgette had stowed beneath the pillow. She held up the piece of paper triumphantly, yellowed and crinkled as if with repeated readings.

"My Georgie," she read in a sing-song voice.

Georgette squeaked indignantly and lunged across the bed, dress forgotten and falling to a heap on the floor. Even as she grabbed for the letter, Scarlett stepped back and held it aloft.

"I am travelling to Paris to ask my father for my share in the family business," Scarlett kept reading. "Once he does, hopefully I will return to you with a fortune more suitable to marry a lady—"

Georgette jumped, succeeding in wrenching the paper for Scarlett's grip.

"Ah, so you're waiting for dear Leon?"

Georgette smoothed her fingers over the ink on the page, as if checking the words were all still present, before folding it neatly on the well-worn creases.

"I'm not exactly in a hurry to rush to the altar with somebody else if that's what you mean," Georgette agreed.

"But he's been away for a while," Scarlett clarified, to which Georgette nodded. "That would explain why I haven't run into him sneaking down the trellis when I've come to visit recently."

"That was one time!" Georgette's voice was little more than a high-pitched squeak, and Scarlett chuckled. Seeing a pantsless Leon fall into the snow drift below the bedroom window in his hurry to escape notice had been the highlight of an otherwise dreary winter.

"Besides, I thought he'd be back by now." Georgette's voice dropped low. Scarlett leaned in and put a hand on her shoulder.

"That man is crazy about you," she said sincerely. She didn't know Leon well, but she had passed secret letters between the lovebirds enough to see what any blind person could: that Leon was smitten. "I'm sure he hasn't run off and abandoned you."

"Yes, but he has all these noble ideas. I'm afraid his father isn't going to agree to give him his rightful stake in the business, and he won't come back until he can make me a proper bride." Georgette's fingers fluttered anxiously as she tucked the paper back under the embroidered cushion.

"Paris is a long way," Scarlett said. "He's probably just traveling. Besides, maybe hearing that you're being courted by Lord Pearce will make him hurry home."

At that, Georgette's smile returned, wide enough to crinkle the corners of her eyes.

"Then we better get you dressed to impress."

Even with stopping to drop off a large bundle of dresses and cosmetics at Granny's, Scarlett still made it to the Roost earlier than she did the night before. The sight that greeted her when she entered made her glad of her punctuality.

"Ah, there you are!" Amos called from where he held court, sitting on the bar. "I hope you're ready for a bit more action than delivering unfriendly messages tonight."

Scarlett slid between two familiar brawlers who made room for her as she approached Amos. He leaned back, resting on his hands with his legs thrown wide in arrogance, the smile on his face as oily as his slicked-back hair.

"And here she is, the ace up our sleeve!"

In response to Amos's proclamation, the brawlers cracked their knuckles and flexed brawny biceps in anticipation. Scarlett resisted the urge to shift nervously in response to the crackling promise of violence in the air. You didn't survive as a Talented in the lower city by showing fear.

"What game are we cheating at tonight?" Scarlett asked, folding her arms.

"The Scorpions think they can carve out some of the Lions' old territory for themselves," Amos explained, his excited tone riling up the nearby Raptors even more. "The Wolves may have taken the majority of the territory left by the Lions, but we've claimed the factories down by the port. It's time to remind the Scorpions what's ours!"

"A fight?" Scarlett clarified, mentally checking for the weight of all her knives against her skin. One in her boot, two up her sleeves, two against her ribs, and a short blade against the small of her back.

"A negotiation." Amos's smile, wide enough to display several chipped teeth, held no reassurance. "Brandon has agreed to meet with me and three of my lieutenants at midnight in the alley off broad street to negotiate our territory. But if he doesn't agree to our terms, we're prepared to make him see things our way."

"Looks like you have your three lieutenants ready to go," Scarlett said, glancing at the men gathered around her. While they weren't Amos's most influential enforcers, they were certainly the largest. What they might lack in cunning they made up for in crushing strength.

"Oh Scarlett my darling, I don't intend on this being a fair fight." Amos chuckled in a way that indicated he thought he was being charming. Scarlett's top lip inadvertently pulled up into a snarl at the way he casually threw around pet names with her, and she willed her face into neutrality.

"You're going to work your magic and hide on the roof next door until the negotiations take a turn for the physical. Then you'll jump into the fray, and we have a one-man advantage." Scarlett nodded silently. She was used to this kind of task. The invisible lookout, the unseen reinforcement.

With that the small group set out of the tavern to hearty cheers and encouraging slaps on the back. Despite her apprehension, the encouraging whoops and pats on her shoulders relaxed some of the tension in her stance. The Raptors were as much of a family as she had these days.

The group made their way through the darkened streets towards the few blocks of warehouses and factories they would be fighting to claim tonight. The area had once been under the protection of the Lions, but since the end of the Inquiries and the pardon of the Lions' leader, Nathanial Woodrow, the gang had all but disappeared. Rumor had it that Mr. Woodrow and his wife were working to get all their former gang members legal work, or at least the appearance of it. As the only people to be officially pardoned for their actions during the Inquiries, Mr. and Mrs. Woodrow seemed determined to publicly distance themselves from criminal activity.

Now all the remaining gangs rushed to divvy up the abandoned territory. "Negotiations" like this were becoming weekly occurrences. The power vacuum left by the dissolution of the Lions and the death of the Rattlesnakes' leaders had lit the fuse on the powder keg that was the lower city.

The Royal Police, left in disarray after their former chief had been revealed as a murderer and sentenced to a life in prison, didn't have the manpower to suppress the infighting. As hard as the young Chief Joseph Thorne tried, much of the populace had lost faith in the police.

Approaching the alley where the meet-up was to take place, Amos motioned silently to Scarlett. With a nod, she broke off from the group, the cool whisper of her shadows brushing against her skin as she cloaked herself in darkness. Practically invisible, she darted over to the building bordering the alley. The climb up to the roof was quick thanks to an open window and the fact that it was only a single story high. Scarlett was grateful that the building was low enough that she likely wouldn't twist an ankle when she jumped down into the fray.

Once on the roof, Scarlett didn't straighten, instead sliding across the roof on her belly to peek over the edge. She kept the shadows pulled tight around her but left as much of herself hidden behind the ledge of the roof as possible. The darkness made her nearly impossible to spot, but the Scorpions would be expecting a betrayal, watching the surrounding areas closely. Scarlett scanned the surrounding rooftops in turn. The Raptors weren't the only ones known to be less than honorable. She only picked out four figures entering the alley from the far side to meet Amos and his enforcers.

Voices rumbled in the alley below, and Scarlett barely drew breath as she listened, alert for danger.

"—Wolves have taken most of the territory for themselves, even though our gambling dens are the closest," argued a voice that Scarlett didn't recognize. It must be Brendan, the leader of the Scorpions.

"Sounds like something you should take up with the Wolves." Amos's silky voice was unperturbed.

"We all know you're working with them, Amos, why else would you give up so much of this area to them without a fight?"

Scarlett's brows drew together. She hadn't heard about any agreement between the Raptors and the Wolves. Brendan must be desperate, grasping at straws.

"Please." Scarlett could practically hear the dismissive wave of Amos's hand. "They've started a new operation that's bringing in more money than the Wolves can spend. Even I know better than to challenge Fang when his pocket is newly bursting with unspent coin. That could buy him a lot of manpower."

"Which is why the rest of us need to split up the remaining territory fairly, to keep Fang's head from getting too big for his top hat," Brendan argued.

"How magnanimous of you to assume I'll play fair."

At that, Scarlett bunched her thighs under her, prepared to leap at the Scorpions from behind. What Brendan said next though gave her pause.

"And how stupid of you to assume I didn't know you were a double-crossing bastard."

Scarlett thinned her shadows enough to let her see out, just in time to catch a flash of silver from the roof across the way.

As the man on the opposite building aimed down the sights of his pistol, Scarlett's dagger flew into her palm. She barely took a moment to aim before flinging it across the gap of the alley. There came the wet thunk of the blade connecting with its mark, followed by the strangled gasp of surprising pain. The man made to turn and see where the knife had come from, but the leg with the handle sticking from it buckled under his weight. For a drawn-out moment, he teetered on the edge of the roof before tipping over the side. The sick crunch as he hit the dirt below raised bile in the back of Scarlett's throat. The world swam as she clambered off the rooftop. She'd done it again. She hadn't checked the surrounding rooftops well enough, and another man had died at her hands.

Barely registering the sounds of fists meeting flesh and grunts of aggression from the brawling lieutenants, Scarlett dropped from the roof and sprang across the courtyard to where her victim lay. Her heart stuttered back into rhythm again as his conscious gaze met hers and he moaned in pain. He was alive, although his ankle bent at an angle completely at odds with his leg. It was only a one-story drop, nothing that would kill a man.

Distracted in her relief, Scarlett didn't register the body encroaching behind her until it was too late. A massive weight crashed on top of her, pitching her forward and banging her head against the ground with a thud that echoed through her skull. The man resting on her back suffocated her even as he pinned her wrists to the ground, one in each meaty fist. Amos's brutal training kicked in without thought.

Scarlett shoved one of her arms forward, wrenching to the side as hard as she could. The sudden shift of weight forced her assailant to drop to his elbows. Pressing the advantage, Scarlett jammed her thigh up into his knee where he pinned her down, gaining the leverage to flip their positions. As she pinned him beneath her, Scarlett flung out a hand, curling tendrils of darkness leaping from her fingers to cling to his face.

He instinctively clawed at the ethereal blindfold, but his fingers found no purchase. As he was distracted, Scarlett took the opportunity to ram her knee into his groin, leaving him incapacitated on the ground. Leaping to her feet, she whirled around to see how the rest of the Raptors fared.

Thomas, one of the Raptors' brawler twins, licked blood from a split lip as he faced off against the last Scorpion still on his feet. With the Scorpion's attention on Thomas, Scarlett unsheathed her blade. Just as the Scorpion swung for Thomas, fist whistling through the air with the force of his punch, Scarlett leaped on his back. With all the force she could muster, she clocked the bruiser on the temple with the hilt of her knife. He teetered for a moment, and Scarlett managed to jump clear before he crumpled to the ground.

The alley fell silent, and Scarlett glanced around to see all the Scorpions sprawled on the ground, blinking the sting of dust from their eyes. Timothy, Thomas's twin, pinched a bloody nose, but the Raptors all still stood. From how unrumpled Amos looked, Scarlett doubted he had even joined in the fray, his grin looking even slicker now than when they had left the roost.

Sauntering over to where Brendan lay on the ground, cradling a swollen wrist, he spoke down his nose at the fallen Scorpion. "This is our turf, and you better remember it. We have big plans, and you bugs will be stepped on if you don't get out of the way."

Chapter Four

As much powder as Scarlett patted on her face, she couldn't fully cover the bruise on her brow where it had met the cobblestones the night before. She winced at the press of the powder puff as she dabbed it against her brow, trying to pack on enough product to obscure the purpling blotch. Looking in the warped shaving mirror propped on her rickety bed, Scarlett sighed in defeat. Her attempts to beautify herself only succeeded in making her face look drawn and dirty.

Thankfully, Georgette had also lent Scarlett a feathered hat to add to her disguise. She would just pull it lower over her face than was fashionable to disguise her injury, as well as the fact that her features weren't quite as delicate as Georgette's.

For now, she tucked it under her arm, not wanting to don such a fine piece of clothing until she was closer to the park. As she tromped down the stairs, all the children milling about Granny's stopped what they were doing as they caught sight of her before dissolving into giggles. Scarlett tugged at the bodice of the lilac dress, overly conscious of how tight it nipped in at the waist where she usually hid herself in overly large shirts and bulky jackets. Her efforts only succeeded in pitching the already dangerous neckline of the dress even lower, exposing skin that rarely ever saw the light of day. As Scarlett huffed in defeat, Granny herself came around the corner, the sound of her cane rapping on the aged floorboards quieting the urchins back into their chores or games.

"It's nice to see you dressed up for once," Granny said, the corners of her already weathered eyes crinkling further in what was her version of a smile.

"Another day, another scheme." Scarlett shrugged.

Granny responded with a noncommittal grunt, but Scarlett could have sworn she saw the amused twinkle fade from Granny's eyes before she hobbled off to scold a ragamuffin for the way he wiped down a table.

Scarlett pushed out the door and into the bustle of the cobblestone street. Lifting her skirts, she picked carefully through the road so as not to damage Georgette's dress. Walking dressed as she was in the lower city drew lots of stares, and Scarlett's skin prickled in discomfort. She itched to cut through the side alleys and pick through the shadows where no one would spare her a second glance, but that only worked in her normal getup of a gang runner or messenger boy. Dressed as a fine lady, in all the regalia of the jewel of the season out for a stroll, there was no escaping curious eyes.

Luckily, she only had to walk a few blocks to the fringes of the middle city where Mr. Ward's carriage driver picked her up.

"Miss Ward," he greeted with a knowing nod, hopping down from the driver's seat to give her a hand up into the carriage. Scarlett narrowly avoided catching and ripping the lace trim of the dress on the stair as she pulled them up into the box of the coach. She didn't wear so much fabric—or ride in carriages—very often anymore.

As the driver tapped the horses into motion and the wheels began clattering across the cobblestones, Scarlett spotted an envelope on the bench across from her. Upon examination, it had her name printed neatly across the back and carried Mr. Ward's seal. Breaking it open she read the contents, printed in Mr. Ward's impeccable cursive.

Lord Pearce has accepted Georgette's invitation to a promenade in the park today. She is sure to be the talk of the town after accepting his attentions in such a public manner.

Scarlett nodded and tucked the letter away in her skirts, pleased that Benedict was playing along with their ruse. Pushing aside the drape across the window, Scarlett watched the passing houses as the horses pulled the carriage into the upper city. Servants running errands for their distinguished families occupied most of the street here, bustling about with baskets of vegetables or wrapped parcels sure to contain the most fashionable dresses for upcoming parties. A few fine ladies strolled down the street, parasols shielding their delicate complexions from the reedy sunlight.

As Scarlett watched, a lone child with grubby hands slipped unnoticed through the busy street towards the pack of ladies. As he darted past the ladies and closer to the Wards' carriage, he tucked a scrap of fabric into his shirt. Seeing the pickpocket tuck away an embroidered handkerchief that would fetch enough coin for several meals niggled something nearly nostalgic in Scarlett's mind. The days of merely pickpocketing for the Raptors had been simpler, before the stakes were raised as Amos realized her Talent's usefulness.

The carriage turned off the road and into the drive of the sprawling park that occupied a large swath of the upper city. As it pulled to a halt, Scarlett spotted the man of the hour milling near the rosebushes at the edge of the path. He wore his dark hair loose, and it curled at the base of his neck beneath his top hat, a bit longer than was fashionable, but it suited him.

Scarlett shook herself and busied her hands with pinning the hat into her wig, pulling it forward while trying to push the feathers out of her face. When Mr. Ward's driver opened the door and sunlight pierced the darkness of the carriage, she could only hope she looked as elegant as Georgette would in her place.

Benedict turned from the rosebushes and greeted her with a smile that almost convinced her she could pass as one of the most desirable matches of the social season. He was a good actor, for all his bungled plans so far.

"Ah, Miss Ward." He offered an arm to her with great ceremony, and Scarlett laid her hand in his elbow as delicately as she could manage. That part at least wasn't too difficult, as the one thing Scarlett did share with Georgette was a petite build. Where it made Georgette seem like a porcelain doll, it enhanced Scarlett's ability to slip under the radar. Now though, she felt multiple sets of eyes on her as Benedict led her onto the garden path.

"I'm glad to see you again so soon," Benedict continued conversationally. "You left me with a lot to consider after our last meeting, and I've thought of further questions."

"I'm sure those questions can wait." Scarlett surreptitiously dug her nails into his sleeve and glanced around at the others in the park. While they all gave her and Benedict a respectful berth, she wasn't convinced they couldn't eavesdrop if they wanted to. The gossips of the upper city were incorrigible. "After all, it's such a lovely day, and it would be a shame to distract ourselves from it."

Benedict chuckled, a free and musical sound like bells. It startled Scarlett enough from her inspection of their surroundings to look at him. He stared at her with open amusement.

"Of course. This outing is for pleasure, not business." The corners of Benedict's eyes crinkled in amusement.

Scarlett huffed. "Do you ever take anything seriously?"

"Not if I can help it." Benedict shrugged, his arm flexing under Scarlett's fingers.

"If you're not careful, it's going to get you into trouble one of these days," Scarlett said, a hint of very real caution underlying her generally light tone.

"Trouble seems to have a way of finding me whether I take things seriously or not. I refuse to give it the satisfaction of not seeing me enjoy everything to the fullest," Benedict argued.

"Is that how you came by your reputation of being a rake?"

"Oh no, I got that simply by being a rake."

Scarlett let out a short, surprised laugh for the second time in as many days at Benedict's antics. He looked down at her with a smile, seeming proud of her amusement. Seeing him for the first time in sunlight instead of a shadowy alley or hedge maze, she realized that his eyes weren't as dark as she had originally thought them, but instead a warm honeyed brown.

As she examined him, Benedict frowned.

"Let me help you with your hat," he offered. Scarlett moved to object, but Benedict was already adjusting the ornamental hat pin. "You know, you're supposed to show off the feathers, not pull them over your face like you're trying to mug somebody."

Scarlett bit her tongue to avoid shooting back that she didn't need to bother with a such a ridiculous hat to rob somebody.

As he repositioned the hat on Scarlett's wig, he pulled it off her brow, revealing the shadow of her injury under a thick layer of makeup. A frown creased his brow, and for a moment his hand drifted towards her face as if he planned to brush his fingers over it. Scarlett tensed, thinking that she should brush his hand away but standing as frozen as one of the statues scattered around the gardens instead.

A sudden wave of tittering passed through occupants of the path like a cat running through a flock of birds, and Benedict dropped his hand, Scarlett's injury apparently forgotten. Refocusing on their surroundings, Scarlett found the epicenter of the tittering to be a couple strolling down the path towards them. The wide brim of the man's hat partially obscured his face, but as he tilted his head to listen to something the lady was saying, Scarlett stiffened.

The thick scar running from his chin through his mouth and eye, distorting his face into a permanent snarl, marked him as Nathanial Woodrow. The former Beast himself, now the personal bodyguard to King Byron. The only other time Scarlett had encountered him, she hadn't seen much of his face, only his fearsome prowess with a knife as he quickly dispatched a mob of Rattlesnakes intent on taking more than money from a woman they were mugging. Even then, he couldn't be mistaken for anybody else with that scar and hulking build.

Scarlett didn't recognize the woman with him, but she would bet Benedict's purse it was his wife, Mrs. Contessa Woodrow. The lovely blonde on Mr. Woodrow's arm wasn't what Scarlett had expected for the woman who had discredited the police captain and was recognized for putting an end to Inquiries. Even now, she supposedly had the king's ear when it came to controlling violence in the lower city. From the way Mr. Woodrow's ruined face twisted into a smile as he listened to her talk, it was clear she was more than the delicate lady she seemed.

Everybody else on the garden path seemed equally curious about the couple, whispering shared rumors behind gloved hands.

"Advisor to the king—"

"—can read minds."

"Shouldn't be among decent society."

Benedict leaned in to murmur in her ear, close enough that Scarlett felt his breath on her skin. She shivered despite the warm sun warming the garden path. "Is Mr. Woodrow an...acquaintance of yours?"

Scarlett shook her head slightly, not taking her eyes off the couple, just as curious as everybody else. As she did, Mr. Woodrow's eyes darted to hers, and her breath froze in her chest for a second. His golden gaze met her own, and for a moment she wondered if he really could read her thoughts, so intense was his expression. His eyes narrowed and then darted between Mrs. Woodrow and Scarlett once before relaxing. Then they had walked past, the whole interaction only having lasted a second.

"I thought you might have run into him before in your...line of work?" Benedict murmured once more as he led them down a side path towards a trickling fountain.

"I only ever saw him in passing once," Scarlett admitted, keeping her voice hushed. "And he wouldn't have seen me."

They entered what was nearly a room made by hedges, deserted but for the statue of an angel standing at the center of the fountain, endlessly pouring its pot of water onto the tile flowers around its feet.

"Rumor has it the Lions were awash with Talented. I'm surprised you never worked for them."

"I wasn't so lucky," Scarlett admitted, the barest edge of bitterness creeping into her casual tone. The Lions had earned a reputation as a safe haven for Talented youths during the Inquiries, but Scarlett hadn't been wise to the ways of the lower city and ended up with a Raptors tattoo out of desperation. Other gangs would give you a haven from the

Royal Police as long as you used your Talents to line their purses. If you refused, the reward for turning in a Talented to the police would be a fine consolation prize.

"Lucky?" Benedict echoed, bringing Scarlett's thoughts back to the garden path. "I'm not sure I would be able to consider working for Nathanial Woodrow as lucky. Most people still don't trust the Woodrows. I can't blame them either. He looks like he could rip you apart. Still, I don't suppose I envy them being the first openly Talented members of polite society, even if people don't actually know exactly what their Talents are."

Scarlett nodded thoughtfully. If the Woodrows couldn't integrate into the upper class with the king's explicit support, then there was no hope for anybody else.

"We should get back to the main path," Scarlett commented, tearing her mind from that grim train of thought. "If the whole point of this charade is to be seen, we aren't doing much good back here."

Benedict obligingly turned them back towards the hedges demarking the main concourse, lacy parasols just peeking over the top. Still, he chuckled. "True, but people wouldn't believe us having a proper courtship if I didn't try to sneak you away to steal a kiss. I do have a reputation to uphold after all."

Scarlett's cheeks felt warmer than was warranted by today's temperature at the mention of kissing, and she had to chide herself for reacting to Benedict's flirtatious manner. She wasn't some innocent noble woman, and he wasn't really flirting with her anyways.

"Be that as it may," she countered to distract herself, "I don't want to ruin Georgette's impeccable reputation."

"I suppose it is a challenge to balance my status as a known rogue and Miss Ward's as an angelic flower. We will have to settle for fluttering eyelashes and gazes full of longing," Benedict concluded.

The laugh that tumbled from Scarlett's lips seemed a little more natural this time, if a bit truncated still, as if Benedict's presence somehow reminded her body it had the capability of making such a noise. On the other hand, Benedict's responding chuckle was warm and easy, as if joy just bubbled up naturally inside of him so often it had to spill out of his mouth.

"So, what do you do for amusement?" Benedict asked, so sharply changing the topic that Scarlett blinked in confusion for a moment.

"Are you really asking me that?" she asked. "I would think you wouldn't really want to know the answer."

"Well it's the type of question I would usually ask of a woman I'm courting, so it seemed appropriate."

"Why don't you ask me a question I'm less likely to answer with something...incriminating," Scarlett hedged. She was loathe to admit to both herself and Benedict that amusement hadn't been a part of her life for several years now.

"Alright." Benedict ran his fingers along the brim of his hat as he thought. "What is your favorite thing to eat?"

"Kipper."

A barking laugh tore from Benedict and several people strolling nearby turned to look at the sound. Scarlett ducked her head as if in amusement, letting the loose curls on the wig partially obscure her face in case anybody near was familiar with Georgette.

"All the wonderful foods out there, and you choose kipper?" Benedict asked in disbelief, "Not toffee, or petit fours, or even fine cheeses...but kipper? Seems rather mundane."

"I will not have my favorite breakfast besmirched." Scarlett turned up her nose as they strolled. "They're buttery and salty. When they're cooked just right with herbs they melt on your tongue and warm your bones perfectly on a chilly morning."

"I've never heard somebody wax poetic about kipper, but I guess when you put it that way..." Benedict shrugged.

They walked along for a few minutes in companionable silence, drawing interested glances from other couples and groups of ladies strolling around the park. If Scarlett's skin prickled under the scrutiny, Benedict seemed to bloom with it, offering easy smiles to those they passed. As aware as she was of the eyes of others, she was still more aware of the flex of Benedict's arm under her fingers as they walked. Even separated by his jacket and the lacy gloves Scarlett wore, her mind kept circling back to the casual touch.

Scarlett reminded herself that she touched people plenty for missions, whether she was punching them or bumping up against them to distract from her hands slipping their purse from their belt. Still, her mind insisted that this familiar touch was something else entirely.

As she stared at other couples to distract herself, Scarlett's gaze caught on a well-dressed woman standing on the edge of the path. On a gloved finger of an outstretched hand perched a sparrow, and the woman cooed to it softly. Scarlett frowned at the sight, wondering how the lady had coaxed the flighty creature. Perhaps it was a Talent with animals, one that she could risk people observing now that it wouldn't mean a march to the gallows. Still, it wasn't nearly as obvious as Scarlett's Talent, and people would take much more kindly to tame birds than curling darkness. Even if some were bold enough to subtly use their Talents in public, Scarlett was unlikely to ever be so lucky—not after using her shadows for so much harm. She tore her eyes away from the lady and the sparrow with gritted teeth.

With relief, Scarlett saw they had circled back to where the main path met the road, in view of where the Wards' man waited with the carriage. They stopped, and Scarlett wavered, but Benedict took the moment into his own hands.

"It was a privilege to accompany you on your turn around the park, Miss Ward," he said, a little louder than the rest of their conversation had been but not loud enough to arouse suspicion that he was putting on a show. Then he lifted Scarlett's gloved hand from the crook of his arm before raising it to his lips.

Something about the mischievous twinkle in his eye and the way his breath warmed her fingers even through the gloves she wore locked Scarlett in place. His lips brushed across her knuckles, and Scarlett held her breath until he let go of her hand and stepped back. A stillness stretched between them before Scarlett finally inclined her head and turned to step into the carriage behind her.

As the Wards' manservant shut the door behind her, she reminded herself that Benedict was pretending to court her—not even her but Georgette. Still, if the way his gaze sent warmth skittering through her chest was any indication, he came by his reputation of being a rake honestly.

Chapter Five

Scarlett rested her chin on her knees and wondered about her decision-making skills. She sat with her legs tucked up, arms around her to hold herself in a tight ball as she sat in the rapidly lengthening shadow of a chimney.

When she had sent the note to Benedict via the Wards' servant, disguised as a letter from Georgette, this had seemed like a logical place to suggest a rendezvous. After all, the city square was easily found and not an area it would draw suspicion to be seen coming and going from.

Still, as Scarlett looked out over the open space below the roof she sat on, she regretted her choice. Despite how hard she tried to keep her gaze on the comings and goings of people from the square, colorful socialites and grime-crusted urchins alike, her focus kept darting to the dark patch in one corner. A stain marring the vibrancy of central London. The charred remains of the gallows.

For several decades, the gallows had stood tall, casting judgement over London during the Inquiries. The city would gather to watch the Talented hang, shouting at them that they were abominations—Cursed. It was in this very square where Scarlett had stood, clutching Georgette's hand tightly in her own, as her parents' lives were snuffed out before her eyes. She sometimes wished she had been able to squeeze her eyes shut like Georgette did as it happened, but she hadn't been able to bring herself to take her gaze from her parents even as their necks snapped.

She hadn't returned to this spot until just last year, the day King Byron declared an end to the Inquiries and made being Talented legal once more. Scarlett ran with the mob from the lower city that charged into the square with torches, setting the gallows ablaze. She cheered until she was hoarse as the flames reached high into the sky, covering the middle city in a blanket of smoke. Still, as the wooden beams broke and collapsed in on themselves, the crowd grew quieter as collective realization dawned on those of them who had lost loved ones—entire families—to the Inquiries.

Burning down the gallows couldn't bring anybody back from the dead. It couldn't undo things that had already been done. Just as the charred chunks of wood and soot stained the main square, the Inquiries had permanently stained lives, and the blackness couldn't be scrubbed clean. It seemed a little piece of that blackness had wormed its way into Scarlett's soul, living as the anger she constantly tamped down.

A panting from the edge of the roof behind her drew Scarlett from her reverie. She recognized the cadence as belonging to Benedict, despite having only encountered him a few times. Her time spying for the Raptors from her shadows honed her observation skills, and Benedict had somehow managed to permeate her awareness uncommonly fast. Probably because he had already caused her so much trouble.

"Do you simply fly up to these rooftops, little bird? Because you seem to have a habit of perching up high, and I'm not very accustomed to this much climbing."

Scarlett glanced over her shoulder and blinked at the sight that greeted her. Benedict had forgone his normal ensemble of velvet waistcoat and cravat, even leaving off his top hat. He had attempted to pull his hair back into a tail at the base of his neck, but the strands that weren't long enough to reach dangled in his face, and he swiped them out of the way. He was clearly sweating from the climb, and his light shirt clung to his chest and biceps.

Scarlett blinked and returned her gaze to the square. She saw plenty of Raptors strip their shirts entirely to fight or tend to scrapes and bruises. Still, for a gentleman like Benedict, it seemed borderline indecent to see him in such a state, perhaps because he was usually so meticulously dressed. Her mind seemed to catch on the flex of his arms as he wiped sweat from his brow, and she wrenched her thoughts free with great discipline.

"I've had a lot of practice," Scarlett said with a shrug as Benedict sat down beside her on the roof. Where she kept herself confined to as small a space as possible, he sprawled out next to her, legs extended and flung unnecessarily wide as he leaned back on his hands.

Scarlett sighed and with a jerk of her head extended the shadows of the chimney beside them to blur his silhouette. The ease with which she did so in another's presence after years of hiding her Talent surprised her, but Benedict had already seen much more impressive shows of her shadows. Besides, she didn't want anybody watching them if they happened to look up.

"So where are we going to start our investigations?" Benedict asked casually, swiping his fingers through the misty shadows that danced around him as if they were cobwebs. His manner was almost curious, not scared like many were by Scarlett's darkness. Then again, he had already proven his sense of self-preservation to be suspect.

"I was reminded the other day that the Wolves have recently gained a fair bit of territory, and coin to go with it." Scarlett quickly filled Benedict in on the situation of the turf disputes in the lower city, purposefully vague about her involvement in the brawls over coveted ground. Benedict nodded along as if he were listening to her assessment of which horses to bet on, seemingly unscandalized by the rough and tumble nature of gang life.

"So you think their newfound power has emboldened the Wolves to track down bigger prey?" Benedict asked.

"It seems plausible," Scarlett huffed. "But it doesn't tell me anything about why they've targeted Georgette in particular. Amos—I heard somebody mention something about a new operation though."

"What kind of operation?"

"If I knew, I wouldn't be sitting here picking the brain of somebody clearly better equipped for flirtation than criminal politics," Scarlett snapped, irritated by her lack of progress.

Benedict chuckled, seemingly unoffended. "Is that your way of telling me you want me to flirt with you instead of coming up with ideas? Because I was going to suggest that we start investigating the Wolves new territory to find this 'operation.'"

Something about Benedict's teasing eased the seed of frustration in the pit of Scarlett's stomach. She nodded.

"I'll comb the area and see if I can find anything. If I do, I'll send you another message via Georgette."

"*We* will comb the area you mean," Benedict insisted. "I didn't dress like this because it's the new fashion you know."

"You'll only slow me down," Scarlett argued, pushing to her feet, debating leaping over to the next roof and off into the twilight, knowing she could easily lose him. "I think we proved that last time when your grand plan was castrating enemies with a letter opener."

"Ah but I have this now, and I promise you I know how to use it." Benedict stood as well, producing his pistol from the waistband of his pants with a flourish. "And I'll be able to point out anybody that ah...recruited me...for the business with Georgette."

Scarlett hesitated, muscles bunched and ready to dart away and leave him to wait for her next message. Still, he could prove useful if he recognized any Wolves who were part of the scheme on Georgette's life. Her shadows could conceal both of them if he managed to keep that mouth of his in check.

"Alright," Scarlett agreed, "but you'll have to be quiet. And if you give us away, you'll find out exactly how much pain one can inflict with a letter opener."

Scarlett turned away to climb down the roof the way Benedict had come, suppressing the warmth in her stomach brought on by Benedict's triumphant smile. It had just been such a long time since anybody besides Georgette had seemed happy to be in her presence.

To his credit, Benedict behaved admirably as Scarlett led them through the streets towards the blocks of warehouses down by the wharves that had once been the purview of the Lions. They clung to the edges of the street, the thickening twilight especially dense around them. Benedict stayed silent, although he continuously dragged his fingers along the shadows subtly clinging to their silhouettes. He seemed mesmerized by the way they afforded the slightest resistance in this form, as if the air itself had congealed. Scarlett would have to summon much denser darkness to make it as solid as the mass that had cushioned their fall from the windows. She stuck to ephemeral darkness for times like this though, knowing this use of her Talent was less likely to leave her debilitated with a splitting headache the next day.

Scarlett internally debated telling him to stop touching them, but she didn't have it in her to tell Benedict that she could feel his fingertips as a phantom touch in the part of her mind that controlled her Talent. It seemed an oddly intimate thing to admit.

Soon enough, they crept into the blocks bordering the Port of London, newly claimed by the Wolves. Scarlett hadn't ventured down here often when it was under Lion control, mainly sticking to Raptor territory, but even she could tell that it seemed different. Before, it had been relatively quiet, a few urchins on the corners alert for anybody not keeping a keen eye on their purse. Now, it was quiet, but undercut with a dangerous vibration, as if the neighborhood waited with bated breath. The few pedestrians scurried quickly to their destinations, keeping their eyes on the ground. Nobody loitered on street corners.

Not wanting to stand out, Scarlett pulled Benedict briskly down the street and around a corner. They stood on a narrow stone ledge where the last building on the street backed up against the Thames. The murky waters ran sluggishly between the banks, the gurgling noise obscuring Scarlett's voice from anyone walking on the street.

"We'll climb up to that window." Scarlett gestured to an open sill on the third floor. "You go first and I'll keep a look out."

"What's wrong with front doors?" Benedict huffed, even as he began inspecting the uneven stone before him.

"When I'm spying on people, I generally don't like to announce my presence," Scarlett hissed.

With a resigned sigh, Benedict began to climb. His progress was slow, but Scarlett had to commend him for not complaining further, even as she was sure his well-manicured nails were shredded by grappling for purchase in the rough mortar. Just as he was an arm's reach from the open window, a loose stone broke from the wall where Benedict's foot had rested. Even as it fell to the ledge beside Scarlett with a dull clatter, Benedict began to slide down, toes scraping against the wall. Just as he looked as though he were about to lose his grip, pitching back into the murky waters at her feet, Scarlett grit her teeth and a patch of shadows formed a lip under his boot. His weight landed on it and the force of it jarred like a gong at the base of her skull. The sensation passed quickly as Benedict regained his footing and disappeared through the open window.

Not hearing any commotion from his entrance and seeing nobody watching on a quick study of her surroundings, Scarlett followed up the wall. In about half the time it took Benedict, she perched on the windowsill. She found him waiting for her in what appeared to be an uninhabited storage room and hopped down lightly to the wooden floor.

After ensuring that the room was deserted, she turned her attention towards the rest of the building. Creeping towards the door into the rest of the building, Scarlett strained her ears for sounds. Sure enough, rowdy voices filtered up from the floors below. She motioned for Benedict to stay put as she eased the door open, thanking luck for quiet hinges. Sneaking out into the hallway, she felt a presence behind her and suppressed a grunt of annoyance. She would have scolded Benedict for not doing as he was told if it wouldn't make so much noise.

Instead, she led the way down the hallway towards the stairs. There, they peeked over the rickety wooden railing to find a dozen men milling about below, laughing boisterously. Several empty bottles tipped over on the rickety table and a rather one-sided arm-wrestling match added to the impression of some Wolves enjoying their spoils. Getting the impression they wouldn't learn anything here from drunken brawlers clearly not thinking of business, Scarlett made to head back the way they had come and try a different building.

Before she could take a step, Benedict tapped frantically on her shoulder. When she looked over her shoulder, she found him gesturing emphatically between him and the men below, before pointing at his neck.

Turning back to the scene below, she squinted and found that one of the thugs had his tattoo of the howling wolf across the side of his throat. She jerked her head towards him and raised her eyebrows in question, to which Benedict nodded emphatically.

At his confirmation, she chanced sneaking closer, trying to get close enough to make out their words.

"—never had it better."

"Living like kings," the one with the neck tattoo agreed. "And it's only going to get better."

"The operation is already raking in the coin. How are we going to get better than that?"

Scarlett chanced stepping down another stair at that, not wanting to miss a word.

"Fang has some friends in high places. They're going to spread the word at the viscount's ball next week, see if we can't reel in some bigger purses."

"Even bigger fish? We better have some good fighters," the first commented, worry creeping into his tone.

"Don't you worry, we've got that part under control. Fang knows how to keep them under his heel," neck tattoo assured with an air of superiority, leaning back in his chair and folding his hands behind his head. "Now why don't you quit questioning Fang's plan and get us some more drink to celebrate another lucrative night. There's some whiskey in the storeroom upstairs."

With a grumble, the first thug pushed back from the table and Scarlett's heart accelerated in her chest. Not waiting to hear more, she turned around, nearly knocking over Benedict where he crouched on the stairs behind her. Grabbing his arm before he could fall, she yanked him back down the hallway the way they had come. Prioritizing haste over stealth, she dragged them back into the room they had entered, closing the door behind them.

By now, the Wolf's footsteps were audible on the stairs. Glancing at the climb down, she cursed, knowing they only had a matter of moments before they were discovered. Benedict couldn't climb down that fast. Still, the ledge three stories below them was narrow, dropping off into the turgid waters of the Thames.

"Phillip, you up here? Better not be stealing the drink," a voice called from the hallway. The Wolf must have heard the door shut.

Scarlett chanced a glance beside her at Benedict, finding him wide-eyed and reaching for the pistol in his belt. With a bolt of resignation, Scarlett knew she wasn't willing to risk his inexperience in a fight.

"Hold your breath," was all the warning she gave him before she grabbed his arm and jumped out the window, towing him behind her.

They hit the sludgy surface of the Thames with a slap, the pollution making it thicker than the usual consistency of water. As they surfaced, Benedict spluttered beside her. Scarlett couldn't hide her grimace either as she dashed mud from her eyes.

Thankfully, Benedict seemed able to swim. Not wanting to climb out of the river right next to the building they had just exited with so much gusto and arouse suspicion, Scarlett paddled in the direction of the sluggish flow towards a nearby dock. Reaching the outskirts of the port, she clambered up onto one of the rickety docks, Benedict heaving himself up behind her.

"That is—" he paused to spit out the remnants of a mouthful of river water "—the second time this week you have thrown me out of a window."

They both clambered to their feet on the wooden planks. Thankfully, at this edge of the port, nobody was watching them.

"The word is defenestrated." Scarlett gathered as much of her short cropped hair as she could to squeeze the water from it. Moments like this made her grateful she had taken to lopping it off with her dagger, knowing it would make it easier to wash the muck from it.

"I didn't know they taught lower city gangsters such big words," Benedict responded.

Scarlett opened her mouth the retort that she wasn't from the lower city, but snapped her mouth shut. That wasn't something she needed to share with Benedict. Instead she said, "I don't really think you can accuse me of throwing you out a window when I went with you both times. Besides, it was worth it."

"Your ears are sharper than mine, because I didn't quite catch anything. But as excited as I am to hear your revelations, I'm even more excited to get this river water off me." Benedict swiped at his muddy face with equally soiled hands, only succeeding in smearing the sludge around. A patch of mud clung to the prominent arch of his nose. "Why don't we go back to my home to regroup and get clean."

"I'm not sure—" Scarlett started.

"I refuse to think about you trying to get clean after that using a rag and a basin," Benedict insisted, already tromping up the dock towards the street, dripping a trail of brown water. Scarlett had to take a few steps at a jog to keep up with his longer strides. Her boots squelched with every step, punctuating how much she really could use a hot bath. They were hard to come by at Granny's.

"It'll draw attention for the two of us to come in like this," she argued anyways.

"You think that I, a younger son infamous for my improper behavior, don't know how to sneak in and out of my own house?"

"Your family—"

"Won't be home," Benedict cut her off, his tone curt. "Now spend your breath walking and not arguing. I want to get these clothes off and incinerated as fast as possible."

As Benedict led the way through the back carriage entrance and into the kitchens of the duke's grand estate, Scarlett blinked to find them completely empty. It seemed that not only was his family away, but all of their staff as well. Benedict didn't seem surprised by this, tramping up the stairs to the main house without a comment.

He continued through a richly appointed sitting room to a much grander staircase leading to the upper levels. Scarlett trailed him, blinking at the moonlight sparkling off the unlit chandelier, affording the main hall a haunted look.

"Pick any bathroom at the end of that hall you like." Benedict gestured vaguely to the left as they reached the top of the stairs. "They're all just wasted space right now."

Scarlett hesitated, but Benedict didn't even wait for her to turn away before he started shucking off his shirt. Catching the barest glimpse of dark curls leading down from his navel as he lifted the cloth, Scarlett whirled around to contemplate the row of doors at the end of the hall.

Walking past them, she reached out and opened one at random. She found it to be a bedroom, although rather bare. The mattress was stripped of any linens and the walls and mantlepiece devoid of any decoration.

Scarlett moved to the next door and almost moaned in relief when she found it to be a bathroom, most of the space dominated by a clawfoot tub. Although somebody as tall as Benedict might have to bend his knees to soak, Scarlett would be able to sink right to her chin. The image of Benedict in the bathtub jumped back into her mind, and she shook her head to be rid of it. His ceaseless flirting and comfort with undress was turning her mind.

Instead, she shut the door behind her, gratefully shucking off her clothes and removing the weapons beneath. Knives fell with a clatter to the tile at her feet. She tried to bathe as quickly as she could, scrubbing dirt from under her fingernails and rubbing at her face until it was positively raw. After all, she was only here because of her mission to keep Georgette safe. And she was only bathing here because she was sure Benedict didn't want her making his house smell like the Thames. Still, as she rubbed the bar of floral soap she found on the shelf through her hair and let the grime from her skin turn the water brown, she found herself involuntarily relaxing. A luxurious bath like this was almost like something from her life before...

Scarlett shook herself from that train of thought and finished cleaning with brutal efficiency. Stepping from the tub, she looked down at her pile of muddy clothes in disappointment. She didn't relish putting them back on, but her only other change of clothes was in her trunk back at Granny's. She washed them as best she could in the tub, even sacrificing some of the expensive soap to the cause. Wringing them out, she pulled the sodden clothes back on with a shiver. They may be cold, but at least they were cleaner. She ran fingers through her hair quickly, declaring it good enough as soon as it stopped sticking out from her head in every conceivable direction.

Trying not to think about how much mud she had left in the tub, Scarlett ventured from the bathroom. The door at the end of the hallway in the direction Benedict had gone was still closed, and she saw no trace of him.

It didn't do to linger outside his door while he bathed, so Scarlett picked her way downstairs, taking in her surroundings more thoroughly than she had on the way in. While the house itself was certainly grand, bedecked with carved woodwork and impressive fireplaces, it seemed rather sparse. There was very little art on the walls, and even the furniture seemed scarce. It was almost as if the Pearces were moving out. Perhaps they had purchased a different house here in town.

As Scarlett wandered through the living room to the front parlor, her breath caught in her throat. Positioned under the window was a pianoforte, dimly illuminated by the light from the rising moon. Sheet music was strewn in haphazard piles on the bench, and the cover lay open, ivory keys gleaming as if invitation.

Ignoring the feeling that she was doing something forbidden, Scarlett approached the instrument. Reaching out, she let her fingers just brush over the keys, a featherlight touch, not even enough to make a sound. She itched to sit down on the bench but didn't want to leave a watermark on the satin cushion.

Holding her breath, she cautiously picked out the first few notes of a familiar melody, the memory hidden in the recesses of her memory coated in dust and cobwebs. As the opening tones of the song echoed through the empty room, a lump rose in Scarlett's throat. She swallowed thickly to dispel it, even as she found herself blinking rapidly. Her soul shuddered within her body as if trying to escape the confines of her skin, trying to force her to want things that were long gone.

Even as she willed herself to step away and not lose herself in the song from her past, her fingers continued to play unbidden, just a few more stilted bars. There were so few things Scarlett allowed herself to miss from before her parents were killed, focusing instead on surviving. But music—it awakened a part of her heart she had long considered dead.

"You play?"

Scarlett snatched her hand from the piano as if burned by it, whirling on her heel to find Benedict leaning on the doorframe. His still-damp hair clung to his neck in dark swirls. While he had put on pants, his top half was clad only in a burgundy dressing robe, the angle of his body causing it to drape open and reveal a triangle of chest dusted with dark hair.

Scarlett blinked, Benedict's single raised eyebrow reminding her he had asked a question.

"A little," she answered noncommittally, stepping away from the instrument.

"Well aren't you full of surprises." Benedict stepped closer. "I would say you should accompany me, since I haven't had anybody to play with my singing in quite a while."

"You sing?" Scarlett asked in disbelief.

"How else am I supposed to serenade my lovers on their balconies?"

"Then I guess you will have to recruit one of them to play for you, assuming they're not too busy swooning at your feet."

Benedict grinned wide, revealing a chipped bottom tooth. "Now you understand my struggles. Come on, let's get something to eat." Benedict led the way back down to the kitchen before rummaging through cupboards as if he did so all the time. He lit the stove and put the kettle on with practiced hands while Scarlett leaned against the wooden counter, looking on with her head cocked.

"The son of a duke makes his own tea?" she questioned.

"Younger son," Benedict clarified as he pulled out two cups. "We don't warrant quite the same bowing and scraping."

"I would have assumed that you would have been able to charm your servants into the same sort of service."

"Alas, my brother has a whole regiment under his command at his post in the army, and they seem to be immune to my charms. What is left of our bare-bones staff is in the country with my mother and younger sister. We have only a carriage driver here now, and he'll be out for the night." Benedict imitated Scarlett's posture, leaning on his hands behind him as they waited for the water to boil.

"And your father?"

"He'll stumble in sometime well after dawn, most likely after getting kicked out of several gambling halls. I got my roguish ways from somewhere after all." Benedict offered Scarlett another crooked smile, but this one lacked the dazzling effects of his usual grins. His eyes weren't in it.

"Is...is that how you got entangled with the Wolves?" Scarlett asked haltingly. She had told herself it didn't matter why Benedict was entrapped with lower city scum, only that he could help her save Georgette. Still, the empty cavern of a house combined with emptiness of Benedict's perpetually dancing gaze pushed her to ask.

"Like me, Father doesn't know how to quit," Benedict said with a lopsided shrug, staring at the ground. "While I tend to be tenacious in pursuing beautiful women though, Father is likely to double-down in games of chance whenever he's losing. First we had to sell off some paintings, and then let go of some staff. Eventually though, the Wolves demanded he pay his debts in full, and when he didn't have the money...well..." Benedict shrugged.

"What about your brother?"

"He's been stationed abroad for so long, being a responsible heir by serving king and country. I had hoped to be able to handle things without bothering him, be more than the middle sibling only good for throwing parties and telling jokes. Alas, I don't seem to be having much luck being the child who can solve problems, only make them." Benedict seemed to be attempting to plaster his rakish demeanor back in place, but it was slow to adhere after his moment of vulnerability.

Scarlett searched for something to say to his admission, looking for kind words to soothe Benedict's guilt and finding them difficult to grasp. As if she had spent so long being a shadow for the Raptors she couldn't remember how to offer words of comfort. The whistling of the kettle saved her from her ineptitude as Benedict turned away and busied himself with the tea. By the time he faced her again, offering her a teacup, his confident demeanor was back.

"As much as our most recent escapades might have ended in trouble, we are also making steps to solving our shared problem it seems," Scarlett commented as she took it from him. She lifted the cup to her lips and let the steam warm her face, combating the chill from where her damp clothes clung to her skin.

"I was too busy trying not to breathe so as not to draw attention to hear what was being said below," Benedict admitted sheepishly.

"They mentioned the viscount's ball. Something about hunting down bigger purses there. It appears that they're targeting more socialites than just the Wards."

"Well then it would seem to me that our next stop should be the viscount's ball. I can't say I'm disappointed that our next expedition should not involve a swim in the Thames. And it can serve a dual purpose if you attend as Georgette. I can put on an excellent show of wooing you on the dance floor." Benedict sipped his own tea.

"Just make sure you aren't so busy waltzing me into a stupor that we don't keep our eyes peeled for a stray Wolf."

"So you admit I could waltz you into a stupor? Don't worry, I shall be prepared to catch you if you swoon," Benedict teased.

Scarlett hid her smile in her teacup. As much as she dreaded the heat of a wig and the stress of pretending to be Georgette, spying on the Wolves at a ball didn't seem to be the worst turn this investigation had taken.

Chapter Six

Amos was in the type of dark mood that made Scarlett itch to wrap herself in shadows until she could disappear, slipping from the Roost and the violent atmosphere brewing within. Instead, she planted her feet and crossed her arms as she stood before where Amos sprawled across his wooden bar stool as if it were a throne.

"Tonight is going to be a good haul for the Raptors," Amos declared with his signature oily grin. Scarlett ground her heels into the rough wooden floorboards to avoid shifting her weight in discomfort. Still, she longed for another night of slipping threatening notes onto people's pillows. After all, she preferred delivering threats to actual violence.

"In fact, tonight, we will be paying a house call to Mr. Davies."

Scarlett's stomach twisted into a knot at the name. She had slid a note onto Mr. Davies' pillow, between him and his sleeping wife, not three nights prior. A repeat visit could only mean the debt remained unpaid. From the bruisers surrounding Scarlett, it appeared that Amos planned to extract his payment in other ways.

Scarlett furrowed her brow.

"Mr. Davies has the ear of the king. Are you sure roughing him up wouldn't cause more trouble than it's worth? I could always tack on some interest in the valuables I steal, to drive home our message." Scarlett added the last bit on with a shrug.

"Oh, he won't call the Royal Police on the Raptors if he knows what's good for him." Amos waved a dismissive hand. "After all, he would have to tell them why we were paying him a visit in the first place."

Scarlett nodded, keeping her face blank. A warning bell rang in the back of her mind though. After all, Mr. Davies likely owed the Raptors money after a few unlucky hands of cards. While gambling was generally the purview of the gangs, it wasn't technically illegal. The worst the Royal Police would do to Mr. Davies for gambling would be to give him a disapproving look.

"Timothy and Thomas will be coming with for security. The three of us will pay a visit to the upstairs bedroom while Scarlett combs the downstairs for appropriate offerings to resolve his debts," Amos ordered, drawing Scarlett from her thoughts.

"How much does this man owe? If it's not that much, I could always slip in and relieve Mrs. Davies of her jewelry without risking the Raptors being implicated." Scarlett aimed for nonchalance.

"I'm starting to think you don't want the Raptors to get their due. Are you saying we should let our marks just skip out on their payment?"

Scarlett shrugged one shoulder, resisting the urge to squirm under Amos's stare. He contemplated her with one eyebrow raised, head cocked to the side like a predator. Shadows coalesced at Scarlett's fingertips, just bare traces of smoke that took significant willpower to disperse.

"You spend a few days running around the upper city and you think you're one of them now? That you're better than us?"

The blood froze in Scarlett's veins. Did the Wolves mention her and Benedict's deal with them to Amos? He would not be pleased with her making promises to other gangs behind his back—especially ones she didn't intend to keep.

"Oh yes, we've seen you leaving Granny's in those fancy dresses, probably trying to charm some man out of their purse, thinking you could pass as a lady."

Scarlett's heart stuttered to a hesitant start in her chest again. Amos didn't seem to know about her arrangement with the Benedict. Still, he pressed on.

"You know, you've always acted like you're better than the rest of us—renting a room at Granny's instead of living at the Roost. But putting on a fancy dress doesn't change anything. You're a killer like the rest of us. Your neck would have been stretched with the rest of the Talented in the Inquiries if you weren't under the protection of the Raptors."

Scarlett reared back as if she had been slapped in the face. She only managed to avoid sneering at Amos by gritting her teeth so hard they creaked in her skull. His words burrowed under her skin like knives heading straight for her heart, because she knew they were true.

Her room at Granny's was the one shred of separation Scarlett had left between herself and her life with the Raptors. Going home to her own space, no matter how tiny, allowed her to compartmentalize her nocturnal crimes. It didn't change the facts though. She had too much blood on her hands to ever be anything other than what she was now. It didn't make a difference how many strolls through the park she took or balls she attended with Benedict.

Amos seemed to sense his victory in her silence, offering a slimy smirk. "Now be a good shadow and help us take our due."

Scarlett nodded, mentally tallying the weight of her knives strapped against her skin and offering up a silent prayer that they wouldn't be spilling blood tonight.

Scarlett's lungs screamed for air as she held her breath, waiting for the night watch to pass her hiding spot where she crouched under a hedge. Her shadows coalesced around her in a cool mist, dense enough in the dark of night that they wouldn't see if they happened to glance this way. Still, Scarlett had learned the hard way that her ability to avoid being seen didn't help if her enemies could hear her panicked breathing.

The polished standard boots of the Royal Police tromped by before disappearing around the corner. Scarlett inched out from beneath the brambles, thoroughly dusty and covered in tiny scratches. She waited a moment for the officers to get far enough away that they wouldn't hear her boots scrape along the cast iron before launching herself at the fence surrounding the Davies' garden. She made quick work of the climb, her wiry muscles long since having developed the strength to lift her slight frame.

Dropping lightly to her feet inside the fence, she unlocked the gate from the inside so the rest of the Raptors could follow her without having to replicate the climb. Thomas and Timothy might be strong, but their muscles were more useful for punching than climbing. Darting past the sterile hedges towards the house, she fell into a crouch just in front of the main door and pulled her shadows tight to her back. Even if Scarlett wasn't the quickest lock pick in the Raptors, she had the advantage of being able to avoid detection while she worked, making her a valuable advance guard for the gang.

Several attempts later, and a bitten tongue to avoid cursing audibly, the pins clicked into place under her picks and the knob turned. In place of an exclamation of victory, Scarlett let out a low trill like that of a nightingale to signal the Raptors that the way was clear. Even as she glanced back towards the gate to shield the bruiser's passage, she winced at her own birdcall. It felt on the nose for the Raptors to imitate the calls of birds to signal each other, and Scarlett struggled to master the sounds.

As the thugs and Amos did their best to sneak across the lawn, Scarlett slipped inside, finding herself in a marble entrance hall. Although the impressive chandelier wasn't lit, the moonlight streaming in through the tall windows reflected off the marble, bouncing of the crystals in the light fixture, casting a strangely ethereal glow considering that she was breaking and entering.

Amos and the thugs ruined the stillness of the house as they pushed in the door, tramping where Scarlett had tiptoed. Now that they were away from the potentially prying eyes on the street, Scarlett let the shadows drip away from all of them, the darkness slipping away back into hidden corners.

With a jerk of his chin, Amos indicated that Scarlett should begin raiding the ground floor.

"We're going to greet our unknowing host and his lovely wife," Amos growled. The violent grins Timothy and Thomas gave in response sent shivers down Scarlett's spine. She turned away to focus on her task as the men headed up the stairs.

The first room off the hall was a parlor. An enameled clock shimmering with inlaid crystals glimmered on an end table, and Scarlett snatched it up to shove in the satchel slung across her back. She picked her way through the richly appointed room, stepping past silk upholstered chairs and velvet curtains in her search. She nabbed an engraved silver plate off the mantle and a snuffbox inlaid with what appeared to be jade.

She was about to search for an office, hoping for a safe she could crack, when movement at the window caught her eye. Scarlett ducked behind the heavy velvet drape. She poked her head around just in time to see five men walk through the still-open gate, the shape of their helmets giving them away as Royal Policemen. Scarlett stood frozen for half a second before turning and bolting. Forgoing any illusions of secrecy, the soles of her boots slapped the ground as she crossed back through the marble foyer and bounded up the stairs. Seeing light at the end of the upstairs hall, she sprinted towards it.

"Police!" she shouted as she rounded the corner.

The sight that met her in the bedroom was a grim one, Mr. Davies sprawled on the ground, pitiful groans escaping from behind his hands where he clutched his nose. Timothy held Mrs. Davies by the hair, keeping her pinned and unable to help her husband.

Amos froze, his foot already pulled back as if to kick Mr. Davies in the spleen.

"You're sure?"

"They're here! We need to make ourselves scarce," Scarlett panted. She thought she could hear the front door slamming open downstairs.

Instead of running, Amos snarled, focus turning back to the man cowering at his feet. "You thought you could get the Royal Police to protect you? As if you're innocent yourself?"

"Had to stop you..." Mr. Davies mumbled, voice clogged as if he were speaking through a broken nose.

"Nobody crosses the Raptors," Amos declared, voice as sharp as the blade that sprang into his hand. A wet *shink* filled the room as Amos dragged the blade across Mr. Davies' throat before his wife's ear-piercing scream split the air.

Scarlett stood frozen in horror as his body slumped to the floor, the floral design of the rug darkening as it was soaked with blood. Then time picked up again double speed as a battalion of police officers crashed through the door.

The leader shouted, but Scarlett couldn't make out his words through Mrs. Davies' screaming. Timothy lost hold of her as she thrashed, throwing herself to the ground on top of her dying husband as she wrenched herself free.

As the police officers charged forward into the mayhem, Amos grabbed Timothy and Thomas by their collars, shoving them towards the officers like human shields. Scarlett's shadows sprung up around her without a thought, instinctually shielding her from the violent scene. The police grappled with the bruisers, struggling to subdue them with their clubs. One officer pulled out a pistol and waved it around helplessly, seemingly hesitant to fire in such close quarters. Another threw himself down next to Mr. Davies, using his hands to try and staunch the blood streaming from his neck. His efforts were hindered by Mrs. Davies clinging to him desperately, leaving crimson handprints on his crisp uniform.

Scarlett shoved herself back into a corner, seemingly unnoticed in her thick patch of shadows that the two lit oil lamps were unable to disperse. In the mayhem, she almost missed the flutter of Amos's coat as he launched himself from the window to escape the scene, unsurprisingly indifferent to the fate of Timothy and Thomas.

Scarlett looked around for her own escape route, desperate to get away before she was noticed. Thomas grappled with the officers between her and the windows, fists and clubs flying in a violent whirlwind. Scarlett fingered the blades at her wrists but knew joining the fight would mean getting arrested. She couldn't go to prison—not when Georgette was still counting on her.

Her gaze snagged on the empty fireplace on the wall next to her. Only ashes lay in the grate, no fire necessary in the warm spring weather. Scarlett glanced towards the chaos of the room one final time, the sight of Mr. Davies limp on the carpet searing into her mind before she ducked below the mantle and crouched in the fireplace.

Reaching up, rough bricks scraped her fingertips as she traced the edges of the chimney. It would be a tight fit, and she would have to leave the bag of stolen trinkets behind, but she could make it. She dropped the satchel and braced her palms on opposite walls. Levering herself up, she wedged the back of her shoulders against one wall, arms bent tightly against herself to brace her palms on the brick in front of her. She squirmed determinedly, worming her way up until she could find purchase with the toes of her boots on the edge of the chimney.

The passage was too tight for her to climb properly. Instead, she had to shimmy, pushing herself up with her hands and feet as the majority of her weight was supported by her back pressed flush against the wall behind her.

Scarlett bit her lip to suppress a yelp as a sharp brick raked across her shoulder blade, not wanting to ruin her escape by making too much noise. Still, her shirt loosened around her indicating that it had ripped, and a warm trickle down her back told her she was bleeding. Still, she wriggled onward, gaining ground by inches. Her movement knocked loose soot and ash, making it fall onto her face and into her eyes. She desperately tried to blink it from her burning eyes even as the smokey air and compression on her ribs made it hard to breath.

Scarlett looked up, the hint of stars in the hazy sky peeking through the top of the chimney seeming impossibly far away. Even as she tried to calm herself and get her muscles to cooperate, panic rose in the back of her throat. Shoving it down, Scarlett clawed at the brick before her, ignoring broken nails and scraped skin as she gained another foot.

Long moments passed, and Scarlett had the hysterical thought that she would die in here, her body only to be found when the smell attracted crows or somebody lit a fire and noticed the smoke wasn't escaping properly. Just before she burst into a horrible combination of laughter and tears, fresh air brushed Scarlett's face. The top of the chimney was just inches away.

Redoubling her efforts, Scarlett managed to reach up and grab the lip of the chimney, levering herself up and out. Her arms trembled with the effort as she slumped over the edge, shoulders hanging out as she gulped down fresh air, legs still dangling in the chimney. She rested there a moment, the hysterical sobs of Mrs. Davies still filtering up from the room below. Scarlett needed to get away—as far away as possible from the corpse below.

She kicked her legs to get herself the rest of the way out of the tight passage, only to find her arms too unsteady to hold her weight after the climb. With a yelp, she tumbled from the chimney stack to the slate tiled roof below. Scarlett twisted in the air, and bright pain flashed behind her eyes as her left ankle landed under her, wrenching at an unnatural angle.

She lay on her back for a moment, panting through the sharp sensation until it faded to a manageable throbbing. Gingerly she sat up before using the chimney to haul herself up, keeping her weight on her uninjured side. She slowly tested her left foot and let out a sigh of relief as she found that it held her weight. Still, it throbbed angrily enough that it would keep her from running or jumping.

Weighing her options, Scarlett searched around from her vantage point on the roof. There was no trace of Amos, indicating he had fled the scene while leaving the rest of the Raptors to fend for themselves—not that she expected anything more from him. However she did spot figures moving on the street, the gleam of moonlight off helmets indicating that more Royal Police were coming. Her chances of getting out of the upper city unnoticed dwindled before her eyes. Shadows could conceal her somewhat, but injured as she was, Scarlett would move too slowly to go completely unnoticed. She wasn't in good shape for a fight either.

She cast about the roof frantically. It wouldn't be ideal to hide here until the police left the area, but she might be able to wait them out. As she searched for a place to hunker down, her gaze caught on familiar gables a few houses over—the duke's house.

Scarlett chewed her lips as she considered and then immediately stopped as she choked on a mouthful of ash that still dusted her face. Benedict had seemed sure that his family and servants wouldn't be home last night, so it was likely the same was true tonight. If Benedict was the only one in the house, she could sneak in the window and hide out there until morning without him even noticing. And if he did notice her—well then she would solve one problem at a time.

Hobbling across the tiled roof, Scarlett searched for an easy climb down and was lucky enough to find a trellis facing away from the street. With some hopping and slipping, she managed to climb down mostly using one foot. The pain when she did step on her left side nearly scattered her shadows, leaving her completely exposed, but she managed to keep herself cloaked enough to avoid notice from anybody not staring directly at the house.

Once her feet landed on the manicured lawn, Scarlett hobbled through the garden to the back fence. Another torturous climb later, she found herself in the adjacent gardens with a straight shot to the back of the duke's house.

When Scarlett reached the familiar home and picked a window, she was surprised at the quality of the locks securing them. It hadn't looked as if the Pearces had much valuable left to steal, but she remembered Gil's threatening words, and Benedict's mother and younger sister. She didn't blame the Pearces for increasing their security when the Wolves were out for their blood. Scarlett plucked the right picks from her boot and got to work.

A few minutes of concentration later, the window swung open on blessedly silent hinges. Carefully, Scarlett lifted herself into the library at the back of the house, feet landing softly on a rug that had once been soft and rich but had clearly seen better days. Turning back to the window she eased it shut behind her.

As the latch clicked, tension faded from Scarlett's shoulders, leaving her feeling heavy and limp. She leaned her head against the cool glass of the window pane and closed her eyes, only to immediately snap them open again. The image of Mr. Davies bleeding on the carpet as his wife desperately tried to keep his life force from spilling out seemed etched into the back of her eyelids. Nights like this were why she craved evenings of creeping around in the darkness alone, her only job to deliver letters, when she could feign ignorance to the violence of their contents. These missions with the Raptors, though, reminded her how far into the life of the lower city she had fallen. Amos was right: She was no better than the rest of the Raptors, whether she slept at the Roost or not. After all, she had the same blood stains on her hands.

"Little bird?"

Scarlett jolted so hard she knocked her forehead against the window pane. Her knives flew into her hands before she could think, spinning around and falling into a crouch as her ankle screamed in protest.

Benedict stood in the doorway, clad in his nightclothes. His hair was rumpled as if from restless sleep, but he clutched a cut crystal glass of brown liquid in one hand, indicating he hadn't been in bed. If Scarlett's heart hadn't hammered in apprehension from being found, she might have been breathless from how undone he appeared.

As it was, she hissed in pain as her ankle nearly gave out under her. She clutched at the embroidered footstool beside her as Benedict took a step towards her, setting his glass down on a nearby end table.

"You look terrible." His tone was concerned, surprisingly devoid of any anger from finding her trespassing in his home.

"You would too if you just climbed up a chimney," Scarlett shot back through gritted teeth. Before she could react, Benedict slid under her armpit, slinging her arm around his shoulders to act as a crutch on her weakened side.

"Silly Scarlett, that's not how St. Nicholas works," he chided. "He's supposed to come down the chimney and give you gifts, not take your things before climbing out the window. Let's go get you cleaned up."

Scarlett tried to pull away once she had her footing, cringing at the soot smears appearing on Benedict's thin nightshirt, but he stayed with her.

"How do you know I was stealing?" she retorted, distracting herself from the way Benedict's muscles bunched under her arm.

"Because I'm the one of us more likely to be sneaking in to visit a lover," Benedict countered easily.

Scarlett's snort of laughter came out as a grunt of pain when the cut on her back brushed against the edge of the doorframe they squeezed through side by side.

"Did you decide jumping out of windows lacked flair or something?" Benedict continued, carrying the conversation for her.

"There were...complications."

Now they stood at the bottom of the stairs. Scarlett stared up them with a look of dismay. Before she could grit her teeth for the trek up, gravity shifted and her feet swept out from under her.

She squawked inelegantly and flung her arms out, nearly punching Benedict in the nose as he swept her into his arms. He jostled her bumps and scrapes, even bumping her sore leg against the banister as he maneuvered up the grand staircase, but Scarlett was stunned into silence.

Her brain searched through memories for the last time she had been held and came up blank. Even when Granny had patched up her injuries when she first started running for the Raptors and ended up tumbling from roofs more often than not, she had treated her clinically. Granny's affection was practical and gruff. Benedict held her to his chest as if she were a bride he was sweeping over the threshold on their wedding night. Although his breath came faster as they trudged up to the bathrooms, he didn't utter a word of complaint.

In her shock, Scarlett's hand had come to rest on his chest, fingertips brushing bare skin at the edge of his loose neckline. She snatched it back and rubbed her fingers on the filthy cloth of her trousers to banish the feeling of his heart fluttering beneath her touch.

"I'm getting your shirt filthy," Scarlett protested. Indeed, his shirt, which had been fine and white when he found her, now was streaked with grime. Scarlett swallowed heavily at the sight of a crimson smear on one of his shoulders. She hoped the blood was hers.

"I don't get a chance to sweep ladies off their feet very often. I'm not going to pass up the opportunity when one tumbles through my window," Benedict huffed. Scarlett was glad she didn't weigh much more because Benedict was clearly unused to this much physical labor.

"I'm not a lady," she shot back.

"Clearly, or you wouldn't be letting me hold you like this." Benedict leaned in conspiratorially as he spoke, his breath tickling across her neck.

Scarlett shook her head. The delirium of her narrow escape and Benedict's incorrigible flirting were a combination headier than the Roost's strongest brandy.

They'd made it to the top of the stairs, and Benedict turned down the hall towards the bathroom he had disappeared into a few days earlier. He still didn't put her down until he could deposit her gently on the sink. Once he was sure she wasn't going to slip off, he turned to light a lamp, revealing pale blue tile and a massive clawfoot tub taking up one half of the room.

"So can I ask why you broke into my house looking like you were on the business end of a flock of angry hummingbirds, or should I just enjoy the midnight visit and not ask questions?" Benedict questioned as he rummaged around in the cabinet behind the mirror.

Scarlett bit her lip. She had managed to distract herself with finding a place to hide and tending her injuries, and Benedict's question reminded her why she had visited this part of town in the first place. Why it was a very bad idea to be sitting on a nobleman's sink when she had just been engaged in very un-noble things.

Benedict turned back to her with a brown glass bottle and a roll of bandages in hand. He cocked his head to the side, still waiting on her answer.

"I had to pay a visit to one of your neighbors," Scarlett hedged.

"I take it this wasn't a social call?"

"I wish it were, but my acquaintances get very finicky when people lose money at the gambling tables and don't pay up." Scarlett sighed.

Benedict unstoppered the brown bottle, pouring some of the contents onto a clean cloth. As he approached Scarlett, the sharp tang of rubbing alcohol assaulted her nose.

"It seems that my father isn't the only one on this street who wagers more than he has then," Benedict commented as he picked up Scarlett's hand where it lay on the counter and began dabbing at the ripped skin with the cloth.

Scarlett's wince wasn't just from the sting of the alcohol as it touched open wounds. Benedict's current predicament was caused by lower city gangs' intimidation tactics when it came to collecting debts. Mr. Davies' death would only prove that he was right to be scared and comply with the Wolves' demands.

Scarlett should pull her hand from his and tend to herself. It seemed wrong to let Benedict care for her when people like her were the reason his life was in danger. He held her hand gently though, wiping at it with a level of care that Scarlett hadn't experienced in a long time—that she likely didn't deserve. In the aftermath of the night's chaos, Scarlett didn't have it in herself to deny herself the moment of comfort.

"I didn't mean to wake you," Scarlett admitted. "I was hoping I could hide here until the Royal Police had gone. I thought you might not even notice."

"I was awake anyways," Benedict commented.

"You keep later hours than I thought."

Benedict shook his head, loose hairs brushing against his neck. "I don't sleep much these days. Too busy worrying about my mother and sister...my father. Wishing I was better equipped to help them. Alas, dancing and flirting don't do much to get us out of the mess we've found ourselves in."

"I'm sorry," Scarlett murmured as Benedict finished with her hands.

"For what?" He motioned to her ankle, and Scarlett held out her leg for him to inspect.

Scarlett shrugged, unable to articulate exactly what she was apologizing for. For breaking in through his window in the middle of the night? For further entangling him in the violence of the lower city? For being a murderer?

"You know, I knew you were in the gangs when I agreed to work with you," Benedict said, beginning to wrap a bandage around her ankle, tight enough to stabilize the weak joint. "It's not like it comes as a shock to me that you're involved in some...unsavory happenings. Although to be fair, many members of polite society are involved in unsavory dealings too, although they're just less open about it, but that's beside the point. My point is, the first time I met you, you were risking your life to save Georgette's. The next time I saw you, you put your head on the chopping block to save mine. So even if you do make a habit of breaking into people's homes in the dead of night, I have no reason to hold it against you. Besides, I was willing to kill to save my family. I can't blame you for the same."

Scarlett swallowed thickly, glad that Benedict's gaze was cast down at where her foot rested against his chest as he tied off the wrap. She didn't think she could handle meeting his eyes right now. He might be wrong, but Scarlett didn't have it in her to shatter this image he had built of her. She couldn't bear to mar this view of her as somebody kind and virtuous with the smear of her guilt.

"How's that feel?" Benedict asked, gesturing to her ankle.

Scarlett gave it an experimental wiggle and found the bandages did a good job at keeping it immobile. The makeshift splint would offer enough support for her to limp back to Granny's.

As she let her foot dangle again, Benedict stepped forward, thighs nearly brushing her knees where they hung off the edge of the sink. Scarlett had to tilt her head back to see his expression. Shadows under his eyes marred his handsome face, betraying an exhaustion which echoed in Scarlett's bones. Where she hid her weariness with shadows in the dark of night, Benedict disguised his with jokes and dazzling smiles. Now though, in the quiet of the bathroom, his face serious, the worries that weighed on him were as clear as day.

His hand drifted up to brush her temples, pushing stray hairs away from an abrasion she sustained during the climb.

"I'm glad you weren't seriously injured," he said. His voice was quiet but echoed loudly in the tiled bathroom.

"It would certainly have put a damper on our plans," Scarlett agreed.

"That's not what I meant." Benedict braced on hand on the counter next to Scarlett's hip, the other still lingering on her hairline, near the cut on her forehead.

Without her telling them to, Scarlett's legs opened so he could step into the gap between her thighs. He encroached on her space, near enough now that his chest brushed against her tattered shirt as he inhaled. Scarlett breathed in as well, Benedict's scent of citrus and earth and the whiskey clinging to his breath enveloping her as he stood so close.

Scarlett's breath stuttered. Benedict's gaze drifted from her forehead her mouth at the sound. She should push him away—he wasn't even supposed to know she was in his house, let alone treat her injuries. Let alone look at her mouth with something warm and intangible in his gaze.

Unable to meet those eyes that held something far too close to softness, Scarlett's gaze drifted down to where his shirt lay open across his chest. The red smear of blood across one shoulder snapped her back to reality so forcefully she nearly heard the crack in her mind. She jerked back, bumping against the wall behind her.

As her injured shoulder blade made contact with the tile behind her, she hissed at the stinging cold, shattering the charged moment. The tension had probably only been in Scarlett's head anyways, a product of fading adrenaline and Benedict's relentlessly flirtatious nature. While she was no stranger to brief romantic liaisons, she shouldn't encourage Benedict. After all, he couldn't possibly be interested in Scarlett as more than a useful ally. She was a criminal covered in soot, smearing her grime all over his home and his life. As soon as they disentangled themselves from the Wolves, Scarlett would slip back into the shadows of the lower city, never to see him again. She shouldn't leave any stains on Benedict's life, or any loose ends her mind would cling to.

"Where else are you hurt?" Benedict asked, focus returning to the task at hand. Scarlett drew her gaze from the lines of concern knitting his brows to display her back to him.

"I think I cut my back," Scarlett explained.

"You really did a number on it." Benedict inspected the wound through the rip in her shirt before moving in with his cleaning solution and bandages. Scarlett had a brief moment of gratitude that the cut was on the opposite side of her Raptors tattoo, so she wouldn't have to reveal that tonight too. If Benedict's fingers lingered on the nape of her neck as he wrapped the bandage around her shoulder, it was probably just Scarlett's imagination searching for comfort after such a chaotic night.

Chapter Seven

The bright light of midday assaulted Scarlett's eyes, even as it filtered in through the tiny window facing the shadowed alley in her room. She felt like she had been run through a mill, muscles filled with a heavy ache and tiny cuts stinging her skin from head to toe. Something familiar but unexpected pulled at the back of her mind, and she peeled her eyes open further to see shadows dancing around her form where she huddled under a threadbare blanket. She gasped, and they dispersed like mice frightened by a cat, skittering away to meld back in with the darkened corners of the room.

Scarlett took several deep breaths, carefully walling off the part of her mind that controlled her Talent. It had been years since she had lost control of her shadows in her sleep, having carefully tamped down her Talent during the years of the Inquiries. Not since she had first come to Granny's had she summoned shadows in her sleep, emotion overcoming her in her dreams as her unconscious mind replayed the image of her mother and father being dragged from their home on repeat.

Her dream last night had been very different. The ephemeral image of her sitting at the piano in the Duke of Pearce's house, playing a familiar melody as Benedict watched, smiling, slipped farther from her mind as she thought about it.

With a groan, she pulled the threadbare blanket over her head and took a few deep breaths. As she did, she noticed her hands were still carefully bandaged, evidence that her midnight visit to the Duke of Pearce's house had not been a dream, although it had been far less pleasant than her imaginings. In the bright light of day, it seemed hard to believe that the younger son of a duke had tended injuries she sustained while breaking into his neighbor's house. Perhaps the night had seemed like a dream to him too.

Thinking of Benedict, Scarlett shoved the sheets down with a huff. They had an appointment today, and Scarlett needed to get to work if she was going to transform herself into a lady that could pass as Georgette by the time she was supposed to meet him in the market.

It ended up taking Scarlett the better part of an hour to scrub off the remainder of the soot from the night before, and even then black crescents lingered under her torn nails. Scarlett hid them under long white gloves, covering the rest of her injuries with a powder blue dress featuring long lacy sleeves. A flowered hat completed the ensemble, and by the time she looked in the warped mirror propped on top of her trunk, Scarlett could almost convince herself that she hadn't spent the night before sneaking around covered in ash and blood. Almost. The rage and revulsion at Amos's careless spilling of blood was harder to disguise.

As she tromped down the stairs, heavy footfalls at odds with her ladylike ensemble, Granny met her at the bottom of the stairs.

"Bad dream?" the wizened woman asked as a good morning.

Scarlett shook her head, but Granny looked her up and down appraisingly.

"It's just been a while since I woke up to darkness curling under my door," Granny said, voice heavy with meaning.

Scarlett swallowed thickly, nodding. Granny had risked the wrath of the Inquiries by helping Scarlett hide her Talent years ago. Even if it wasn't illegal anymore, she would do well to keep it under control.

Granny hobbled away without another word, and Scarlett hurried out the door. Thankfully, the square where she planned to meet Benedict wasn't more than a ten-minute walk from Granny's, although it took her almost double that with her sore ankle. Still, Benedict's wrap from last night held, and it seemed not to be broken.

When she arrived in the square, Benedict stood next to the sleek black carriage, leaning against it casually.

"I have a treat," he announced as Scarlett approached, dipping his head and sweeping off his hat in greeting.

"A treat?" Scarlett inquired, glad that their rhythm didn't seem any different than it had before last night. The intimacy of the quiet moments in the bathroom stayed hidden in the dark of night, where it belonged, away from the harsh scrutiny of daylight.

"I figured that you might not be in the mood to walk today, and so I prepared a bit of a diversion for us." Benedict opened the door of the carriage for her and pulled down the step. He held out a hand to help her inside, and when Scarlett leaned on it more heavily as she put her weight on her tender ankle, he didn't comment.

Once Benedict stepped up after her, he took the bench opposite and rapped sharply on the roof to tell the driver to set off.

"You know, hiding us in a carriage won't get the word out that you're courting Georgette," Scarlett pointed out.

"That's true, but there's a bit of an outing planned at a nearby estate. It'll be the talk of the town that I brought you with. I even set up a bit of a picnic for us," Benedict responded with a self-satisfied smile.

Scarlett had to admit it was a good idea. Not to mention, people would give them a wide enough berth that they could speak without being overheard.

The carriage left London behind them, trundling out into the countryside. It surprised Scarlett how quickly the dense shuffle of the city gave way to gentle hills, covered with grass the pale green of early spring. She couldn't remember the last time she had left town, escaping from its constant noise and pollution. The air seemed lighter out here, and Scarlett's soul lifted as she pushed back the curtain to let in more fresh air. Benedict smiled at her antics, the sun warming his dark eyes to a honey color.

It didn't take long to reach the estate in question. Scarlett spotted fine ladies playing lawn bowling and couples sitting at tables set for tea scattered around. The carriage dropped them off at the edge of the festivities, where the manicured lawn gave way to a sparse wood.

"So I have another surprise," Benedict admitted as he helped her down from the carriage. Scarlett only teetered a bit on her unsteady ankle as she balanced on the stair. "My friend who owns this estate said I could use his hunting dogs for the day. He knows I like to impress ladies with my aim."

Scarlett glanced over at the picnic table set up nearby, and her heart sank as she spotted two fine hunting rifles propped up against the table.

"I hope you are ready to be thoroughly disappointed by my skills," Scarlett admitted as they approached the table.

Benedict hefted the weapons in practiced hands, handing one to Scarlett with a raised eyebrow.

"I would have thought you would be comfortable with guns," he said, not pointing out where he would have gotten that impression. Scarlett swallowed.

"Guns don't lend themselves to secrecy very well. Too loud," she admitted. Knives were more befitting of a silent assassin.

"I guess that explains why I prefer guns. I tend to make a lot of noise," Benedict said with a grin.

A short while later, it became clear that Scarlett's assessment of the situation had been right. As the dogs chased the birds from the brush, Benedict landed shot after shot with casual ease. Dogs cheerfully deposited a growing pile of pheasants at his feet, and he gave them affectionate scratches behind the ears.

He nodded at Scarlett to take her turn, and while she leveled the sights and pulled the trigger, she couldn't even be sure she fired in the direction of the bird as it flapped off into the woods. She propped the gun at her side with a sigh.

"I told you I wasn't any good," she said.

"I suppose at some point I had to be better than you at something," Benedict commented lightly.

Scarlett cocked her head at him.

"I must admit, this is good for my wounded pride after following you around the city feeling rather useless the past week," Benedict admitted sheepishly.

"I suppose you're a good shot with a pistol too then." Scarlett considered him, thinking of the dueling pistol she had snatched from him the night they first met.

"Well I wouldn't like to brag, but I can do a few neat party tricks with one. I generally avoid shooting at people though."

Scarlett appraised him thoughtfully. Perhaps he wasn't as helpless in the lower city as she would have liked to believe him to be, if his skill with the rifle was any indication. He could be a threat with the pistol he carried if worst came to worst. She was grateful he hadn't fired when he first encountered her in the hedge maze.

"I could show you?" Benedict offered, jerking Scarlett from her thoughts.

"Excuse me?"

"Here. You're coordinated enough that I'm sure you could be a good shot too with a little practice." Benedict approached, stepping up behind her.

He motioned for her to raise her rifle, which she did. He laid his hands over hers, helping her position it against her shoulder. Stepping up close, he put his head in the gap between her cheek and his shoulder. At the feeling of his solid chest at her back, Scarlett closed her eyes, steadying herself. A stolen moment like this would do wonders to convince anybody who saw them that Benedict and Georgette's courtship was progressing.

"Look down the sights, little bird," Benedict instructed, and Scarlett peeled open her eyes to do as he asked.

As the dogs darted through the underbrush, the birds took to the air, flapping and squawking. Benedict guided her hands, tracking their movements with the barrel of the gun. As his breath caressed the skin beneath her ear, Scarlett's hands shook so hard she barely managed to pull the trigger.

Her ears rang with the crack of the bullet, even as the birds fluttered away unscathed. Benedict dropped his hands and stepped away, letting Scarlett breathe again.

"Ah well, maybe I'm a good shot but not a good teacher," Benedict said with a shrug. "Why don't we stop terrorizing pheasants and have some refreshment?" he asked, gesturing to the low table set up on a nearby patch of grass.

Scarlett nodded her agreement, glad for the reprieve. As Benedict busied himself with the picnic basket, Scarlett took a deep breath to steady herself. This was all an act.

"I said I had a treat," Benedict turned around with a covered dish in his hands.

"Hunting and a picnic with your fine self isn't treat enough?" Scarlett found herself teasing, immediately biting her lip. Put her in a fine dress and apparently she was about to turn into an insufferable flirt, fluttering eyelashes and all.

"Well, it is, but I brought something especially for you." With a flourish, Benedict whipped the cover off the plate to reveal a kipper, topped with herbs and melting butter.

Scarlett's heart fluttered in her chest like a hummingbird even as her mouth watered at the delicious scent wafting off the plate. It was easy to pretend that a picnic like this was meant for Georgette and that Scarlett was just playing a part. But the kipper—Benedict had brought those for *her*.

"They aren't a particularly romantic picnic food, I'll admit. But you said they were your favorite, so I figured, why not? I think I did a good job with a wine pairing for such an unconventional dish too." Benedict passed the plate to Scarlett and turned to the basket to dig out a bottle, completely oblivious to the odd warmth blooming in Scarlett's chest and radiating up to her face. She took the reprieve to compose herself.

In a matter of moments, they each had a plate of kipper with a piece of fluffy white bread and a full glass of wine.

"Cheers." Benedict lifted his glass to Scarlett before taking a healthy sip. "I have to say, this is quite lovely. I feel bad that Georgette is missing her opportunities to have this for real."

Scarlett glanced around, but the only people she could see were several ladies playing croquet across the lawn. Even though they shot curious glances at the couple, as was the plan, they were well out of earshot.

"I would think so too," Scarlett admitted. "But she's glad to escape from the matchmaking of the social season."

"She isn't interested in making a good match? Isn't she Mr. Ward's only daughter?"

"It's more that she's already set her sights on somebody," Scarlett hedged. These weren't her secrets to tell.

"Well then, she's still missing a proper courtship with him. What's an engagement without being preceded by secluded picnics and wild rides through the countryside?" Benedict argued.

Scarlett avoided saying that was unlikely to be the case, given that Leon came from significantly less money than Benedict. Still, something in the pit of her stomach grew heavy at the reminder that he and Georgette weren't engaged yet. Leon had not returned from his trip to collect his family's blessings.

"Do you know Leon Blayford?" Scarlett blurted before she could think better of it.

"The art dealer?" Benedict asked, taken aback by what must seem to be an abrupt change of subject. "He's purchased some of the paintings my family had to...liquidate."

"When was the last time he bought a painting from you?"

"Probably several months ago. Why? Is he about to receive a visit of an unsavory sort?"

Scarlett shot him a look. "No, but he's traveling and has been gone quite a bit longer than was expected."

Understanding dawned on Benedict's face. Scarlett was unsure whether or not she was relieved that Benedict had figured out the purpose of her questioning without her having to explain it.

"And you and Georgette are interested in seeing him return safely I take it," Benedict clarified, to which Scarlett responded with a nod.

"There is a statue in the house that I've been trying to hold onto but may need to sell. I might put in an inquiry with his assistant and see when Mr. Blayford might be available to take a look at it."

Scarlett nodded her gratitude. As much as it twisted her gut to be relying on Benedict both to help her find Leon and to protect Georgette, she was glad she'd have some good news for her friend next time she visited.

Chapter Eight

A groan bubbled up in Scarlett's throat as Georgette held up a tiara in the mirror. The wig of chestnut curls was heavy enough without an additional headpiece.

"How do you stand having your hair pinned up and bejeweled all the time without getting a headache?" Scarlett bemoaned as Georgette worked the shimmering accessory into the wig.

"You've just gotten so accustomed to short hair that your scalp isn't used to it anymore," Georgette commented. "Honestly, I'm a little jealous of how pretty you look with hair that barely covers your ears. I don't think I'd look good if I lopped mine off."

Scarlett bit her tongue. Her hair had been waist length before she hacked it all off with a dull knife. Without a lady's maid to help her manage it—or even a hairbrush for that matter—it had become a veritable rat's nest, unable to be salvaged. Only weeks after her parents' deaths, she knelt in a back alley and hacked at her hair viciously, gritting her teeth to suppress her anger. It had been about survival.

Now she smiled at Georgette in the mirror as she admired her handiwork. Something about Georgette's sweetness was a balm to the anger that bubbled under her skin, making it easier to shove down in her presence.

"This tiara is my favorite," Georgette explained as she fetched her box of cosmetics from her drawer. "It was Mother's, and it's what I would wear if I were trying to catch the attention of a duke's son."

"Younger son," Scarlett said as she closed her eyes so Georgette could apply paint to her lids.

"So all the money with none of the responsibility," Georgette teased.

Scarlett kept her mouth shut, loath to admit to anybody that the Pearces currently flirted with bankruptcy. Benedict's admission of vulnerability was something she felt the need to keep to herself.

"I've heard he's the more handsome one too."

Scarlett opened her eyes to find Georgette staring at her with mischief in her gaze.

"Not as handsome as a certain art dealer, I would say," Scarlett deflected, not wanting to think about how handsome Benedict may or may not be right now. She regretted changing the subject when Georgette's shoulders slumped.

"I still haven't heard from him," she admitted.

"Benedict is going to help me inquire after him. I'll let you know as soon as I hear anything." Scarlett patted Georgette's shoulder in comfort.

Georgette smiled softly but remained deflated.

"You're doing so much for me. I hate sitting here doing nothing. Like I'm just waiting on other people to fix my problems or something," Georgette admitted.

"You're being my friend. That's something."

"Yes, but that's hardly work."

Scarlett bit down the urge to disagree—to say that these visits with Georgette were sometimes the only thing that calmed the ball of anger that lived locked in her chest, even if it was only temporary. And Georgette risked her future by associating with Scarlett, seemingly uncaring of the scandal that would arise if the world knew that she had tea with a gangster most nights.

Now Georgette moved onto her lips, painting them a deep crimson that would generally be too eye catching for Scarlett's taste, but was perfectly in character for Georgette.

"There you go," Georgette declared with a satisfied smile. "Now he won't stop being able to think about how much he wants to kiss your lips all night."

"You mean your lips," Scarlett corrected. She was going to be pretending to be Georgette after all.

"No, I mean yours," Georgette said matter-of-factly as she stowed her cosmetics back in her vanity drawer.

"This is all an act," Scarlett reminded even as something akin to excitement fluttered in her chest.

"Yes, but that doesn't mean you can't have a little fun with it."

Scarlett busied herself with collecting a fan and handkerchief from Georgette to avoid thinking about what Georgette was implying.

While the first ball where Scarlett met Benedict had been out in a garden, open to the cool night air, the dance floor at the viscount's ball was indoors. The grand space was large enough to hold the Roost twice over, and it was packed with every member of polite society, their gossiping filling the hall with a deafening buzz. As Mr. Ward led her into the room, taking care to avoid those who would recognize her as an imposter,

Scarlett couldn't help but mentally mark all the exit points. It would be a challenge to find the Wolves' agents among the glittering masses. At least having less darkened corners to hide in and observe would mean the Wolves had fewer places to hide as well.

"Miss Ward, may I request the pleasure of having the first dance of the evening?"

A familiar voice pulled Scarlett from her contemplation of the surroundings. Benedict stood in the path of her and Mr. Ward, holding out his hand in offering.

Scarlett had seen Benedict covered in mud and in his nightclothes in the past week, but now seeing him in all his finery, she had a visceral appreciation for how he managed to leave many a heartbroken lady in his wake. His emerald green cravat matched his waistcoat, golden buttons gleaming almost as brightly as his eyes. He had kept his hair loose, letting it curl at the nape of his neck and frame his angular face. His nose, which might be considered too large by common standards, seemed to fit perfectly with his lopsided smile and eyes that danced with amusement even in the direst situations.

"She would love to," Mr. Ward answered, nudging Scarlett and giving her a stern look, probably worried about why she had been standing there motionless for several long moments.

"Of course," she demurred, doing her best impression of a flattered young lady. Benedict tucked her hand into the crook of his elbow and led her across the room to the dance floor where a string quartet played a lively tune.

Letting the volume of the music cover her words, Scarlett leaned in to murmur to Benedict, "I don't think the dance floor is going to be the best vantage point for spotting any funny business from the Wolves."

"Yes, but it would look suspicious if I didn't take several turns around the floor with you. I am known for being on the dance floor all night you know." Benedict leaned in conspiratorially. "Unless I've convinced the lady who has my attentions to duck out with me for a different sort of escape that requires far more privacy, that is."

He spoke the last words directly into the shell of Scarlett's ear, sending a subtle tremor down her spine. She brushed it off by shooting him a glare that she hoped conveyed the need to focus. He smirked back before his face fell.

"The dances, you don't know them—"

"I know enough to get by," Scarlett interjected. "I'm just...out of practice."

Benedict raised an eyebrow at her, but she didn't elaborate. He huffed in amusement.

"Dancing, playing the piano...you could pass as a proper lady if you didn't toss me out of windows so often."

"I told you, if I'm jumping out too then it hardly counts as throwing you," Scarlett argued.

At that moment the music drew to a close and the couples currently dancing on the floor parted ways with polite bows and curtsies. Benedict led Scarlett onto the floor, leading them to a place where they couldn't be missed.

As the violinist began the new song, Benedict swept Scarlett into his arms. She gulped as she recognized the opening notes of a dramatic waltz, and they were off.

Even if it had been years since Scarlett last danced, nights of running over rooftops and dodging punches had honed her coordination and balance. While Scarlett could outpace Benedict in the back alleys, he blew her away on the dance floor, just as he had while hunting. With a firm arm around her waist, Benedict swept them around in a graceful arc. Perhaps it had been too long since Scarlett had danced with a man, her parents having died before her first season out in society, but the feel of Benedict's fingers splayed across her ribcage stole her attention. As her focus zeroed in on their warm pressure, her faced warmed in a way that almost drove away the awareness of a ballroom full of gazes fixed on them.

As the musicians built to a dramatic crescendo, Benedict took the opportunity to brace both hands around her waist and lift her around him, making Scarlett's stomach swoop in a way not altogether unpleasant. She might tease him about his upper body strength compared to her when they climbed through windows, but he clearly knew what he was down on his home turf.

Placing her on her feet again, Benedict maneuvered Scarlett in a small dip, his face dropping dangerously close to her throat, near enough that his breath tickled her hammering pulse.

"Remember, you're supposed to be falling madly in love with me," he murmured low enough that nobody else could hear.

Scarlett blinked in confusion to dispel the odd feeling of drunkenness working its way through her mind.

"You look so stricken, I'm afraid people watching might think I'm stomping on your toes," Benedict continued.

Right, this was part of their elaborate show, proving to the guests—and any Wolves who might be spying—that Benedict was seducing the hapless Miss Ward out of her sizeable dowry.

"I'm afraid you're the one having to deal with bruised feet," Scarlett countered as Benedict saved her from stumbling through a turn she hadn't practiced in quite a while.

"An injury I'm more than willing to bear for uninterrupted time with a beautiful woman," Benedict responded easily. He certainly knew how to act the part of a charmer when the job demanded. It was no wonder he was starting to turn Scarlett's head.

With that, the waltz drew to a close, and Scarlett offered a wobbly curtsy. The strings began to strike up a lively quadrille, and Benedict inclined his head in question. Scarlett shook her head forcefully enough that she felt her wig shift ever so slightly. If a sedate waltz tested her muscle memory, then anything involving more coordination was sure to end in disaster. Not to mention, dancing with Benedict didn't seem conducive to keeping her wits about her.

"I could use a glass of punch," Scarlett admitted.

"Of course. You need fuel to have a properly good time at any of these balls." Benedict tucked Scarlett's gloved hand into his elbow once more. As he led her through the crowds to the adjacent parlor, Scarlett could feel the weighty gazes of dozens of London socialites trailing them. She tightened her fingers around Benedict's biceps to resist the call of her shadows, wanting to shield her from the eyes of those long considered to be unfriendly. They might not look kindly on those they considered lower city dirt, but right now she was Georgette Ward, jewel of the social season and a lady Benedict would be proud to have seen on his arm. The fashionable dress she wore, plunging low at the neckline and adorned with silvery ribbons, served as both armor and disguise.

As if hearing her thoughts, Benedict's other hand came up in a proprietary gesture to cover where she clutched his arm. Even if it was for the benefit of their audience, it helped Scarlett relax her grip and push down the beacon of safety offered by the shadows at the edge of her mind.

Once they each had a glass of punch in hand, Scarlett situated them in the alcove of a bay window where they could observe the room as a whole while also being seen by any gossip who might look their way.

As Scarlett settled herself into the window seat, she took a moment to glance out the window. Through the glass, the darkened city looked peaceful and quiet. From the top of the hill, the viscount's house had a view of a vast swath of London, twinkling street lights leading down to the middle city until they trailed off into the darkness of the lower city. Shadows covered the streets until they reached the Thames, where moonlight glittered off the sluggish water. Even though Scarlett could see the lower city from here, imagining the brawls and thefts that would occur on a night like this, it seemed a world away from the glittering spectacle of this ball. It felt impossible that bloody-knuckled gangsters could exist on the same streets as these refined socialites, living such different lives in the same space. It gave Scarlett whiplash to run jobs with the Raptors one night and then dance in the arms of a duke's son the next.

"Where do you think the Wolves would plant their agents at a party like this?" Benedict murmured, pulling Scarlett's attention away from the window and back to the party where it belonged.

"It's hard to say," Scarlett admitted. "As far as I knew, Nathanial Woodrow was the only gangster ever to frequent society balls. I doubt the Wolves have an undercover agent like that on the guest list. My guess is that this is a surreptitious backroom rendezvous situation."

"We could always pretend to sneak off for a rendezvous of our own and see if we find anything," Benedict suggested.

"And risk missing our lead because we were wandering around the house? I think not," Scarlett retorted. "Besides, I'm here to make it seem like you're courting Georgette, not to ruin her status."

"You think a man of my reputation hasn't learned how to be discreet?" Benedict clapped a hand to his chest in exaggerated offense.

"If you were discreet, then you wouldn't have the reputation." Scarlett took a delicate sip of her champagne.

Benedict's responding chuckle was low and warm. "Can't get anything past you, can I?"

Scarlett grabbed his arm to indicate he should be quiet as she spotted movement across the hall. While most of the crowd churned aimlessly, flowing and eddying into pockets of conversation only to break up and regroup in new arrangements, a few figures cut through the crowd in a direct path. The dark silhouettes of three men in suits trailed from the ballroom towards a door leading off to what appeared to be a study.

Scarlett jerked her head towards the figures. Benedict's gaze scanned the crowd, brow creased in confusion a moment before it settled. With a quick nod, he sprang to his feet, Scarlett right behind him.

She took the lead as they began weaving through the partygoers. Although her height caused her to lose sight of their targets as soon as she entered a throng of tittering ladies, she managed to slip through the clusters of partygoers relatively easily, used to going unnoticed and hindered only by the voluminous skirts she wasn't accustomed to. Benedict wasn't quite as agile, but his stature allowed him to keep sight of their quarry, and he directed Scarlett with a soft hand on her shoulder.

Soon they were across the room, standing before the door the men had disappeared through. Benedict blocked Scarlett's form with his frame as she leaned in close. The door had been left ajar, but the room beyond seemed to be empty. If there were voices, they could not be heard over the general hubbub of the party.

Cautiously, Scarlett inched the door open further, revealing a darkened library. Seeing it was empty, she opened it just wide enough to slip inside before yanking Benedict in after her.

"What are—"

Scarlett moved to press a hand to Benedict's mouth to silence him and ended up flopping her hand against his jaw in the darkness. Still, he got the message and fell silent. With the door closed behind them, muffling the music and din of conversation, the low cadence of several voices became audible. Creeping across the room, Scarlett could just make out the shape of another door, outlined in light seeping through the cracks near the floor and at the hinges.

Benedict trailed her towards the source of the voices, and Scarlett unconsciously wreathed them in even deeper shadows, despite the darkness of the room. Reaching the door, Scarlett nearly pressed herself against the wall, straining to hear the voices within.

"—hear you like games of chance," came a grating voice that plucked at something in the back of Scarlett's memory.

Benedict wedged himself between Scarlett and the bookshelf next to the door to listen as well. The warmth of his breath tickled the nape of her neck as he pressed behind her to eavesdrop.

"You're not wrong, but why go to the lower city when there are plenty of good hands of cards to be played at parties with far more creature comforts?" asked a voice with the polished accent of a society gentleman, followed by another chuckle of agreement.

"I don't think the hands of whist you play at balls have quite the same stakes the Wolves can offer you," the first voice responded, sounding like his best approximation of a posh businessman despite the natural gruffness of his tone.

"I attended two weeks ago, and I can assure you that games of dice in polite society don't hold the same...entertainment value as what the Wolves offer at their new establishment," another voice cut in.

General rumbles of agreement drifted through the door, but Scarlett couldn't manage to catch any words as multiple conversations occurred at the same time.

"So what do you say?" the Wolf asked. "Can I tell Fang to save the best seats in the house for you lovely gentlemen on Friday?"

Murmurs of ascent ran through the room.

"I better go squeeze in several dances with my wife then. Help placate her before I excuse myself from her sister-in-law's party on Friday."

Before Scarlett had time to retreat from the door, footsteps approached and it began to swing open. Benedict seemed to realize they were about to be discovered at the same moment she did, and he yanked her back into him, pulling them both behind the narrow bookshelf by the door.

Instinctually, shadows coalesced around them, making the darkness of their hiding spot denser than the gloom of the rest of the room. Several figures filed out of the back room, but Scarlett couldn't focus on identifying them. Instead, she found her mind fixated on the press of Benedict's body against hers. He had her pinned against the bookshelf, his hands braced on the shelf on either side of her hips. The wooden edge dug into the small of her back, giving her no room to retreat. Even as she took quiet, shallow breaths in an effort to remain silent, the movement caused her breasts to brush against the buttons of Benedict's waistcoat, and an unfamiliar warmth rushed from the crown of her head to the base of her spine. She had the fleeting thought that this dress was daringly lowcut compared to her usual attire.

Even as she battled for control over her racing heartbeat, Scarlett found herself enveloped by Benedict's scent as her nose lingered mere inches from his neatly tied cravat. Fresh citrus undercut by deep earthiness invaded her senses, making it impossible to focus on the murmured words of the men now pushing back into the party.

Alone in the study once more, Benedict didn't move away immediately. Scarlett peeled her hand away from where it gripped the edge of the shelf behind her, finding that she had dug her fingernails into the wood, to push Benedict away from her. She hesitated as his head dipped. As his face came closer to the space behind her ear, she could swear his breath sounded as ragged as hers had suddenly become. He seemed to shudder, shaking himself free of the moment before quickly stepping back.

With a snap, the spell was over and the sounds of revelry from the next room over rushed back in as if Scarlett had just surfaced from underwater. The light filtering in from the cracked door silhouetted Benedict's profile as he ran a hand through his hair, seemingly uncaring if he disturbed its careful styling.

"So the Wolves have started some sort of gambling operation," he remarked, for once his tone empty of its usual levity. Perhaps it was the harsh shadows cast by the backlighting, but Benedict looked uncharacteristically tired. Scarlett frowned.

"The gangs have always run gambling operations though. It's not even illegal—although the amount the house cheats is usually not above board," she reasoned. "So why all the secrecy? And what does it have to do with Georgette?"

Doubt weighed heavy in Scarlett's stomach, turning the punch there into acid. Perhaps she had gotten off track and whatever the Wolves were doing in the Lions' old territory had nothing to do with their threats towards Georgette. Maybe she and Benedict were just wasting precious time unraveling this mystery when her friend's life was still in danger. Soon enough, the Wolves would grow impatient, waiting to hear that Benedict had acquired the dowry and Georgette could be disposed of.

The soft brush of fingers on her wrist drew Scarlett from her spiraling worries.

"Knowing what the Wolves are up to can only help us keep Georgette safe," Benedict assured, as if he could read Scarlett's thoughts. He must have been able to feel her pulse hammering in her wrist, both from frustration and the lingering effects of their close proximity.

Scarlett nodded, pulling her wrist from his grasp and subtly scrubbing it on her skirt to dispel the odd sensations still surging through her. She wasn't going to be able to help anybody if she couldn't stay focused.

"I guess we will need to find this...event on Friday then," she mused.

"I think I might be able to help with that," Benedict commented. "I recognized Baxter's voice in that room. We've hunted together often, so if I play my cards right, I'm sure I can persuade him to bring me along. Especially if I play on how a love for gambling runs in my family. For all I know, this *operation* is what landed my father in such deep debt with the Wolves anyways."

In the dim light, Scarlett could just make out a muscle in Benedict's jaw tick. Her hand twitched as if to comfort him in turn, but she kept it at her side.

"We'll get both of our problems solved." *And then we'll go our separate ways.* Scarlett added to herself as a reminder. This partnership with Benedict was only temporary, and when it was over, she would be moving into the Roost to live out her life as a Raptor until she was either killed or thrown in jail. The thought filled her with a heavier sadness than usual.

"I'll go catch him before I lose him, and regroup with you in a minute," Benedict said before slipping back out into the party. Scarlett took a few moments alone in the dark to regroup as well, making sure her wig was still firmly affixed and her wits were gathered.

When she slipped back out into the ballroom, she quickly found Mr. Ward. He smiled warm and broad as she approached, as he would if she were Georgette. Slipping into his radius, Scarlett positioned herself between Mr. Ward and the wall, so any other of Georgette's admirers would have to get past a scowling father to ask her to dance.

They stood in companionable silence for a moment, not uncommon for the two of them on the rare occasions they were left alone. Most of their understandings were better left unspoken.

"You do only seem to have eyes for Lord Pearce." Mr. Ward broke the silence.

"I'm glad to find out that acting lies among my talents."

"That's the odd part. I got the distinct impression you weren't doing much acting, despite being fully costumed," Mr. Ward observed, his voice even.

Scarlett froze, glancing around them, but by now everybody in attendance seemed to be deep in the punch and paying them no mind.

"I wouldn't know what you mean," Scarlett deflected.

Mr. Ward sighed heavily, the expression on his face drawing attention to the streaks of gray in his sideburns and the lines around his frown.

"I know I haven't exactly…protected you well since—" Mr. Ward cleared his throat looking more uncomfortable than Scarlett had seen him before. "But maybe I can change that just this once. I recognized the expression on your face when you danced with Lord Pearce, and it wasn't just for the benefit of the onlookers. I have no doubt you can dodge a knife, but the kind of hurt you're setting yourself up for here isn't as easily avoided."

Scarlett swallowed, not moving to deny his claims. She was all too aware of the battle with her attraction to Benedict, but Mr. Ward's comment made it clear that she was denying the severity of her predicament. Even as her heart wrenched with the realization, it warmed in her chest.

Any resentment she held towards Mr. Ward for not taking her in when her parents were killed was buried deep with all her other hurts. After all, she hadn't given him the chance to offer, disappearing into the shadowed alleys of the lower city at the realization that her Talent would put anybody who tried to shield her in danger, and unwilling to pile any more burdens onto her conscience. But Mr. Ward's concern for her soothed a wound inside her even as it made her realize it still festered.

"The son of a duke is expected to marry well, and you've long since discarded your own good name," he pressed on, echoing the thoughts that ran through Scarlett's subconscious but she had avoided thinking because they would mean acknowledging that Benedict had become more than an inconvenient partner.

At that moment the gentleman in question appeared in the crowd, cutting through the throngs to where they stood. His hopeful expression and the way Scarlett's own frown involuntarily softened in response confirmed what she already suspected—she had inadvertently thrown her own feelings into the line of fire.

"I'll tell you what I learned while we dance. After all, the night is young and we must make the most of it." Benedict swept Scarlett towards the dance floor, and she went without protest. She spared a glance over her shoulder at Mr. Ward's grim expression before they were engulfed by a cluster of partygoers. Even if he was right to be concerned, Scarlett suspected that she was in too deep now to disentangle herself from Benedict easily.

Chapter Nine

"**M**essage for you," Granny said by way of greeting as Scarlett stumbled bleary eyed down the stairs the next morning.

She barely managed to grab the folded piece of parchment Granny shoved at her, clutching it to her chest in surprise. Not even Georgette sent notes to Scarlett, Mr. Ward hesitant to send a man to the lower city on a regular basis on the off chance somebody connected Georgette with the gangs and besmirched her reputation.

"You got an admirer?" Granny asked in her typical blunt fashion. She didn't even look up from the counter she rubbed with a cloth ragged enough that it looked as if it might disintegrate in her hands.

"You know I don't," Scarlett said, turning the paper in her hand to find it sealed in blue wax, emblazoned with a sparrow.

Granny's responding hum was unconvinced, and she fixed Scarlett in her beady gaze. "That lip paint smeared on your face tells me otherwise. Besides, you could use somebody to show you a good time. You've been wearing that scowl more and more for years now."

"You're one to talk," Scarlett snorted, racking her brain for a memory of Granny smiling and coming up blank. "Maybe you should get an admirer."

"You don't know what I get up to at night," Granny argued, giving up on scrubbing the counter and bracing her hands on her hips. "Now go upstairs and read your little love letter and get me my rent money while you're at it. Due on Friday."

Scarlett froze. She had emptied the last of her dowry onto Granny's counter a few weeks back. With as busy as she had been dashing around the city on the Wolves' tail, she had nearly forgotten about her decision to move into the Roost. She thought she had come to terms with the inevitable, but facing it down, Scarlett felt the world shift under her feet like sand. She was about to take the final step into being a lower city gangster. As many stairs as she'd descended to get to this point, this last leap had a foreboding sense of finality to it.

Somehow, her time with Benedict in the upper city had approximated her old life—even if she was living it as somebody else—and thrown into sharp relief how far she had fallen. It was one of the reasons she relegated her time with Georgette to stolen midnight visits. Being reminded of all she had lost only made her angry, the feeling a luxury that Scarlett couldn't afford in the lower city where the constant objective was survival.

"See, now I know you've taken a lover. I've never seen you stand and daydream like that before," Granny cut in with a shake of her head, drawing Scarlett from her contemplation.

Scarlett shot a glare at her before bounding up the stairs to open her note in the privacy of her room, another luxury she wouldn't have for much longer.

Once the door closed behind her, she pulled a dagger from the sheathe under her sleeve to use as a letter opener. Without consciously deciding too, she slid the edge under the wax seal and popped it off without cutting through it. The sparrow embossed in Emerald sparked the memory of Benedict calling her *little bird*. Putting the seal in her pocket she unfolded the letter and read the elegantly looping script.

Scarlett,

While I managed to secure an invite to tonight's festivities, Mr. Baxter has informed me that it's not the type of event I should bring a lady friend too. I can lead you to the location, but you may have to use your own unique charms to invite yourself inside.

I also made the inquiry you asked about for selling the marble bust. It seems that Mr. Blayford has been back in town for several weeks and is happy to come by and appraise the statue at my earliest convenience. Shall I schedule a meeting with him, or do you wish to make your own arrangements?

Yours,

Benedict

Scarlett twirled her still-unsheathed dagger in her hand as she frowned down at the letter. It was a habit she often made fun of brawlers for but had picked up when she found it kept people away from her, where they couldn't cause her trouble. Now it was a subconscious distraction as she mulled through Benedict's letter.

The first part wasn't an issue. As long as she knew where to go, she should be able to sneak inside. After all, she had gotten used to creeping into enemy territory over the last few weeks. What caused her brows to crease was the second paragraph. She couldn't think why Leon wouldn't contact Georgette if he were back in town. It seemed as farfetched as Amos throwing a tea party to imagine that he wasn't interested in her anymore. Even if Leon hadn't been successful at securing the money for their marriage, he had to know Georgette would want to be assured he got home safely.

Scarlett chewed her cheek hard enough to taste blood as she considered the information before her. It wasn't her place to tell Georgette about Leon, but it rubbed at her nerves to leave her in the dark when she knew he was back. Scarlett could lie to a lot of people, but not Georgette. Either way, Scarlett wouldn't have to decide right away because she wouldn't be seeing Georgette until tomorrow. Tonight, she had a date with the Wolves.

Benedict's warm chuckle echoed down the sidewalk to where Scarlett hid in the shadow of a doorway. He was all charm and easy smiles as he and Mr. Baxter climbed out of their cab in front of an unassuming building in Wolf territory. The only sign that anything unusual was happening inside was the bruisers flanking the entrance and the excited chattering that spilled out into the darkened street whenever the door briefly swung open.

As Benedict approached the men at the entrance, she could have sworn his eyes darted to the patch of shadows where she crouched, as if to ensure she hadn't had issue following them here. His gaze flickered over her briefly before returning to his companion, who retrieved a piece of paper from the inner pocket of his waistcoat. After inspecting the document briefly, one of the thugs opened the door and beckoned them inside.

The carriage clattered away, the driver no doubt searching for a place to have a drink of his own before coming back to pick up his charges. As it rounded the corner out of sight, Scarlett eyed the task before her. There weren't many points of entry, the building almost intentionally windowless as it hid the illicit activities within. Given that she didn't know what kind of situation she'd be entering, Scarlett decided on the front door.

Keeping herself shrouded in a swirling miasma of darkness, Scarlett crept as close as she dared to the entrance, pausing just outside the pool of light cast by a streetlight. From here, she could hear the bouncers conversing in low grunts.

"Shame we don't get to watch the fun."

"True, but if we watch the entrance, then we get a cut of the winnings."

Looking at the size of the first one's bicep as he crossed his arms with a disappointed huff, Scarlett decided against fighting them. Steeling herself, she focused on the patch of darkness on the far side of the streetlamp. With a deep breath she focused on the shadows there until they began to shimmer, coalescing until they morphed into the shape of a woman. Scarlett grimaced against the high-pitched ringing in her ears that always came when she forced the shadows to do something so dramatic.

"Who goes there?" one of the bouncers barked, only for the other to jab him in the ribs with an elbow.

"May we help you?" the second one added on, clearly trying to prove his manners to the darkened lady.

Screwing up her face, Scarlett forced the silhouette of the woman to fall to the ground as if in a dead swoon. Instantaneously, the thugs jumped into action, rushing towards her figure. It was all the opening Scarlett needed to dash towards the unattended door and slip inside.

The sight that greeted Scarlett inside took her off guard. As soon as she slid through the door, she plastered herself against the wall, unsure if she would be confronted as she entered. Instead, nobody paid her much mind, only sparing her a glance as they milled about a large open space, some with drinks in hand.

Scarlett cautiously drifted further into the room and away from the exit, in case the bouncers came to check if anybody had entered un-invited. She slid through clusters of people, predominantly men, more well-dressed than she would expect for most lower city haunts. The general atmosphere buzzed with excitement, so thick it hovered in the air like mist, as palpable as Scarlett's shadows. She craned her neck, trying to find Benedict, when she caught sight of what was to be the evenings attraction.

In the center of the large open room was a roped off ring, surrounded by low benches, with plenty more room for spectators to stand behind them. A small cordoned off area held more comfortable-looking seats in one corner. As she watched, a man with a Wolf inked on his forearm beckoned Benedict and Mr. Baxter inside to where several other finely dressed gentlemen already sat.

Scarlett frowned at the arrangement. Boxing matches were a common entertainment, even in the upper city. They might be lucrative for the Wolves—indeed, stacks of cash were already changing hands as Wolves prowling through the crowds collected bets—but they certainly didn't warrant this level of clandestine security.

"Gentlemen, please get your drinks and place your final bets!" Scarlett recognized the Wolf with the neck tattoo, standing in the middle of the ring, arms raised as he grandly announced, "The first match of the evening will start soon, and tonight we have a great lineup, but if you blink, you might miss it!"

Scarlett frowned even as the buzz in the room hit a crescendo. The Wolves meandering through the room hollered for final odds, thick stacks of cash being shoved into their already overflowing hands. Who did they have fighting that could raise this sort of ruckus?

As the crowds clamored to get a good view of the arena, Scarlett glanced around for a good vantage point. A roped-off staircase in the corner led to a landing that would afford a good view of the ring. It was child's play to avoid the notice of the Wolves collecting bets and slip up to the second floor, barely having to use the aid of her shadows.

No sooner had Scarlett hidden herself in the corner of the landing so as not to be immediately noticeable from below but still have a good view of the proceedings, that the familiar Wolf stepped into the ring once more.

"Ladies and gentlemen!" he pontificated as if announcing for a traveling circus, "tonight, we have a special warm-up match between a returning champion and a new challenger. Stepping into the ring for the first time, let's hear it for Bartholomew, the bladed wonder!"

The man who stepped into the ring was everything Scarlett would expect from a boxer. Clothed only in a pair of trousers, every one of the ropy muscles of his torso was on display, leading up to a neck as thick as Scarlett's thigh. The mean glint in his eye and the stern set of his brow signaled a tough fight for his competitor. The crowd cheered as he stepped into the ring, but Scarlett frowned at the tattoo of a scorpion, poised to strike, inked across his chest. Perhaps he had defected from the Scorpions to join the Wolves when they expanded their territory, although a second inspection revealed no marking of the Wolves. If he really was a Scorpion, this boxing ring involved more of the lower city than just the Wolves.

The furrow between Scarlett's brow only deepened as the Wolf announced the second fighter. "And our returning winner from last week's opening match, let's hear it for the Jumper, Jim!"

Despite Scarlett's wonder at what kind of name that could possibly be, the crowd went wild as a twig of a boy stepped into the arena. He held up his hands to bask in their whoops and applause as if unconcerned by the man twice his size clearly about to beat him to a pulp.

The opponents squared off against each other, Bartholomew falling into a defensive crouch, fists up before his face. Jim stood up straight, not even adopting a fighting posture. Scarlett's teeth creaked in her skull as she ground them. She had more experience than she cared for fighting somebody bigger than her, and normally the trick was taking them unawares.

The announcer stepped up to the bell just outside of the arena, his hand hovering on the rope. An anticipatory hush swept through the room as every gaze fixated on the pair in the arena.

Clang!

The echoes of the bell still rang through the hall when the bigger man lunged. He charged forward, flinging his arms out as if to tackle Jim to the ground, but Jim wasn't there. Scarlett blinked at Jim standing on the far side of the arena. She was quick in a fight, but not even she could move that fast.

Bartholomew growled, whipping around to find his opponent standing casually by the wall of the ring. With a snarl, he lunged again. This time, Scarlett was watching for it. Right before Bartholomew reached him, Jim evaporated from existence, blinking back into being a few feet to the left.

Scarlett's stomach dropped all the way through the bottom of her boots and into the jeering crowd below. These competitors weren't boxers. They were Talented.

Obviously growing frustrated with the game of cat and mouse, Bartholomew rounded on his evasive opponent. At first, Scarlett thought he was shaking with rage, until she realized it was just his skin shifting. The crowd roared as spikes emerged from his knuckles, his elbows, even the backs of his shoulders. They were pale like bone but came to lethal points, turning the competitor from an intimidating brawler into a fighter bred for destruction.

His powers unleashed, Bartholomew began swinging in earnest, and the pace of the fight picked up. Jim continued to flash step out of the way of every blow, not making any swings of his own, clearly trying to tire his opponent out. While Bartholomew's chest began to heave, and even Scarlett could see the sweat dripping down his back from this distance, he came closer to connecting with Jim every time. The manic gleam growing in his eyes made bile rise in the back of Scarlett's throat. She had inched forward out of her hiding spot as she watched, her fingers gripping the railing on the edge of the landing with blanched knuckles.

The crowd gasped as Bartholomew's next blow skimmed against Jim's shirt, tearing the fabric before he disappeared. Jim seemed to have been thrown off his rhythm by the contact, stuttering in his next dodge. As Bartholomew threw his next bladed punch, he threw his other arm behind him. As Jim blinked back into existence behind his opponent, he froze. The room grew quiet, as if collectively holding their breath. In the resulting stillness, a haunting gurgle slipped from Jim's lips.

He staggered backward, revealing that he had impaled himself on the elbow spike of Bartholomew's opposite arm. His hand came to his stomach, blood already dripping onto the floor. As Scarlett watched him collapse, she realized that the entire floor of the ring was littered with rusty stains. This wasn't the first puddle of blood to be seen in this arena.

The ringing in Scarlett's ears at the realization was nearly loud enough to drown out the screams of the crowd. With growing horror, she realized that they weren't screeching in horror at the violence before them, but cheering on the victor who now wore a look of triumph on his face. Rivulets of crimson dripped from the bone blade still protruding from his elbow, running down his arm, but he didn't seem to care.

The Wolf who served as an announcer jumped into the ring, grabbing his fist and hoisting it into the air in victory.

"We have a first-time winner!" he shouted, the announcement met with stomping feet and applause.

In the crowd, Scarlett saw more money changing hands as some celebrated their winnings and others bemoaned their losses. Either way, the house always won.

Without orders, several figures emerged from the crowd. Two picked up the now limp form of Jim and hauled him into a back room—to get him medical treatment or let him die in private, Scarlett didn't dare to hazard a guess. Another Wolf jumped forward with a rag to attend to the blood stain, mopping up most of it even while rubbing the red stain into the rough-hewn floorboards, a permanent mark of the carnage wrought there.

Scarlett stared dumbfounded over the scene before her, something she hadn't imagined in her nightmares. As if drawn by gravity, her gaze traveled to Benedict. He was already looking at her, the horror she felt at what they had just witnessed mirrored in his expression. These were gladiator matches, pitting the Talented of the lower city against each other for the amusement of well-paying spectators. No longer were the Talented just the muscle of the lower city, they were its entertainment.

Heat built under Scarlett's skin, bubbling in her veins as if an angry bird were trying to claw its way out from under her skin. She screwed her eyes shut, blocking out the sight of Benedict's wide eyes that somehow only made her angrier. She counted measured breaths through her nose, trying to get the sensation under control. They had to get out of here, and causing a scene wasn't going to do her any favors. She could retreat to the shadows and find a way to fix this. For now, she just had to endure, just as she had when her parents died. Thinking kept you alive; anger got you killed.

Opening her eyes, Scarlett found Benedict still staring at her. She jerked her head towards the exit, and he offered her the smallest nod before turning to his friend. Scarlett couldn't help but be impressed by the unbothered façade he put on, as if he too were enjoying the evening and was sorry to duck out.

"Ladies and gentlemen, it's time for the main event!" The announcer stepped into the now empty ring once more. "It's time for the match you've all been waiting for. We have our undefeated champion, the king of ice himself, Ivor!"

Scarlett watched in morbid curiosity as she edged towards the stairs, another musclebound man stepping into the arena as if drinking in the enthusiasm of the crowd around him.

"Facing off against recent fan favorite, the boulder who can take a beating, Leon!"

Scarlett turned to stone where she stood as a familiar figure stepped into the ring. Last time Scarlett had seen Leon Blayford, his sandy hair was shiny and his face lit with a smile as he handed her a love letter to deliver to Georgette. Now his hair hung in dirty strands around his face, framing gritted teeth and a bruise across one cheekbone.

"No one has been able to stand up to Ivor's icy punches yet, but Leon here has shown himself capable of hanging in there even when things get rough."

Scarlett was pressed against the railing once more, paying no heed to if she could be seen from the floor below.

Ivor's face split in a wicked grin and breath puffed from his nose in a visible cloud, as if he were outside in winter. Leon remained stoic, but the briefest flicker of fear in his eyes combined with the lingering fire under Scarlett's skin spurred her to action.

Bracing her palms on the banister before her, she leaped over it. She sailed through the air for a fleeting moment before landing in the center of the fighting ring, breaking her fall with a roll that made the rough floorboards scrape along her still-healing shoulder blade. She ignored the sensation, letting the momentum of her tumble carry her to a crouch among a cacophony of shouts and gasps.

The Wolf who served as the announcer jumped back into the ring, advancing on Scarlett. She straightened and backed up, putting herself between him and Leon.

"Just who do you think you are? You don't look like you came with an invitation," he asked, his tone holding none of the bravado it had when announcing the fights, instead going low and cold.

"I'm—" Scarlett stammered, her gaze flickering to Benedict over the Wolf's shoulder. He would know how to fast-talk his way out of this situation. "I've come to challenge him." Scarlett jerked her chin at Ivor, who watched the proceedings with a scowl and folded arms.

"Scarlett?" Leon asked from behind. She didn't spare a glance over her shoulder. It wouldn't help to have the Wolves know that she had jumped in to protect him.

"You know her?" the Wolf asked.

"We've run into each other before," Scarlett cut in before Leon could answer. "What matters now is the fight at hand."

"The fights are only for Talented girl, as much as I might enjoy seeing Ivor beat you to a pulp," the Wolf snorted.

With a smile that she wore like a snarl, Scarlett unleashed her shadows, letting them drip from her fingers and crawl up her arms until she wore them like shadowed talons. The angry beast within her seemed to crow in approval, but she snapped it to heel. This was a precarious situation, and she didn't need to jeopardize it with clouded judgement.

The Wolf hesitated, clearly intrigued with the display. Scarlett's gaze flickered to Benedict over his shoulder once more. His complexion was pale, and his dark eyes wide and conflicted. Scarlett raised her eyebrows at him infinitesimally, mentally begging for his help. He seemed to deliberate for a split second before his features smoothed themselves.

"After an entrance that dramatic, I'm curious to see what she can do!" he commented loudly to his neighbors, clear enough to be heard by the announcer. His comment was met with a rumble of agreement.

"Everybody came to watch stone skin though," he argued, seemingly disgruntled by this upheaval.

Scarlett stowed that comment away to ask Leon about later. For now, she racked her brains for what she might say to tip the scales in her favor.

"Let the girl fight, Zed."

A hush fell over the room as an imposing figure emerged from a back room. Although Scarlett had seen Fang from afar in a street fight, back when he had only been a lieutenant in the Wolves, she barely recognized him now. His black trousers and bloodred waistcoat gave him the look of somebody who had recently acquired a large amount of money but not the taste to accompany it. His rested his hands before him on a walking stick topped with a silver snarling wolf's head and smiled at Scarlett in a way that showed far too many teeth. It didn't reach his narrow, black eyes.

"After all, everybody loves to cheer for an underdog, and she looks like she'd just be a snack for Ivor." The appraising way he looked Scarlett up and down made her shadows thicken subconsciously. It wasn't the lecherous way men sometimes stared, but the look of a man looking at a business venture—at a means to an end.

"You have a name, girl?" Fang asked when Scarlett continued to glare at him, unmoving.

"Scarlett."

"Well then ladies and gentlemen, we have a surprise match for you this evening! Scarlett, the girl with the shadows steps up to challenge Ivor, the reigning champion. Just give us a few minutes to get the competitors set and then you're in for more action than you bargained for," Fang announced, the crowd erupting into titters. "Everybody place your bets! It's sure to be good odds for Ivor, but you could make a killing if you're willing to gamble on a newcomer."

As everybody scrambled to find Wolves to take their money, no longer paying attention to the ring, Scarlett finally turned to look at Leon behind her. Up close, he looked even more haggard.

"Go find Georgette," she snapped. "Let her know you're safe."

"I can't let you do this for me," he argued, paying her order no mind.

"It's a little late for that now."

"You don't know what you're signing up for," Leon insisted.

"I saw the last match. I think I have a pretty good idea." Scarlett walked to her corner of the ring, not looking at Leon. "Besides, I've been living in this world far longer than you have. I think I know how to take care of myself."

Scarlett may have been exaggerating on that last bit. Clearly, if she knew how to take care of herself, she wouldn't keep dramatically hurling herself into situations she had no business in the first time somebody was in danger, although she didn't have time to unpack that now.

"I'll at least wait until the fight is over," Leon insisted.

"I'm here with a friend. He's over there with the blue cravat." Scarlett jerked her head to the cordoned off area, finding that Benedict continued to stare at her with an expression that looked too close to abject terror for her comfort. Another thing to push aside and unpack later.

Leon opened his mouth to speak again but Scarlett cut him off.

"Go."

With a jerky nod, he stepped out of the ring and the crowd engulfed him. Scarlett didn't watch where he went, trying to return her focus to the fight at hand. That was the only way to survive: Take things one fight at a time and worry about the rest when she could, if ever.

The announcer, Zed, stepped up beside her and gave her a quick once over.

"I'll need you to turn in your weapons. And don't try pretending you have less than four blades on you. I'm smarter than I look."

Scarlett nodded, expecting as much. She reached up her sleeves and into her boots as she asked, "What are the rules?"

"Rules?" He sneered. "You've come to the wrong place if you want rules. The only thing we care about is that you make it entertaining. You'll get your cut of the house pot if you win. We skim some off if you kill your opponent, to make up for the fact that they won't be able to fight again. Don't let that stop you though, because more people will come to watch you next time if you make it bloody, and the pot will be even bigger."

A tingle of fear shot up Scarlett's spine as she removed the last dagger from the small of her back and handed it over. It might have been because she was so rarely unarmed, or because the size of the crowd indicated that Ivor generally didn't shy away from a brutal showing.

Once Scarlett had divested herself of all her knives, the announcer moved away. She rolled up her sleeves, bouncing on her toes to get her blood flowing, and sizing up her opponent. She'd fought men Ivor's size before, but rarely did they have Talents—or at least ones they were willing to use openly. Then again, Scarlett tended to conceal her Talent out of habit as well. Now she could let her shadows run free. As she observed, Ivor took a jug of water and proceeded to pour it over his hands. Vapor clouded the air as it froze around his fingers, turning his meaty fists into icy clubs the size of a mace. One direct hit from those could lay her out flat.

Benedict's gaze burned into her like a brand from across the room, but Scarlett refused to look over to where she knew he stood. She didn't want to think about him watching whatever was to come.

"Place your final bets. The fight is about to begin!" Zed stepped up to the bell, resting his hand on the rope connected to the clapper.

Scarlett lifted her fists, wisps of shadows gathering around them like curls of dark smoke. She drew in a breath through her nose and blew it out slowly through her mouth as the room tensed in anticipation.

The bell clanged.

Chapter Ten

The echoes of the bell still rang through the room when Ivor rushed her. Scarlett sidestepped and ducked under the icy club of his fist easily. She bounced backwards on her toes, taking the measure of how he moved. As he spun around to face her once more, he snarled, cold breath clouding his face.

Another swing whistled by Scarlett's face as she spun out of the way, turning her momentum into a sweeping kick. Ivor countered faster than she expected, grabbing her leg as it lashed out at his side. He yanked her forward by her ankle so hard that Scarlett's head snapped back. Even as he dragged her towards his oncoming fist, Scarlett dropped to the ground, falling out of his grasp and rolling out of the way.

Coming to her feet in a crouch, she took a sweeping kick at Ivor's ankles, knocking his legs out from under him. The thud of his back against the wooden floor was drowned out by the gasps and cheers of the crowd.

Pressing her advantage, Scarlett sent a wave of shadows to cover his eyes with a flick of her wrist. As he was blinded, Scarlett aimed a kick at his flank, causing him to grunt in pain as her foot connected with his kidneys.

Before she could rear back to land another blow, Scarlett gasped as pain penetrated the base of her skull, the feeling an icy shock as if she had just jumped into the Thames in the dead of winter. A coat of frost encased the shadow clinging to Ivor's face before it shattered apart.

He took advantage of her surprise by grabbing her ankle, pulling her to the ground next to him. The impact stole the breath from her, and he moved to pin her as her vision swam before her eyes. Still gasping for air, Scarlett pulled her knees to her chest, pushing her feet out as he rolled on top of her, forcing him backwards. As her feet connected with his chest, she pushed against him to roll backwards over her shoulder and put distance between them.

In a matter of moments, they were both on their feet again, circling each other warily once more. Her ankle still protested from its injury last week, but Scarlett ignored it in favor of tracking her opponent's every move. With a jerk of his arm, Ivor sent a shard of ice like a dart hurtling at Scarlett's face. She threw up her arms, creating a shield of shadows. The ringing in her ears from the effort of making the darkness solid nearly distracted her from the tooth-aching cold as the ice shattered against her shadows.

Scarlett let the shadows dissipate just in time to see Ivor charging. She dodged out of the way, not quite fast enough as the frozen club of his fist clipped her ribs. Her back slammed into the ground as heat bloomed in her side. She escaped the paralyzing grip of pain just in time to wriggle out of the way of Ivor's oncoming fist. It crashed into the floor next to her head, the encasing ice shattering like thrown glass, razor shards scattering across her face. She blinked blood from her eyes, metallic copper coating her tongue.

Unable to see, she couldn't block the kick that Ivor aimed at her knee, throwing her arm up just in time to take the punch aimed for her face on her forearm. The next kick to her already bruised ribs had black spots dancing across her bloodied vision.

As Scarlett blinked to regain her sight, she found Ivor pacing around the ring, arms up as in an act of showmanship. The jeers of the crowd pressed in around Scarlett, drowning out the feeling of blood on her face and the pain beating at her consciousness. This audience reveled and cheered at her pain. As she lay there the hoots and shouts of encouragement telling Ivor to finish her off changed. They morphed into a sound that haunted her dreams, the jeers of the crowd waiting for her parents to hang. The end of the Inquiries might have meant the end of the hangings in the square, but people still showed up in force to watch the Talented bleed.

Heat boiled Scarlett's blood, burning away the pain of her injuries in a rush of adrenaline. The wild animal under her skin reared its head, and this time she didn't call it to heel. She had compressed her rage into a ball of molten rock in her heart when it meant survival, but she hadn't endured this long to be beaten for entertainment.

Ivor approached Scarlett where she still lay on the ground, the ice still encasing his one fist lengthening into a lethal dagger. He drew it back, ready to plunge it into her throat. As he swung it down, Scarlett's hands shot out, catching him by the wrist at the same moment she kicked up with her legs, throwing Ivor over her head. By the time he hit the floor, she was on her feet again.

As soon as he stood, Scarlett was on him, fists flying and teeth bared. She hit him everywhere she could reach. He tried to return her blows, but Scarlett blocked them with walls of shadow, barely feeling the pain of his ice in her head as adrenaline raged through her system.

Before she could think on it, darkness curled around her fingers, hardening into an obsidian set of brass knuckles. She could no longer hear the cheers of the crowd over the ringing in her ears, but she didn't care. Even as her fists pummeled at Ivor, he met her blows, so much larger than her that her inferior strength couldn't drive him to his knees. She took a step back, reevaluating her target, determined to bring him down.

The beast inside Scarlett screeched in frustration, and she answered with a matching snarl. Charging at her opponent, she threw out a solid step of shadow using it to launch herself into the air. As Scarlett flew over Ivor's head, she twisted, grabbing him around his thick neck and driving her knee between his shoulder blades. She bore him down into the ground, landing atop him. At some point, her shadows had formed into dagger in her hand, which she now pressed to the back of Ivor's neck, right in the hollow at the base of his skull.

The world fell still. Ivor tapped at the ground with his free hand, indicating his surrender. For a moment, Scarlett's eyes lingered on the point of her dagger of darkness, pressing against Ivor's skin just hard enough to draw a single drop of blood, bright red against the black of her blade. She looked up, her gaze instantly meeting a set of wide brown eyes. She had almost forgotten Benedict was watching this fight, so consumed was she by the heat of her anger.

Without a thought, Scarlett's shadows dissolved into nothing, the ringing in her ears disappearing with them to leave a painful silence in its wake.

"—have a new champion!"

Scarlett shoved away from the prone body pinned beneath her. She didn't quite make it to her feet, instead falling to her knees in the middle of the arena. As the anger within her retreated to the recesses of her mind, Scarlett began to feel cold. Pain rushed to the forefront of her consciousness, and she swayed, beginning to pitch forward.

Before she could topple over, arms came around her, and the smell of citrus and earth engulfed her as she was hugged to a familiar chest. She squeezed her eyes shut against the onslaught of emotions that rushed in on the heels of her retreating anger. Her mind was too fuzzy to form a protest, even as she squirmed against Benedict, knowing he shouldn't be holding her after what she had just done.

He paid her no mind, shifting her in his arms so he could carry her properly.

"You can't— People will think…" she started, not able to put together a coherent sentence but knowing she should object to what was happening.

"They'll think that I've fallen for a lower city brawler? Let them." His perpetually laughing tone was gravelly. Scarlett shook her head in confusion even as the world quieted around them. Benedict had carried her out onto the street, the silence of the night deafening compared to the cacophony of the ring they had left behind.

Benedict shifted Scarlett's weight, and she let out an involuntary gasp of pain as his forearm pressed into her ribs. The stabbing sensation that radiated through her chest spoke of bone deep bruises.

"Apologies." Benedict winced as he looked down to regard her. "Would it make you feel any better to know you look beautiful like this? All bloody teeth and bruised knuckles?"

"I didn't take you for a sadist," Scarlett gasped through the pain, scrabbling for their normal joking cadence. Anything to distract her from the fact that Benedict had just seen her at her most feral—fully possessed by the dark part of her mind that she had walled off in the months after her parents' deaths.

"It's not that." Benedict shook his head, gazing at her with something much too close to care. Scarlett squeezed her eyes shut to block out his expression. "From the moment you held me at gunpoint, I knew there was so much you kept hidden. Back in the ring...it was one of the first times I got to see more than a glimpse of what lives under your skin. Even as I feared for your life, I couldn't look away."

The world tipped around Scarlett. She struggled to remain conscious as Benedict's words penetrated her mind. Had she taken a blow to the head? She didn't remember.

Her thoughts were interrupted by the familiar clatter of hooves and carriage wheels. She clung to the familiarity of the noise, which was the only thing that seemed real in this fever dream of pain and confusing words. Using her shadows more than she ever had before left her feeling drunk and unbalanced, barely clinging to awareness.

Benedict lifted her into the carriage, placing her gently on the velvet-upholstered bench before sitting across from her. As the carriage jerked into motion, the jolting of the wheels over the cobblestones jostled Scarlett's injuries. Benedict's worried face swam in her vision as she tried and failed to hold onto consciousness. As her eyes slid shut and she began to tip sideways onto the bench, arms came around her once more.

"Rest little bird, I've got you."

Chapter Eleven

Scarlett couldn't remember the last time she had felt this comfortable, or this hungover. Her brain pounded against her skull as if it were trying to beat itself to death, and aches and pains scattered over her body competed for attention. Still, she couldn't bring herself to spare them much attention as she luxuriated the cloud-soft mattress cradling her aching bones. She inhaled deeply to revel in the scent of citrus and earth permeating her soft surroundings, regretting her actions immediately as her bruised ribs made their displeasure known.

Her eyelids snapped open at the sensation before squinting in protest to the bright light streaming in a window much too large to be the one in her room at Granny's. As she puzzled out her surroundings through slitted eyes, the reason for her current sorry state came back to her. Using her shadows as much as she had the night before always made her feel as if she had downed an entire bottle of whiskey—one of the many reasons she tended to use them subtly.

She took stock of her body from top to bottom, wiggling her fingers and toes. At her movement, a figure stood from the window seat and rushed over. Scarlett froze, not having realized she wasn't alone. Benedict's face swam into focus as he leaned over where she lay, and she relaxed again.

"Did you take me to your home?" she asked. Or rather, she attempted to ask, but it came out as more of a croak as she tried to maneuver her tongue, which was currently as useful as and similar in texture to a lump of wool.

"I wasn't just going to push your unconscious body out of my carriage on some random street, and I don't exactly know where you live." Benedict poured a glass of water from a pitcher on the stand next to the bed.

As he did, Scarlett pushed herself to a seated position, the process not as painful as she feared it might be. A bandage covered her battered forearm, and even her perpetually bruised and split knuckles were meticulously dressed, something she rarely bothered with anymore.

Benedict handed her the glass of water and scrutinized her as she took a few grateful gulps. In her eagerness to parch her aching throat, she spilled a few drops, dripping down her chin to her neck.

Before she could move to mop them up, Benedict's hand darted out to capture the rogue droplets, brushing against the tendons of her neck and lingering in the hollow of her throat.

Scarlett blinked at him, her sluggish brain still catching up to what was happening, and Benedict snatched his hand back before she could process his touch.

"You didn't sleep for as long as I was afraid you might," Benedict commented as he took the glass from her. "You were in a pretty sorry state, but I was afraid of the type of attention calling a doctor would draw."

"I don't need a doctor. I've had worse," Scarlett objected. Benedict raised a single eyebrow at her, and she conceded, "Well not much worse."

As her eyes continued to adjust to the sunlight, she took in her surroundings. The bed she was in took up one half of a large room, not nearly as sparse as the rest of the Pearces' house she had seen. A painting of a horse dominated the wall over the mantel, and several books were stacked haphazardly on an end table, boots kicked off underneath the legs.

"Is this your room?" Scarlett blurted out.

"Well...yes." Benedict scratched the back of his head. "None of the other rooms had sheets on the bed and well..."

As he trailed off, the warm look in his eyes brought her back to the night before as he cradled her to his chest and told her she looked lovely. Something soft stirred beneath her ribs—something she didn't want to examine too closely until she sorted through this mess. Still, she couldn't shove it aside completely, as if loosening the reigns on her anger last night in the fighting ring had broken the dam keeping all her other feelings at bay.

"This situation with the Wolves. It's..." Scarlett buried her face in her hands, finding the cuts on her face had been treated with some sort of salve as it smeared on her bandaged fingers.

"A mess bigger than a brisk gavotte at a holiday ball where the punch was far too heavily spiked?" Benedict filled in.

"I suppose that's a polite way of saying it," Scarlett admitted.

The more they dug into the Wolves business, the deeper it seemed the conspiracies went. She needed the truth, or at least some version of it, if they were going to untangle this web of violence.

"I need to talk to Leon. And Georgette for that matter," Scarlett thought out loud, already swinging her legs out of bed. It was then that she realized her legs were bare, her pants and shirt from the last night removed. All she wore was an oversized nightshirt, large enough to come to her knees. Her time in the lower city had seared away most of her modesty, but something about Benedict undressing her made her uncomfortably warm. Benedict took advantage of her stillness to argue.

"You're not going anywhere before you've eaten something."

Scarlett chewed her lip, anxious to get to the bottom of things while still wholly unbalanced by the image of Benedict running his hands over her skin to check for injuries.

"How about you write them each a note, and I'll have a courier deliver them while you eat?" Benedict suggested, pushing further. "Suggest Leon meet us here. It's the least he can do after you took a thrashing for him last night."

As if to agree with Benedict, Scarlett's stomach rumbled audibly.

"Alright."

Benedict showed her to a writing desk against one wall, producing pen and paper from the drawers before disappearing downstairs to see about some breakfast. Before leaving, he grabbed a dressing gown off the hook and draped it over the back of the desk chair. Scarlett slid it on, tempted to sniff at the citrus sent that clung to the collar, but forcing herself to focus on the issue at hand.

Scarlett quickly scrawled out a note for Leon, asking that he meet them at the Pearces' house at his earliest convenience. Over the letter to Georgette, Scarlett hesitated. Her friend had known they were going to investigate a lead last night and probably anxiously awaited any news. Still, Scarlett wasn't sure what this meant for Georgette, only that it couldn't be good. In the end, she wrote a brief note saying that they had made progress but there had been a complication, and she was recovering at Benedict's home while they made their next plan.

Folding the letters up, Scarlett shoved them in the pocket of the dressing gown. Looking around, her clothes were nowhere to be found.

Considering Benedict had undressed her the night before, it seemed superfluous to worry about him seeing her in a dressing gown now. With that, she pushed out of room and padded down the stairs, having to hike up the fabric of the gown so as not to trip over it as she walked.

Her nose twitched, and she used it to follow the scent of butter and herbs to the dining room. Benedict finished setting a plate on the table as she entered and motioned to it with a smile as she entered.

"Kipper," he explained brightly.

The softness in her chest stirred again, and she tried to smile, only for it to turn into a wince as the expression pulled at the still-healing cuts on her face. She handed Benedict the letters and he passed them to his coachman waiting in the doorway. As the coachman left, Benedict pulled out a chair for her, and she almost giggled at the ridiculousness of sweeping his dressing gown around her to take a seat. It seemed an oddly domestic vignette considering she was there recovering from injuries obtained in an underground fighting ring. The thought sobered her as she tucked into her breakfast with gusto, Benedict sitting down across from her. She moaned appreciatively at the buttery taste on her tongue, and Benedict's gaze darted over to her.

Something about the way he looked at her made her shift in her seat. She itched to break the silence.

"About last night...I'm sorry."

"Sorry for what?" Benedict asked, fork pausing midair on its way to his mouth. "The worst you did was get blood on my shirt, and that's hardly worth mentioning."

"I exposed us by quite literally jumping in from the rafters."

"And it was the dramatic entrance dreams are made of," Benedict pointed out, to which Scarlett scowled. He went on with a sigh, "It's not like I would have expected anything different. The first time I met you, you were impersonating your friend to find out why she was receiving death threats, and the second time I saw you, you dove in a window to get me, a stranger, out of a dire situation. It's not like I didn't know dramatic interference was in your nature, little bird."

Scarlett scowled deeper, shoveling food into her mouth. Something in her rankled that Benedict described her like a hero when she could only think of the depths she had sunk to survive. In favor of pursuing that line of thinking, she asked, "Why do you call me that?"

"Little bird?" Benedict gazed at her pensively. "Well besides the fact that I didn't know your name at first, it seemed like you were so ready to fly away at the slightest movement. But I saw something in your eyes when you pointed that gun at me. I had the feeling I would find something special if I could get close enough—if I could just get a good look at you."

Scarlett blinked, an unexpected lump in her throat making her words tight as she responded, "You might have seen something special from me last night, but not in the way you'd hoped."

Benedict shook his head, putting down his fork, meal forgotten. "I don't think you're as dark as you want people to think you are. Maybe pretending you've fallen too far to climb back up is easier than trying to claw your way back."

"What would you know of it?" Scarlett snapped, unsure where the sudden harshness in her tone came from. The feelings she had unleashed last night continued to tumble forward, and as successful as she had been in suppressing them this morning, Benedict's words caused them to stampede in her chest, beating against her heart like the hoofbeats of racing horses.

"It's clear you weren't always a gang member in the lower city, you know." Benedict took her anger in stride. "Who were you before the gangs?"

"It doesn't matter. That girl is dead. I killed her long ago." It was true. Scarlett had plunged the dagger into the chest of the girl she used to be again and again. The first time she picked a pocket, the first time she ran a job with the Raptors, the first street fight where she broke a man's arm. The time she killed somebody.

"You might surprise yourself," Benedict said softly. "I saw you let out the anger you so clearly carry last night. Who knows what else you might find if you let it out?"

The legs of the chair scrapped against the floor as Scarlett shot to her feet. She didn't remember deciding to stand, but now stood, fists shaking at her sides and teeth bared. It took a deep breath to shove her unexpected anger back into its cage in her chest, the beast under her skin screeching and clawing.

"I need a moment," was all she managed before she turned and pushed from the room. She found herself in the drawing room where she paced across the rug a few times, her knee twinging from a kick the night before. Scarlett welcomed the pain, letting it ground her. She had lived for so long by thinking only of survival, not pulling out her emotions to examine too closely. If she stopped to do so, she surely would never be able to pull herself out of the pit she found herself in. But Benedict had a way of *seeing* her, of looking through the shadows she gathered around herself, without fear.

Deflating, Scarlett slumped down on a bench, finding herself seated before the pianoforte. Hesitantly, she reached out a finger and stroked a key, a single clear note echoing through the room. She did it again, the sound drowning out the clamoring in her head, a welcome change. With slow fingers, she began to tap out a melody.

Her other hand drifted up to join the first, picking out the counter-melody slowly at first before building in confidence. There were some things one never forgot, no matter how deeply one buried the memory. No matter how hard you tried to pretend they were gone.

The music filled the room, melody rising and falling like the breaths in her chest, coming faster now. That newfound softness beneath her breastbone seemed to grow in response. There were many things Scarlett missed about her life before the Raptors, but this was one of the most acute. The need to lose herself in a song, to let the music rise until it drowned out all other thoughts in her mind.

After a dramatic crescendo, the song drew to a close, the last notes lingering in the air like one of Scarlett's shadows, almost dense enough to touch. In the growing quiet, Scarlett heard a shuffle behind her. She turned to find Benedict paused in the doorway.

"That was breathtaking," he whispered, almost as if he didn't want to break the spell of the song by speaking too loudly. He took measured steps into the room, then stopped to stand next to where Scarlett sat at the piano bench. She craned her neck to look up at him.

"Why do you care about who I was so much?" Scarlett whispered. She needed to know why he insisted on trying to crack her ribcage open and pull out all her secrets hidden behind layers of shadows and years of pain. After all, they were only temporary allies, on two separate roads running parallel.

"You have to know little bird," he murmured.

His lips crashed into hers in a way that was both unexpected and also inevitable since her gaze met his over the barrel of a gun. Scarlett only hesitated a moment before throwing her arms around his neck, pulling him down to kiss him more thoroughly. With her emotions as raw as they were, throbbing like an exposed nerve, Scarlett didn't have it in her to deny herself this. Even if it was only temporary, right now, she could have this.

Having to bend over to kiss her like this, Benedict's hands came around Scarlett's waist, lifting her until she sat on the keys of the piano. They let out a cacophony of sounds, a chaotic melody of their own making that echoed the fluttering of Scarlett's heart as she tilted her head to kiss Benedict more thoroughly. Her tongue slicked into his mouth, and his greeted it greedily. He ran his hands from her hips to her neck to cup the back of her head, snagging on the belt of the dressing gown in the process. It fell open, exposing more of her body to the cool air, still not relieving the building heat under her skin.

Scarlett's hands ran through Benedict's thick hair, reveling in its softness. As she let the silky strands twist between her fingers, his lips traveled away from her mouth to the hollow beneath her ear and down to her throat. His tongue darted out to mark her pounding pulse, and he groaned.

"You taste as good as I imagined," he groaned with a nip at the junction of her shoulder.

"You imagined this?" Scarlett asked, her voice breathless as she dared to hope, her heart fluttering against her ribcage like the little bird Benedict always called her.

"Ever since I saw you for the first time." Benedict pushed at the neck of the nightshirt to expose more of Scarlett's collarbones.

"I was dressed as somebody else when we first met," Scarlett said, sinking inside.

Benedict shook his head, nuzzling into the crook of her neck as he did so.

"The more I saw of you, the more I craved you." He punctuated his point by slipping the dressing gown off her shoulders, letting it pool around her on the piano keys.

Scarlett pulled his lips back to hers, needing to silence his words. Words that would make her think of what they were to each other—and what they could never be. For now, she just wanted to let herself feel, a luxury she had denied herself for so long.

As Scarlett kissed him with all the ferocity she contained, Benedict's fingers trailed up her thighs, pushing up the nightshirt inch by inch.

"I want to see you," Benedict murmured into her mouth.

Scarlett hesitated. She certainly wasn't naïve. With the loss of Scarlett's social status, there had been no need to maintain an innocent reputation, and so she had indulged in rushed trysts and excited fumbling with other Raptors on occasion. In the cramped quarters of the lower city though, there was little privacy, and they only undressed as much as necessary.

Now Scarlett nodded jerkily against Benedict, and he pulled back far enough to pull the nightshirt off over her head. Her upper half was left completely bare, only the smallest scrap of fabric around her hips keeping her from being completely exposed.

Not waiting a moment, Benedict dipped his head, instantly dispelling any insecurities in the onslaught of sensations that came with his tongue tracing over her breasts. Her back arched involuntarily, and she braced her hands on the keys next to her, drowning out her stuttering breath in another chorus of disconnected notes. His lips migrated back up to her neck before nipping at her earlobes, hands moving to cover the aching nipples his mouth had just left. Velvety warmth spread from the points of contact, dripping down her body to gather low in her belly. Benedict's fingers followed the heat, tracing down her sides in light strokes that made her shudder even as he took care to avoid the spreading purple bruise over her ribs. They came to land on her hips, toying with the waistband of her underthings.

"Tell me I can take these off. Please," Benedict murmured directly into the shell of her ear, punctuating the request with a light stroke of his tongue.

Scarlett nodded again. If her mind hadn't already been fraying at the edges from the sparks dancing under her skin, she would have taken time to process the ragged huskiness in Benedict's voice.

Now he slid her last piece of clothing down her legs, tossing it forgotten onto the piano bench behind him. He rested his forehead on Scarlett's collarbone to watch his fingers trail over her belly towards the apex of her thighs.

"You're exquisite," he breathed, sending a puff of warm air over her breasts, feeling like a caress.

Her knees drifted inwards subconsciously as he watched his fingers pet through her thatch of curls. They were so close to the where she wanted them, but nobody had ever looked at her like this—watching her as if she were the only thing in the world in that moment as he slowly shredded her composure with gentle touches. Benedict stepped between her legs, keeping them from closing with his hips. He pressed a soft kiss to her shoulder before running his fingers across her center. Her fingers curled at the sensation, and she found shadows springing up around her without being consciously called. They curled around her in dark mist, shielding her skin, littered as it was with cuts and bruises, from Benedict's reverent gaze.

"Don't hide from me, little bird," Benedict chided with a shake of his head, making the ends of his hair brush over her sensitized skin.

With an ounce of hard-won concentration, Scarlett pushed the shadows away, but they still lingered, swirling and pulsing around her hands and at her sides as if barely leashed.

"If you must do something with them, let them touch me instead."

Scarlett hadn't even had time to fully process Benedict's request when he found her most sensitive spot and circled it. Her shadows seemed to have understood without her brain getting involved, leaping forward to coat Benedict's shoulders. They caressed his other hand where it cupped her breast, winding through his hair, even trailing down his shirt to stroke the dark thatch of hair on his chest.

"You want this just as much as I do." Benedict's words sounded almost surprised and a bit questioning, as if the wetness coating his fingers left any room for doubt. While, as usual, Benedict seemed to be able to talk himself through anything, words were beyond Scarlett at this moment, so she settled for another stilted nod.

"I'm going to make you come apart, right here on this piano."

Scarlett didn't doubt his promises in the slightest as he teased her entrance with a single finger. She swallowed, finally finding her voice again, although it came out breathy. "Are you just going to talk about it or are you going to do it?"

Benedict huffed in amusement, fingers still exploring tortuously. "If you thought I was going to be quiet, then you don't know me very well." He looked up with a playful glint in his eye. "Maybe I can find a better use for my mouth."

Benedict's lips trailed over her chest to her stomach, and he sat on the piano bench in front of her. At this angle, his face was level with Scarlett's core, currently throbbing with unrelieved heat. Scarlett desperately wanted to close her eyes, to not exist beyond the feeling of his fingers dragging lightly over her thighs, but those honeyed eyes kept her pinned. He saw Scarlett as she was, and she could not be unseen.

"I want to hear you sing, little bird."

With no more warning, he leaned forward and drew his tongue up her seam in one long stroke. Her shadows jerked with an intent of their own, renewing their caresses of his chest and shoulders.

Scarlett gasped at the onslaught of sensations, biting her lip to stifle the sound as she was overwhelmed by Benedict's mouth, hot and slick against her center along with the odd caress at the back of her mind that came from the touch of her shadows. Emboldened by her reaction, Benedict lifted her knees over his shoulders, licking into her as if ravenous. Scarlett panted through gritted teeth, any sense of composure rapidly slipping.

With another skillful flick of his tongue, he succeeded in pulling a ragged moan from her. Scarlett's fingers scrabbled at the piano behind her, adding to the symphony of desperate sounds now clawing their way from her throat. Benedict only devoured her more enthusiastically, Scarlett's shadows fluttering over every inch they could reach, pushing him away and pulling him closer in equal measure. After the incessant teasing of his fingers and his words, Scarlett's pleasure was already baring down on her, hot and undeniable. There was no stopping the way Benedict undid her.

With a cry, Scarlett shuddered through her release, shaking so hard she nearly fell off the piano, but Benedict's firm hands on her thighs kept her pinned, continuing his onslaught until the only sounds he could pull from her were desperate whimpers.

With one last kiss to the seam of her thigh, he pulled back to look at her with a smile that would have been smug if he didn't look positively dazed.

"I knew you'd be a lovely songbird," he remarked softly.

Scarlett let out a huff that might have been a laugh if she had any breath in her, surprised at how easily he seemed to pull amusement from her, even after such intense feelings.

As she gazed down at where Benedict still sat between her splayed thighs, her shadows lingered around him, tracing his neck and shoulders in lazy circles. He reached up as if to pet one, finding that it wasn't quite solid in this state, fingers drifting through it like water.

"These are lovely too," he commented, admiring them as if he really meant it. Scarlett shuddered. To have somebody touch her shadows and admire them not for what they could do, but simply for their existence was utterly foreign. It felt almost as good as Benedict's mouth on her—almost.

Coming back to herself slightly, Scarlett realized that Benedict was still fully clothed. He could expose her so easily, in more ways than one—even things that she had hid from herself. As the thought dispelled some of the languid haze in her mind, she reached for Benedict, intent on distracting herself from such thoughts by returning his explorations.

The clang of a bell echoing through the house froze her in place, hand outstretched.

Benedict swore under his breath. "That must be Leon."

Scarlett scrabbled for her clothing, the lingering warmth in her veins chased away by cold reality setting back in.

"Your clothes are on the chair by the fireplace in my room. I got them as clean as I could," Benedict said, helping her pull his dressing gown back around her shoulders.

She pushed off the piano and came to her feet, legs a bit wobbly beneath her. At least the morning's...diversion had chased away most of the lingering headache from the night before. Scarlett quickly darted towards the staircase to get herself decent. She spared a backward glance before she left the room though to see Benedict trying to set his own clothes to rights, rumpled as they were by the touch of Scarlett's shadows. Despite her mind already racing with questions for Leon, the image of Benedict's tousled hair played at the softness in her heart as she bounded up the stairs.

Chapter Twelve

When Scarlett made her way back downstairs, she was much more decent, although it was still a relative statement. Her clothes bore several small tears from the night before, and Benedict clearly wasn't as good at getting blood out of clothes as Scarlett was, judging by the dull coppery stains dotting her shirt. Still, she was glad for her short hair, which was easily tamed with a quick finger comb. As she glanced in the mirror above Benedict's washstand, she pronounced herself good enough, knowing there was nothing to be done about the cuts littering her face or the hollows under her eyes from too many nights spent prowling rooftops instead of sleeping.

Scarlett followed voices back into the dining room, where Benedict had somehow embroiled Leon in a discussion on the recent rise of romanticism in paintings. Despite the direness of the situation, it seemed Benedict had an easy time conversing with people, even in the most intimate of situations. Scarlett's cheeks warmed at the thought of the things he murmured to her not ten minutes earlier and reminded herself to focus on the matter at hand.

As she rounded the corner into the room, Leon sprang to his feet. Taking two large steps forward, he stopped abruptly, as if he wasn't sure whether to hug her or keep his distance, looking her over from head to toe.

"That was incredibly stupid," he settled for saying.

"Bold words for somebody I once watched fall out of Georgette's window with his pants around his ankles."

Benedict coughed violently into his teacup.

Leon shook his head. "You shouldn't have done that for me. I would have been fine."

"You can thank me for taking that thrashing for you by explaining to me what exactly you were doing there, and why on earth you haven't contacted Georgette yet. If you've gone off of her, I might just throw you back into that pit and let Ivor have his way with you after all." Scarlett slid into a chair and propped her chin in her hands, looking at Leon expectantly.

Leon looked back and forth between Benedict and Scarlett before resuming his seat with a heavy exhale.

"I assume Georgette told you I had gone to Paris to get my father's blessing to propose?"

Scarlett nodded, and Benedict leaned in with interest.

"When I got there and saw my father, he told me he had no intention of sending me back to London. He wanted to send me to America to expand his art trade. When I refused, saying I planned to return to London for Georgette, well..." Leon ran his hands through his hair, showing that he too bore bruised knuckles. "He disowned me."

Scarlett grimaced. She knew all too well the struggles of being forced to fend for oneself overnight.

"What about your art trade?" Benedict chimed in.

"I'm trying to set off on my own with it," Leon explained, spreading his hands on the table in front of him. "But all our pieces legally belong to my father, and I don't have the capital to acquire many works on my own."

"So how did you become embroiled with the Wolves?" Scarlett asked.

"I was in a pub in the lower city, trying to plan my next move, when I overheard some men talking about how the Wolves were looking for Talented, saying they could make a killing. And well—I've never told anybody about my Talent, and it hasn't been hard to hide, but if there was ever a time to use it, I figured this was it.

"When I asked, they told me about the fighting rings and that any fighters get a healthy cut of the purse. I figured I could do it to get just enough money to get the art business up and running, and then I would propose to Georgette as a successful man. What could it hurt?"

Scarlett huffed. "You could get killed is what it could hurt."

Leon shook his head. "Watch." He reached across the table and grabbed a knife that still lay there from breakfast. Before Scarlett could react, he plunged it into the hand that still lay spread on the table.

Benedict let out a grunt of surprise, but it didn't quite drown out the metallic clang as the knife bounced harmlessly off Leon's skin.

"You're invulnerable?" Scarlett asked once she managed to stop staring with her mouth agape. Some Talents were more powerful than others, but she had rarely heard of any so dramatic.

"Not quite," Leon explained, holding up the knife and finding the tip bent from the impact. "I have to focus on it, and it only affects parts of my body when I'm actively concentrating on them. See?"

Leon now dragged the edge of the knife along the back of his hand, drawing a few drops of blood from flesh that a few moments ago had been as hard as steel.

"That would come in handy in a fight," Scarlett admitted.

Leon laughed humorlessly. "It does, although it doesn't mean I knew how to fight. At first, I mostly just took a beating and watched people break their hands when they tried to punch me. It turns out the crowds enjoyed it though, and I've made a killing."

"Then why haven't you proposed to Georgette?" Benedict interjected.

"I was going to, but it turns out I was making the Wolves too much money."

Scarlett's heart sank as she guessed where this story was going. Greed ran the lower city, and somebody like Fang didn't let go of a valuable asset.

"When I told the Wolves I wouldn't fight anymore, they threatened me. Of course, I told them their weapons were no good on me. That's when Fang played his trump card." Leon's tone was utterly defeated. "The whole time I had been fighting for them, he had been learning all he could about me. He told me he knew about Georgette, and if I stopped fighting, he would kill her. I didn't know if he could do it, but I wasn't willing to risk it. Then I heard Georgette was being courted by the son of a duke—" Leon inclined his head towards Benedict, "and I knew it was over. There was no point in trying to get out anymore."

"Ah you see, that's where your wrong," Benedict piped up.

"Georgette still very much wants to marry you. She's been worried sick," Scarlett agreed.

"Then you're not..." Leon looked between the two with a bewildered expression.

"The Wolves delivered a death threat to Georgette, and Mr. Ward asked me to try and figure out why. I've been disguising myself as Georgette in public to keep her safe while we get to the bottom of this," Scarlett explained. "That's why we were at the fight last night in the first place."

Leon furrowed his brow, clearly trying to process this chain of events. "How did you get involved?" he asked Benedict.

"They were trying to blackmail me into killing Georgette, and I suggested that I seduce her out of her dowry first," Benedict replied cheerily.

When Leon's eyed widened into perfect circles, Scarlett jumped in, shooting Benedict an exasperated look. "It was all a ruse to buy us more time to figure things out."

"Well, I've told the Wolves that I'm in to stay if they leave Georgette alone," Leon said.

"Although they might still expect me to marry her and then dispose of her," Benedict pointed out completely unhelpfully.

"We might have made this even more of a mess," Scarlett admitted, brain churning uselessly through possible solutions. Before she could come up with one, the bell chimed again.

Benedict looked up in confusion. "I wasn't expecting any other callers today."

He pushed up from the table and headed to the front door, and there came some muffled voices before two sets of footsteps approached the dining room once more. Benedict rounded the corner followed by a rather petite footman. Before Scarlett could get a good look at him, there was a shriek, and the figure threw itself at Leon, nearly toppling him out of his chair. In the commotion, the cap fell from his head, letting a cascade of silky brown curls spill out.

"Georgette!" Leon gasped as she leaped into his lap, throwing her arms around him and burying her face in his neck.

"You're here! You're really here." Georgette cupped Leon's face in her hands and stared at him intently, as if verifying his identity. Seeing the bruise on his cheekbone, her eyes widened. "What happened? And why didn't you tell me he was here?" She rounded on Scarlett .

"He wasn't when I sent the letter," Scarlett said. "What are you doing here?"

Georgette squirmed so she sat across Leon's lap more comfortably, apparently having sworn off propriety entirely when she forewent her normal lady's attire. "When you said you were recovering, I knew something awful had happened. I felt so guilty about you taking all these risks by traipsing around as me, especially if you were hurt. Then it occurred to me that if you could masquerade as me, then I could leave the house safely if I pretended to be you. I'm not quite as good at climbing out the window though."

Scarlett blinked in surprise.

"I have to say, I've never worn pants before, and I can see why you do it," Georgette added.

"They are rather freeing," Benedict agreed when nobody answered.

Leon stared at Georgette as if she was an angel who had materialized in their presence, a mix of awe and adoration. Benedict only seemed amused by her appearance. Scarlett's mind whirred, half still occupied by the delicate situation they found themselves in while the other dealt with Georgette's sudden appearance.

"So what happened to you, and how did you find Leon?" Georgette asked, taking a moment to stroke Leon's cheek again and give him a soft smile.

"It's a long story, and I'm afraid we have a bit of a situation," Scarlett hedged, not entirely sure where to begin. How could she tell Georgette that Leon was trapped in an underground fighting ring to keep her alive? Leon didn't seem to be piping up.

"Tell me," Georgette urged. "I might be able to help."

Scarlett chewed her lip. This was exactly the type of situation she didn't want Georgette embroiled in, even if it was too late at this point.

"Oh stop it," Georgette snapped. "I'm optimistic, not naïve. Stop trying to shelter me like I'm some porcelain doll."

The words hit Scarlett like a slap across the face. She had always tried to protect Georgette from the realities of her life in the lower city. It was part of the reason Scarlett kept her distance. Georgette was so kind and so positive—it seemed like wiping muddy hands on a white dress to draw her into the dire politics of the gangs. But here Georgette was calling Scarlett out on it and reminding her that she was the one friend who hadn't cut all ties with Scarlett after her parents had been exposed as Talented.

"Ok, I'll tell you. But first, I want you to know that even though we don't have a plan yet, we *will* find a way out of this," Scarlett urged.

Before Scarlett could embark on the tale of the prior night, the doorbell echoed through the house once more.

"I don't think I've ever had this many callers, and that's saying something," Benedict grumbled as he left the room once more. He was gone for a moment, but when his footsteps approached down the hallway once more, they were followed by another set punctuated by the sharp rap of a cane against the floorboards.

Benedict rounded the corner stiffly, eyes wide. The sight of the figure following him twisted Scarlett's stomach uncomfortably and she lurched to her feet. Out of the corner of her eye, she saw Leon's grasp tighten on Georgette's waist, stony fear etched into the lines of his face.

Fang himself strode through the doorway, once again in an ostentatious waistcoat and a silk top hat, broadcasting just how much cash the Wolves were drawing in these days. He stopped a few steps into the doorway, propping both hands onto the snarling wolf head on the top of his cane. The gesture would have been construed as gentlemanly if Scarlett hadn't been willing to bet the crown jewels that the cane concealed a sword. His eyes darted over the scene before him appraisingly, a spark of interest lighting in their steel gray depths.

"How considerate of you to gather everybody I have business with in the same place," he remarked conversationally.

Scarlett took a step in front of Georgette and Leon, shadows already dancing at her fingertips.

"Come now, I'm not here to fight. Why would I have come alone if I planned to kill you all?" Fang said.

"Then why are you here?" Scarlett bit out, not believing for one moment that Fang was truly unprotected. Surely Wolves were stationed around the house, waiting to crash in and overwhelm them if whatever was about to transpire wasn't working out in Fang's favor. While Scarlett could certainly hold her own in a fight, and Leon might be helpful as well, they wouldn't be able to protect Georgette and Benedict from superior numbers.

"I've come to deliver your cut of the house's winnings last night of course," Fang explained, pulling out a purse. He set it down on the table with a metallic thud that spoke of a hefty amount of money within.

"While that's considerate of you, you're not welcome here. You can take your money and leave," Scarlett protested.

"Come now, you haven't even heard the offer I've come with."

"And what could you offer us?" Scarlett asked, still firmly planted between Georgette and Leon, while Benedict stood with his back to the sideboard a few steps away.

"I would actually call it a...firm request," Fang said with a smile that looked more like bared teeth than an expression of friendship. "You see, the spectators last night loved you. Something about a little scrap like you taking on a behemoth of a man...and with such ferocity!"

Scarlett shifted her weight slightly at the reminder of last night's loss of control but stayed silent.

"As I'm sure Leon has made you aware, I don't like it when fan favorites say they won't fight anymore. I tend to come up with terms that make staying more agreeable." Fangs eyes darted over Scarlett's shoulder to where Leon and Georgette still sat. "Then again, why did you jump in for Leon in the fights last night? Is it just that he's attached to the honorable Miss Ward, who you are most clearly trying to protect?"

Benedict shifted by the sideboard, and Fang's eyes darted to him.

"Your involvement is curious as well. It took me longer than I care to admit to see that you were never actually courting Miss Ward but working with Scarlett here to deceive us. I puzzled out that you were double-crossing us when you jumped so eagerly to Scarlett's rescue last night. I suppose thinking I could get a fighter and a handsome dowry out of this arrangement was a little optimistic of me."

For once, Benedict kept his mouth shut, eyes darting between Fang and Scarlett, still facing off against each other across the dining room.

"So what do you say Scarlett? Keep fighting in the rings, or I'll put a mark on anybody in this room, because you've clearly taken a vested interest in all of them," Fang suggested, as if he were simply haggling over the price of salt cod at the market.

"I'm already with the Raptors. Amos won't take too kindly to me fighting for the Wolves," Scarlett argued.

Fang huffed in amusement. "Amos is already in on it. He's been helping deliver messages to...persuade Talented to volunteer to fight and collecting some debts for a cut of the winnings." Fang tilted his head in thought as he stared Scarlett down. "In fact, I would think you had been helping him with it. Nobody ever seemed to know how the messages were delivered, and I see now that you could be quite the asset when it comes to stealth."

Scarlett swallowed heavily. Is that what she had been doing for Amos? The letters she had been laying on pillows throughout the city in the dead of night—she was just delivering the Wolves their prey. Even Mr. Davies just last week...his debts may have been from the fighting rings, explaining why Amos assumed he would be hesitant to alert the police and admit that he regularly spectated at death matches for entertainment.

"You're saying Amos would be fine with me leaving the Raptors? You clearly don't know him like I do," Scarlett argued.

"He may not like it, but he knows better than to mess with the Wolves. With all the territory and resources we've gained, it's best to let us have our way." His eyes flashed in a dangerous way that reminded Scarlett of the Wolves likely stationed outside the windows and doors. He had Scarlett cornered, but he had also handed her a very valuable card. He wanted Scarlett to fight for the Wolves in the rings.

"I'll fight, but you have to let Leon stop," Scarlett stated.

Benedict made a distressed noise in his throat, but Scarlett didn't spare him a glance.

"Why would I do that?" Fang asked, "when I could have both of you? I'm still willing to dispatch Miss Ward over there if either of you don't do as you're told. Besides, it turns out I won't actually being getting a cut of Miss Ward's sizeable dowry that I was promised, and I think I deserve some compensation."

It was Georgette's turn to let out a distressed squeak, followed by some low murmurs from Leon trying to comfort her.

"You said it yourself. The crowd loves a scrappy underdog, and I put on a better show." Scarlett's shadows pooled down her fingers and crawled up her arms, creating black gloves tipped with glimmering talons for effect. The base of Scarlett's skull throbbed once at her use of solid shadows so soon after overextending herself the night before, but she grit her teeth through the sensation.

Fang tilted his head, as if considering. Scarlett kept pushing.

"And if I leave the Raptors, I'll be able to secretly deliver your threats for you, without you paying Amos a cut. That should make us even for your cut of Georgette's dowry."

She saw in Fang's face that he was softening in his conviction, and Scarlett knew that appealing to his greed was the way to get what she wanted. Her eyes drifted to the bag of coins on the table between them as Fang nodded.

"How much is the normal fighter's cut of the winnings?" she asked.

"Fifteen percent."

Scarlett's eyes darted over to Benedict at the sideboard. "I'll only take five percent if you forgive the Duke of Pearce's debt."

Benedict took a step forward, mouth opening as if to interrupt. Scarlett's heart throbbed as she threw up a shadow to cover his mouth where Fang couldn't see. She could end this all in one fell swoop. Just one shrewd deal and everybody would get what they wanted—everybody except Scarlett of course. The things she desired were impossible anyways.

"You drive a hard bargain," Fang commented, but Scarlett could tell he was tempted to accept. His fingers tapped on his cane as if doing mental calculations.

"You were using Benedict to threaten Georgette's life, but if you let Leon leave the fights, you won't need that anymore. If you take this deal, you'll be repaid the money you are owed over time, as opposed to getting nothing at all," Scarlett pressed.

Fang hesitated only a moment longer. "It's a deal."

He held out his hand and Scarlett grasped it to seal her fate. She kept her gaze on Fang's smug smile, once again revealing too many teeth. If she looked at Benedict over his shoulder, standing frozen, she wasn't sure she would have the composure to shake Fang's hand with a decisive nod.

"I'll be expecting you to fight the night after tomorrow," he announced as he released Scarlett's hand, straightening his waistcoat, "As for the rest of you, I suppose our business is concluded, as long as Scarlett here upholds her end of the agreement."

With one last meaningful look in her direction, he turned on his heel and strode from the room. His confidence in turning his back on Scarlett rankled. He now had her on a tighter leash than Amos ever had, and he seemed to know that he held all the cards. The sound of the front door closing behind him echoed through the house with a sense of finality

"Scarlett," Benedict breathed, a hitch in his voice. Scarlett couldn't look at him quite yet, not knowing what she would find in his eyes and not sure she wanted to know. Instead, she looked at the purse on the table. She picked it up and weighed it in her hand. This would at least pay her rent at Granny's for another few months. Low words drew her gaze over to Georgette and Leon.

"They were threatening me to get to you?" Georgette asked Leon, eyes wide and bright.

He nodded solemnly.

"What did they want from you? Were you...a Wolf?" The hesitant way Georgette asked it, as if being a Wolf were the highest crime, made the beast beneath Scarlett's skin raise its hackles. She was one of them now, but she had chosen that. She would pay the price for her friends' freedom.

Still, she found she couldn't bear to watch as Leon began explaining to Georgette what he had told Scarlett and Benedict, stroking her hair reassuringly. Scarlett turned and strode from the room, into the front hallway. She could leave if she wanted to. Disappear into the lower city as she had when her parents died, this time cutting all ties completely, not holding onto Georgette like a child to a favorite blanket, pretending it was a connection that could be sustained as Scarlett continued to scrabble for survival.

"Scarlett!" Benedict's footsteps echoed across the marble foyer behind her. She stopped but didn't turn.

"Scarlett, look at me," he pleaded.

Finally, she did. When she met his gaze, his eyes were dark, holding none of their characteristic amusement that had endured through many crises. A tenderness in her chest tried to push forth, but she shoved it down. This was why she had kept her feelings on a tight leash for so long. Because wanting was so often at odds with what was needed for survival.

"Why did you do that?" he asked, his voice, barely above a whisper, amplified in the empty vastness of the space.

"It was the obvious solution. One deal, and everybody wins." Scarlett shrugged. "Georgette is safe, and Leon is free to propose, having gotten the money he needs. Your family is free of debt, and you can go find a bride with a healthy dowry to restore your family's wealth." The acidity of the words burned her throat, but she fought to keep her tone smooth.

"You don't win." Benedict shook his head.

"I was already a gang member, what does changing allegiances matter?" she reasoned.

"Is this really the life you want for yourself?" Benedict half pleaded, half demanded, "Fighting and stealing for somebody else just to make ends meet? It's not who you are."

"You don't know that," Scarlett snapped.

"But I do. You wouldn't have gone to such lengths to keep us all safe if you didn't care."

"Better I pay the price than you," Scarlett shot back.

"But why?" Benedict insisted.

"Because its already too late for me," she admitted, voice rising in pitch.

Benedict cocked his head at her. "You clearly belonged to high society once, and being Talented isn't illegal anymore. You don't need to hide away from society. Is it a matter of money? Or connections? I could—"

"It's not that." Scarlett cut him off. She braced herself with a deep breath, needing to explain to him why her life had to be what it was. She needed him to understand, so he wouldn't make this any harder than it already was. "It used to be my Talent, but it's so much more than that now. I joined the Raptors to survive the Inquiries, working for them so they would protect me from the police. But now I'm a criminal in other ways. It doesn't matter if being Talented isn't a crime because my other crimes are numerous. I've stolen, lied, cheated. The end of the Inquiries...it doesn't undo all of that. I'm already a monster, and I'll gladly become more of one if it's for you."

Scarlett swallowed thickly. She hadn't meant that last sentence to sound like it had, but she didn't have it in herself to take it back. Benedict deserved to know that he had made her want more for herself, even if she knew she could never have it.

He shook his head, for once seeming at a loss for words.

"Everything can go back to normal now," Scarlett said. "Your mother and sister can come home, and you can go back to being the most notorious rake at every ball. This can be a fun story you tell at parties."

"What about us?" he asked.

His question shattered something in Scarlett's soul, loud enough she thought everybody in the house could hear the sound of breaking glass. As if "us" was a concept that had existed for a moment and now lay in pieces at Scarlett's feet.

"There never was an us, just a dream," she said. Then she turned and walked out the front door into the afternoon light, but despite the bright sun cutting through the eternal haze from the factories, Scarlett couldn't feel the warmth on her skin.

Chapter Thirteen

Scarlett stumbled back into her room, bruised and battered from her second fight in the Wolves rings. She had been more prepared this time, not taking nearly as much of a beating. Still, the use of her shadows in such dramatic displays left her with a head full of sodden rags. If she were any more alert, she might have noticed the dark silhouette beside her doorframe. As it was, she was taken by surprise when the door slammed behind her and she found herself pressed up against it, forearm against her throat.

A dagger flew to her fingers from the cache on her wrist, having been returned to her by Zed after she collected her winnings for the evening. A quick hand grabbed her forearm, keeping her from stabbing her assailant.

"Did you think to make me look like a fool?" An oily voice cut through the darkness.

"Amos." Scarlett relaxed a fraction. He knew better than to kill her at Granny's. Even he wouldn't violate the neutral ground.

"Working with the Wolves behind my back? Running a scam for them with your upper city friends when you were supposed to be working for me?" Amos was close enough that drops of spit sprayed across Scarlett's face. She would have been disgusted if she weren't already coated in grime and blood.

"I cut a deal with Fang, and you wouldn't cross him." Scarlett's tone held the whisper of a threat. "You can't compete with him when it comes to manpower."

"It's not him I have an issue with, it's you." Amos shook her to punctuate his point, her head knocking against the door at her back. "You were doing a job with the Wolves, targeting Miss Ward with them, when you were supposed to be working for me."

Somehow Scarlett didn't think it would help the situation if she reminded Amos she had been double-crossing the Wolves in that arrangement as well.

"And what do you want me to do about it? Fang won't take kindly to you putting his new prize fighter out of commission."

"You owe me a job," he sneered.

"A job?"

"You worked for the Wolves when you and your Talent still belonged to the Raptors. Now you need to do one more job for me to make things even."

"And why should I do that?" Scarlett asked, debating driving her knee up between Amos's legs. She steadied herself, not wanting Amos's howling to wake Granny at this hour.

"I know you bargained to pay off a certain duke's debt with the Wolves. Makes me think you would be upset if something bad happened to him or his family." Even in the near darkness, Scarlett could make out Amos's feral grin.

"Fine. What's the job?" Scarlett asked. She was already making a spectacle of her Talent, letting people bet on her and jeer at her injuries to keep Benedict and his family out of trouble. One more job for the Raptors was a simple price to pay.

Amos released her and stepped away at her agreement. "You always were too fond of your upper-city friends. What have they ever done for the likes of us?"

"What do you want me to do?" Scarlett asked again, ignoring his question.

"Oh, just something that will make good use of your particular skills."

Scarlett supposed it was fitting that the last job Amos demanded of her was likely to be the most dramatic robbery of her career, and the most likely to go terribly wrong. If she hadn't recently sold herself into a lifetime of Talented gladiator fights, she would have a hard time believing she even agreed to it.

The newly unfurled leaves on the tree branch Scarlett crouched on rustled as she inched along it. She took caution to move lightly enough that the sound was easily mistakeable for the night breeze sweeping through the garden. With an ephemeral coating of shadows, Scarlett dropped to the ground on the far side of the wrought iron fence.

Taking her bearings, Scarlett didn't see any guards or servants about. She didn't expect to, with the bribes Amos had made, but she had been on too many missions where somebody double-crossed them to take that security for granted.

As she glanced around the well-manicured garden, her gaze caught on a hedge maze to the left. It hadn't been lost on Scarlett when Amos told her who the mark was that this was the same manor she had pretended to be Georgette at the month before. An uninvited guest once more, she tore her eyes away from where she met Benedict for the first time and turned back to the mission at hand.

To the right, the carriage house lay partially hidden behind the main manor. Scarlett kept to the walls, crouched below the level of the windowsills as she rounded to where her target lay. She crept closer to the door, finding the latch sealed with a large padlock. She grimaced at the size of the metal she would have to cut through and the noise it was likely to make as she pulled out the bolt cutter stuffed down the front of her jacket. While she was sure she could pick the lock with some patience, it might not leave evidence that the lock was forced, and she hated to implicate the coachman, even if he had taken a bribe from the Raptors.

She worked the bolt cutters around the padlock and waited until the clop of hooves on the street outside could be heard. As the passing horse was at its loudest, she snapped through the metal, hoping to disguise the sound. Still, she winced at the metallic screech as the lock gave and listened with bated breath for a few minutes to see if anybody in the house had heard.

When there was no movement from the direction of the manor, she opened the door and slipped inside, leaving an opening through which a slat of moonlight could illuminate the interior. She sucked in a breath through her teeth at the sight that greeted her. As promised, the coachman had left a horse harnessed to Lord Worthington's stylish new phaeton. The animal stamped and whickered as Scarlett drew closer. Quickly, she slipped an apple out of her pocket and held it forward, hoping to silence him. He eyed her suspiciously for another moment before leaning forward to accept her gift. His warm breath tickled her wrist as he chomped down on the fruit, and she took the moment to inspect the carriage he drew.

The four wheels stood nearly as tall as Scarlett, their royal blue paint job just visible in the dim light. She swallowed thickly as she examined the minimal body, room for just a driver and a jump seat in the back, perched high on the frame. Built for speed, Amos insisted that this carriage was sure to win the Raptors many street races, but she didn't envy the driver. Races in the lower city were rarely clean, and one ram from a competitor's vehicle could easily unseat somebody from a seat so precarious and lightly sprung. Then again, it would be just like Amos to insist on such a flashy vehicle, clearly stolen from a high-profile mark.

The horse butted his head against the middle of Scarlett's chest, nearly knocking her back a step as he searched for more treats. She petted his nose with a light shushing noise, enjoying the velvety softness under her hand and the soft whicker he offered in response. This next part would be easier if she had the animal's trust.

With her focus split between the horse before her and thoughts of driving this deathtrap of a carriage, Scarlett's mind was slow to register the footsteps outside the door. By the time she realized she was about to be discovered, the door was already inching open. Scarlett fell into a crouch, shadows coalescing around her, making the horse snort in discomfort.

The door opened to reveal a figure dressed all in black, scarf pulled over his face just like Scarlett. With the moonlight reflected in his eyes, Scarlett could just make out his gaze take in the carriage behind her before flicking to her. This wasn't a cop or a coachman.

Before Scarlett could think any further than that, he lunged. She rolled out of the way, the silver flash of a knife slicing through empty air where she had been just a moment earlier. Her own knife sprang to her hand even as she backed away with a muttered curse. Of course the time they successfully bribed guards and footmen, another would-be-burglar would set fire to her carefully laid plans.

He lunged again, swiping his knife at Scarlett's face, clearly intent on eliminating his competition. Scarlett sidestepped and grabbed his wrist, twisting in a way she hoped would make him drop his weapon. Instead, he twisted with her and used her momentum to throw her over his hip onto the ground. Dust rose around her in a cloud as the breath escaped from her lungs.

A neigh split the air, shrill with distress. Her assailant, lifting his foot to pin Scarlett in place, stumbled back as the horse reared, striking out at the air. She took the opportunity to roll away, narrowly avoiding hooves slamming back into the ground as she put the horse between her and her attacker. Springing to her feet, she leaped for the phaeton, clambering onto the seat without finesse. With the noise of the confrontation, the residents of the house would soon come to investigate, and she would rather be gone when they did.

As spooked as the horse was, she had barely grabbed the reigns when he charged forward, nearly flinging Scarlett from her perch. She hung on as they crashed through the doors, a shouted curse echoing behind her. She only prayed that Amos had delivered on his promise to have the back gate left open for her. Rounding the curve of the drive to find her way clear, the wave of relief that crashed over Scarlett was quickly washed away by the pounding of hoofbeats behind her. A glance over her shoulder revealed the thief, leaning low on the neck of another of Lord Worthington's horses as they galloped in hot pursuit.

Scarlett urged her horse faster as they barreled through the front gates. Her teeth rattled against each other with the bumping of the wheels over the cobblestones at this speed. Sparing another glance behind her, she found the other horse gaining on them, albeit slowly. A carriage was slower than a rider, but the thief was limited by lack of proper tack.

At the last second, Scarlett pulled her horse into a sudden turn, the phaeton tilting dangerously, skidding around the corner on two wheels. As it slammed back down on all four wheels, she looked behind her again. The rider managed to turn his mount without the direction of a bridle but slipped dangerously to the side as it changed direction. Scarlett cursed as he succeeded in pulling himself back into a proper seat.

Rounding back onto the main road, the few people out at this time of night jumped to the side, pressing themselves against buildings as the chase crashed by. The wind from their speed stung Scarlett's eyes until they watered, tear tracks streaking her temples as she looked for another way to lose her tail. By the time they were in the middle city, the thief was just a carriage length behind her.

Pulling into another sudden turn, Scarlett directed her carriage down a narrower side street. Just wide enough for the phaeton, the thief wouldn't have enough room to pull up next to her. She grit her teeth as she maneuvered through a series of side streets, brick walls coming close enough to touch as she crashed around progressively narrower corners.

She soon ran out of side streets, re-emerging back onto a main thoroughfare in the lower city. More people were out and about at this time of night here, making them harder to avoid.

"Move!" Scarlett shouted repetitively at the top of her lungs, barely able to hear herself over the rumble of the carriage like thunder in her head. Still, she was forced to pull on the reigns, slowing somewhat to not crush those who couldn't jump out of the way fast enough.

The thief, on the other hand, continued at a breakneck pace, more easily able to maneuver his mount. Soon, his horse's head drew level with the back wheels of the carriage. A thud rocked the precarious vehicle as he leaped from his mount onto the jump seat behind her. Before Scarlett could react, an arm wrapped around her neck, forearm pressed brutally against her windpipe. She brought one hand up to claw at it but left the other on the reigns. If they crashed, then they were all dead. Still, her broken nails were ineffectual, and his grip tightened.

The adrenaline coursing through her system and the lack of oxygen reduced her thoughts to a panicked buzz. Still she fought against them, mustering all her concentration to summon a shadow where she thought her attacker's face would be. The slight loosening of his grip told her she had succeeded. She used the ability to move her head to bend forward before snapping it back. The crown of her head connected with something hard. She didn't have time to dwell on the crunch of bone and the grunt of pain. As the arm around her neck slackened enough for her to slip free, she ducked under it at the same time she wrenched the horse into another turn. As they tilted, the man toppled off the jump seat. Scarlett slid to the side of the bench, teetering precariously on the edge. One hand grabbed at the lip, while the other clutched the reigns in a grip so hard, she knew the stitching would be embedded on her palm. For a heart-stopping moment, Scarlett was sure she was going to crash to the cobblestones with the thief. Then the carriage righted itself and she sucked in a breath. Glancing behind her she saw the crumpled form of her pursuer roll over on the cobblestones, but he didn't get up.

Scarlett slowed the horse to a safer pace but continued to trot towards the drop-off point in Raptor territory. She was ready to be off this carriage and done with Amos. Even in the intermittent light of the streetlamps, a sheen of sweat was visible on the horse's flanks and foam from its mouth streaked his neck. Scarlett panted nearly as hard from the fading terror of the chase and lingering feeling of being choked. Her throat throbbed where his forearm had restricted her airflow.

Finally she directed the carriage into an alley in Raptor territory and pulled to a halt. The horse let its head sag in a weary way Scarlett commiserated with. As the echo of hooves faded from the alley where they stopped, it made the clambering in her mind feel louder.

A door opened at the end of the alley, and Scarlett straightened. Amos strode out, beady eyes flicking appraisingly over carriage before rising up to where Scarlett sat.

"I wasn't expecting you so soon, but I thought I heard wheels."

"I wasn't originally planning on galloping the whole way here, but we had some competition," Scarlett explained as she slithered down from her perch. Her legs felt like water beneath her, and she laid a hand on the horse's flank to steady herself, hiding from Amos how shaken she was.

He hummed casually in response, striding up to the horse and lifting its head to look in its eyes. The animal wrenched its head away, and Amos huffed, "I thought the Rattlesnakes might have had eyes on the same prize."

"And you didn't think to tell me?" Scarlett forced out from behind gritted teeth.

"I assumed you'd handle it. Besides, I thought killing a Rattlesnake might be a fitting sendoff from the Raptors. Didn't you kill one in a turf war right when you joined us?" He asked it casually without looking at her. As if the image of a crumpled form at the bottom of a steep drop wasn't etched into the back of Scarlett's eyelids, only fading with years of continued violence. As if the crunch of bones hitting pavement didn't echo in her ears, punctuating the moment Scarlett knew her old life was gone forever.

"All that matters is that we're even now." Scarlett nearly spat, but she contained herself with a slow breath in through her nose. Amos couldn't control her anymore, which was a comforting thought, despite knowing she had traded his assignments in for an even worse job.

"Careful, you might make me think you didn't like us," he responded, finally looking at her.

Scarlett considered him for a moment. While there was no doubt in her mind that she despised Amos with his oily smiles and cavalier attitude towards violence, she couldn't pin down her emotions regarding her time with the Raptors. They were the reason she had survived the Inquiries, and Scarlett wasn't one to discount the value of simply enduring.

With a shrug, Scarlett turned and strode away without another word. Her time with the Raptors was over, but it left more marks on her than the osprey inked on her shoulder blade. She had little hope that her time with Wolves would mar her any less.

Scarlett quietly let herself into Granny's, easing the door open on noisy hinges, only to see that she shouldn't have bothered. The wizened woman herself sat hunched over the counter, the light of the single lamp filtering through the brown liquid in the glass before her. With the flickering shadows dancing across her lined face, Granny looked even more weathered than usual, and Scarlett was struck by the thought that she might actually be aging. Granny always seemed more figurehead than person, an indelible fixture in the lower city with a sense of permanence amongst the constantly shifting borders and alliances within the gangs. So many lieutenants and bruisers had received a meal or shelter from a cold day at one point or another that she had indisputable immunity from the sporadic violence in the streets.

"Back before dawn I see," she commented, downing another sip of the liquor before her.

"Just had one job tonight, but it was more than enough trouble to last me a week."

"Need something to take the edge off?" Granny gestured to the bottle, still open on the counter next to her.

As much as Scarlett had been dreaming about collapsing into her lumpy mattress, she found herself nodding. She slid onto the stool next to Granny, grabbing the bottle and taking a swig straight from the neck, not bothering to dig up a glass. She grimaced as the liquor burned her throat where it was tender from being choked.

"Looks like it." Granny nodded to her neck. "Got a nice purple set of gems for a collar there."

Scarlett took another swallow by way of answer, and Granny pushed off her stool, hobbling to the ice box in the corner.

"You're lucky ice delivery was this afternoon, or you'd be shit outta luck," Granny explained, using a pick to hack off a chunk of ice. She handed it to Scarlett.

Her breath escaped her mouth in a hiss as she pressed it against her bruised skin, the cold a jarring contrast to the warmth of the alcohol.

Still, they both served to numb the ache. Granny climbed back onto her stool and took another sip. They sat like that in companionable silence for a few minutes, drinking and letting the ice go to work.

"I thought you were gonna tell me you were done running jobs," Granny commented eventually.

"What gave you that impression?" Scarlett swirled the bottle in her hand.

"You were leaving in nice dresses, getting fancy letters. I thought you might be leaving us to go back to the upper city."

Scarlett eyed Granny out of the side of her eye. The older woman was staring ahead at the dimly lit common room. Besides Georgette, Granny was one of the only people to know who Scarlett was before she joined the Raptors, although they never talked about it.

"It was just another job," Scarlett murmured, as if she could convince herself.

"Someday you're going to have to stop picking pockets and running cons, you know. You've got a life to live."

"Do I?" Scarlett mused, to herself more than Granny.

"When you stumbled in here and I gave you a place to stay, I was hoping you planned to do more than just survive." Granny shrugged, downing the last of her drink before setting it down with a thunk that felt jarringly loud in the quiet of the night. Then she stood and shuffled towards the stairs. "Rent's due," she shot over her shoulder before disappearing around the corner.

Scarlett dug out her purse and laid it on the counter before grabbing the bottle and carrying it up to her room with her, downing another mouthful along the way. At least what little she won from the fighting rings could pay her rent at Granny's. For now, she didn't have to move into the Wolves' Cave, and that was enough.

Chapter Fourteen

The rickety door on the small room where Scarlett waited did little to block out the noise of fists pummeling flesh filtering in from the next room. She stared down at the floor only to find a rust-colored stain where a puddle of blood had been the night before after another Talented found themselves on the business end of Ivor's icy fists.

Over the past few nights, Scarlett had come to realize that waiting to fight in the ring was the worst part of her new arrangement. When facing down an enemy—usually one much larger than herself—the adrenaline of the fight took over. She could drown out the sounds of the crowd around her and focus on staying alive. But as she waited, the jeers of the spectators pushed in close around her, reminding her that she was no more than a spectacle. It made the angry beast in her chest snarl and snap, although she hadn't unleashed it again the way she had when facing down Ivor. She beat her opponents dispassionately, took her tiny cut of the winnings, and went home.

"There's everybody's favorite underdog." Fang's raspy voice cut through the noise from outside as he came into the room.

Scarlett nodded, not enthusiastic to engage. Fang didn't seem to care.

"I have to say, seeing somebody of your stature taking down my normal bruisers has certainly been a change of pace," he continued, sitting on the bench beside her. Scarlett resisted the urge to inch away from him, even as he took up most of the room on the seat, spreading his thighs and bracing both hands on his infamous cane between them. He leaned in conspiratorially as he continued to talk, unbothered by her lack of response. "Although it occurs to me that the quick way you take them down might be too much of a change of pace. The crowds here have come to expect something a little more...brutal."

Scarlett's eyes darted over to her opponent for the night in the far corner of the room. He currently faced away, wrapping his knuckles, likely unable to hear Fang over the din in the main room.

"You wanted me to fight, and I fight to win," she said with a shrug.

"I have no problem with you winning dear—"

Scarlett ground her teeth so hard she was sure Fang could hear it.

"—but it's more about the way you win. If people wanted to see a polite surrender, they'd go to a regular boxing match and not bother the trek to the lower city."

Scarlett didn't respond, chewing his words.

"I gave you an easy opponent tonight," Fang pressed on quietly, nodding his head towards the man in the corner who had just finished wrapping his hands. "Consider this your chance to put on a bit of a show. Really unleash, and I won't lower your cut of the pot when you kill him."

The urge to punch Fang in the face and the need to vomit warred within Scarlett at the thought that this man was being handed to her like a sacrifice. He was a lamb, and she was the Wolf they expected to tear him apart.

"That's not part of the deal," Scarlett bit out with a sharp shake of her head.

"Deals can be altered."

Scarlett's stomach turned leaden.

"You wouldn't go back on our arrangement. If word got out you didn't hold up your bargains, you'd have a hard time getting the manpower you need to run this place." Even as the words sounded weak to Scarlett, she knew they were true. In a world where cutting deals got you ahead, loss of reputation could be death.

"I won't go back on our agreement," Fang agreed. "But I'm not above adding terms. There are other ways to get you in line."

Scarlett nearly snorted. She knew he wouldn't kill her. It would only put him down a fighter. With her friends protected by their original deal, there was nothing left to take from her. She remained quiet, eyes fixed on her bruised knuckles. Fang pushed to his feet with a heavy sigh.

"Think on it, my dear. I wouldn't want you to have regrets about your performance tonight."

As he pushed from the room, a roar from the crowd signaled an end to the prior match. Scarlett pushed to her feet as well, glad to finally be done waiting. Her adversary stood as well, and she sized him up. He was smaller than some of her prior opponents, and despite him being clad in nothing but a pair of pants rolled up to his knees, she didn't spy a tattoo. He didn't belong to a gang at all, making it seem likely that he was another victim of Fang's blackmailing.

Seeing her looking, he eyed her back warily. Scarlett didn't miss the flicker of fear in his eyes, and bile rose in the back of her throat. Fang really expected her to slaughter a man—barely more than a boy really—who looked like he had never seen a real fight before. Scarlett set her shoulders and pushed out into the main room.

She barely listened as Zed announced her arrival when she stepped over the ropes into the ring. The noise rolled off her shoulders like rain, and she bounced from foot to foot.

"Tonight we have a newcomer, let's hear it for Darius!"

Her opponent stepped up next, and she looked him over for any indication of what his Talent might be. He likely knew hers, having had it on full display in previous fights over the last week. Still, even as Scarlett pulled her shadows close to her hands as they squared off against each other, he gave no indication.

Zed rang the bell, and Darius vanished.

Scarlett blinked once in confusion. Then the air shifted before her and she saw it. Darius was still there but camouflaged against the wall behind him. As he made to dart to the side though, the image warped, and Scarlett could clearly see his outline.

With a grimace, Scarlett swung her fist, connecting with Darius's forearm as he tried to block. Fang was right, her opponent's Talent wasn't hard to overcome in a fight. It would be useful for remaining unseen when one wasn't expecting it, but with Scarlett knowing what to look for, his movement was easily tracked throughout the ring.

Scarlett drew up her knee and threw a sweeping kick at him from the side, sending him stumbling back. He clearly wasn't a trained fighter. Scarlett swung her fist again, putting considerably less force behind the attack than she usually would. Continuing to advance, she let her shadows dance around her to hide her movements even as she drove him back with light attacks. She could put on a show without brutalizing an opponent who was clearly outmatched.

Darius backed into a corner of the ring, trapped by ropes on either side. Scarlett spun around and jumped as she flung her leg out in a maneuver that was impractical against a more experienced enemy but would hopefully entertain the crowd enough for Fang's liking. Just before her kick landed, she froze as her eyes locked on a familiar face among the spectators behind Darius. She tripped on the landing and her opponent took advantage of her momentary shock. Lashing out, his fist connected with her face hard enough to cut her cheek against her teeth.

Scarlett tore her eyes away from Benedict as the taste of copper flooded her mouth. Questions about what he was doing there swirled through her brain even as she fought to focus on the task at hand. In a flash, she swept her leg out, knocking Darius's legs out from under him. She didn't have the focus to put on a show anymore. Not when she could feel Benedict's gaze on her like a brand.

As Darius crashed to the ground, she leaped on top of him, planting a knee in his gut and summoning a shadow in her hand with enough solidity to approximate a blade. Scarlett only held it to Darius's throat for a moment before he tapped the ground in surrender. Scarlett looked up to find Fang standing at the edge of the ring, raising his eyebrows at her. He gave her a small nod as if in permission, but Scarlett's gaze slid away to where Benedict still stood.

The steady gaze he leveled at her calmed her as much as it made her want to leap out of her skin. She pushed off Darius forcefully. Turning away from him, she left him lying there on the ground as she stalked away. The bell rang to signal her victory, but the cheers that followed seemed subdued.

Scarlett didn't bother to look at Fang's reaction as she stepped over the ropes blocking off the platform. Instead, she stalked through the spectators towards the front door. The space felt too small with both Fang and Benedict watching her. She itched to disappear into the night, unseen among her shadows where she could shove all the feelings bubbling up inside her back into their cage. She didn't even stop to collect her cut of the purse. Fang could keep the money if it made him feel better about her not brutalizing her opponents.

She didn't make it two steps out the door before footsteps sounded behind her. She quickened her pace striding purposefully towards a side street where she could disappear.

"Scarlett!"

Benedict's tone made her pause before continuing even faster. She turned around the corner, out of sight of the bouncers outside the Wolves hideout, before stopping. Benedict jogged around the corner, nearly crashing into her when he realized she halted.

"Scarlett," he sighed.

She looked up at him, finding it felt like months since she had last seen him, even though it had only been a week or two. He somehow looked lighter than he had when she had left him before, the circles under his eyes faded, his eyes brighter.

"What are you doing here?" she asked.

"I came to see you." Benedict took a step forward. Scarlett backed away, hitting up against the stone of the wall behind her. Silence stretched between them, a tenuous, uncomfortable thing. Part of her wanted to ask why he wanted to see her, while the other part screamed that it wouldn't change anything.

"Did your mother and sister make it back from the country?" Scarlett asked instead, to remind herself why she had chosen to give herself over to the Wolves.

Benedict nodded. "It's good to have them home again. I sleep better at night knowing they're no longer under threat."

Scarlett nodded this time.

"I wish I couldn't sleep though," Benedict pressed on, his voice pitching low. "It would be easier if I sat up every night again, because every time I drift off, I dream of you."

A choked sound escaped the back of Scarlett's throat. Benedict's eyes were so intensely fixed on her that she felt shadows curling around her fingers, itching to hide her from his penetrating gaze.

"You shouldn't have come." Scarlett's voice was on the edge of cracking.

"Why not?" Benedict stepped forward again, near enough now that the warmth of his body so close to hers contrasted against the rapidly cooling sweat on her chest.

"You make me want things I can't have."

"You already have me," Benedict argued.

Scarlett opened her mouth to say that she couldn't—not in the way that she wanted, but the words were silenced by Benedict's mouth against hers. He pinned her to the wall behind her, trapping her like a bird in a cage. She had no desire to escape. Not when he kissed her rabidly, savagely, tongue slicking into her mouth hot and unapologetic.

For somebody who managed to seem suave when faced with mortal danger, the abandon with which Benedict kissed her now was all the more shocking. Gone was the polished rake of high society, replaced by a man possessed, as if he could right every wrong if he just owned her mouth completely.

The fizzling adrenaline from the fight roared back to life in Scarlett's bloodstream and she gave as good as she got. As Benedict's fingers tangled into the short strands of her hair, she dragged him closer to her by the lapels of his waistcoat, yanking his cravat free in the process. She wanted, *needed* to make him feel the same ache she did and take some comfort in the fact that she didn't suffer alone.

The warm taste of Benedict mixed with the lingering tang of copper on her tongue, a heady combination that made shadows curl around her in anticipation. She sent them skittering over Benedict's skin, stroking the back of his neck, winding through his hair and even skating down his trim thighs. He shuddered against her and broke the kiss with a gasp.

"I realized something last night when I woke from a dream with the taste of you on my tongue," Benedict panted against her lips raggedly.

Scarlett redoubled the efforts of her shadows, forming them into semisolid hands to stroke Benedict all over. If he couldn't concentrate enough to talk, then he couldn't break her with whatever he was about to say.

"I set out to save my family and prove I wasn't the useless party boy everybody thought I was. With my older brother a war hero and my perfect younger sister an angel, this could have been my chance to finally prove myself worth something. Instead, I just lived up to my reputation as a rake by tricking a beautiful woman into taking the fall for me." Benedict dropped his head to her neck, breathing the words against the sensitive skin there. "Now though, I intend to fight for you."

"With a letter opener?"

"With whatever it takes."

Scarlett purposefully ran the most solid of her shadows over the front of Benedict's pants, determined to either silence him with pleasure or drown out his words with the ringing in her ears from such a use of her Talent. The touch in the base of her skull jolted and preened at the hard length her shadows encountered.

"Scarlett, let me fight for you," Benedict nearly begged as he bucked just slightly against her at the ephemeral touches she tortured him with. His teeth dug into her neck, sure to leave a fresh purple mark among the yellow band of bruises around her throat.

"There's nothing to fight for," she murmured.

With what seemed to be a great effort, Benedict lifted his face from her neck and took a step back. It only put inches between their heaving chests but felt like he had created a great chasm between them.

"Stop hiding from me," Benedict grit out, equal parts desperate and angry.

"I'm not. This is who I am," Scarlett insisted.

"I won't have you like this," Benedict argued with a jerky shake of his head. "I won't let you slip away into your shadows, denying that you're anything more than a dog on the leash for the Wolves. I want all of you, that soft heart you've hidden away again, the anger you wear as a shield around it, whatever it is you're still hiding. I won't be satisfied with back-alley fumbling. I want you in my bed, in my home—in my *heart*."

Scarlett's eyes burned. She blinked rapidly, dispelling tears that she hadn't spilled since the fateful night she caused a Rattlesnake to fall to his death. The sudden swell of her emotions at odds with the words that escaped her. "That part of me is gone."

Even as she said it, the tender ache in her heart told her it was a lie. Still, it was easier to believe that the soft parts of her were gone when she had to fight for the Wolves. She still had to work for Fang to keep her friends safe, and peeling back the armor around her heart would make it impossible. She had to keep her feelings hidden behind a wall of shadows if she was going to uphold her end of the bargain to protect those she loved.

"I couldn't save my family, and now I can't save you." Benedict's face crumpled as he looked at Scarlett.

She tried to argue with him, but the words wouldn't come. She wanted to tell him that he had already saved her by showing her that there were things worth fighting for besides survival, and those things were him and Georgette and Leon. The words balled up in her throat, choking her.

Without a word, Benedict turned on his heel and walked off into the night. Scarlett could do nothing but watch as the London smog swallowed the silhouette of his receding figure.

Chapter Fifteen

Hesitant beams of sun crept over the peaked rooftops of the London skyline, barely strong enough to penetrate the thick clouds of smoke belching from the factory chimneys even at dawn. They told Scarlett she had been sitting on her perch for hours, legs stiff from being hugged to her chest as she huddled on the steeply tilted roof. She looked out at the main square, eyes fixed on the blackened scorch marks where the gallows used to stand. For the first time in years, she let her mind wander to the day the girl in her died.

She stood in that very square, Georgette's hand grasped tightly in hers, as her parents were marched up to the gallows. Part of her had hoped until the last moment that somebody would run in, say there had been a mistake. Instead, the crowd watched without protest as proof of her parents' Talents had been read out. Her mother could manipulate light in the way that Scarlett could shadows, and a neighbor had spied her playing with shining balls for Scarlett's amusement and reported her to Chief Cook. Her father had tried to use his Talent of persuasion to get the Royal Police to leave, but when they had realized what he was doing, Chief Cook had ordered his officers to drag him away too.

Scarlett sobbed silently as her parents died, not even able to draw enough breath to scream out her grief. As Georgette held her tightly,

Scarlett could feel the weight of hundreds of gazes fixed on her. She could still feel the phantom pain of her nails biting into her palms as she desperately tried to keep her shadows from lashing out in her sorrow and anger. As Georgette and Mr. Ward led her back to their carriage, Scarlett saw it. Not only did the crowd eye her warily, knowing that Talents tended to run in families, but now they eyed Georgette with suspicion as well.

Scarlett clenched her fists again now, the sharp pain in her palms reminding her that she had disappeared into her shadows to protect her friends, so she would never have to watch anybody hang because of her again. Now Benedict's words swirled in her head too, mingling with the memories of her parents in a dizzying mix.

As the sun grew brighter, Scarlett pushed to her feet, every joint in her body snapping and cracking in protest. Whatever decision she was trying to come to in her head, she knew she would never get there without at least a few hours' sleep.

She hopped over rooftops until she reached the lower city, ready to collapse face first onto her lumpy mattress. After a few minutes, she jumped down to the street level, walking the last few blocks to Granny's. As she turned onto the narrow street that served as the neutral territory around the safe haven, her ears pricked. The ever-present sounds of squabbling children roughhousing and collecting messages to run for various gangs were absent. The street was unnaturally still and devoid of life.

Hairs pricking up on the back of Scarlett's neck, she quietly unsheathed two daggers, padding quietly over the cobblestones towards the door to Granny's. Approaching, she found it hanging askew off its hinges and partly open.

As Scarlett peaked into main room, the sight that greeted her was carnage. Tables were upended, with splintered legs scattered throughout the room. Chairs were smashed to bits, gouges taken out of the paneled walls as if somebody had swung the furniture up against it to break it.

Seeing and hearing nobody, Scarlett carefully stepped inside, shattered glass crunching underfoot. She walked through the room, gaping in horror at the wreckage that used to be the only safe haven in the lower city—the one block that no gang claimed for themselves and weapons were rarely seen drawn.

As she stepped on another broken bottle with a loud crunch, a moan from behind the counter responded. Scarlett hurried over to find Granny's crumpled form. Falling to her knees beside her prone figure, Scarlett sighed in relief as Granny groaned again.

"Granny?" Scarlett carefully rolled her onto her back before blind rage coursed through her at the sight that greeted her. One of Granny's eyes was swollen shut with a purple bruise, and blood dribbled from a split lip.

"Of course you didn't come home until dawn today," Granny scolded, her voice pained but strong even as she clutched her hands to her chest. "They left a note for you." She nodded towards a scrap of paper pinned to the wood of the bar with a knife.

"Who did?" Scarlett demanded even as she reached for the note.

"The Wolves." Finally, Granny let her hands drop, revealing the wound she had been covering on her chest. Burned into Granny's flesh, bubbled and blistered but still recognizable, was a pawprint.

Scarlett saw red as she yanked the knife from the paper, holding it up to read the messy scrawl written there.

These are the new terms. Put on a better show or we'll come up with new ways to make you pay.

The paper crumpled in Scarlett's shaking fist, shadows curling around it as if she could undo all of this by making the note disappear.

"Very intimidating, but I'd rather you help me off the floor than storm off in a blind rage." Granny's voice cut through the boiling anger drowning Scarlett and brought her back to the present.

"I'm going to fix this," Scarlett promised, even as she put her arms around Granny's shoulders to help her up and to her bedroom.

Several hours later, Scarlett crept through the neat rosebushes behind the Pearces' house towards the parlor window. She had left after helping Granny into bed. Scarlett had set to set the frame right side up and shove a considerable amount of stuffing back into the mattress before it could be used. Scarlett had managed to clean and bandage Granny's wounds before the prickly old lady banished her from the room, insisting she'd survived worse.

Scarlett walked straight down the stairs and out the door, letting her feet carry her towards the one person she needed to see more than anybody right now. This time when she approached the window, she found it already unlocked, easily slid open. She vaulted inside before turning to slide the window shut behind her.

A delicate cough sounded behind her, nearly drowned out by the thud of the window against the sill. Scarlett turned, expecting to see Benedict, perhaps in in dressing gown with a glass of whiskey in hand again. She froze at the sight that greeted her.

In the doorway stood a young blonde in a simple white dress that she managed to make look like a priceless gown with her effortless elegance. Her wide dark eyes held something strikingly familiar.

"May I help you?" she asked.

Scarlett looked around her, making sure she had climbed in the window of the right house in her distraught state. Her eyes landed on a piano in the corner forever burnt into her mind, reassuring her she had.

"I'm not sure," Scarlett admitted. "I'm looking for Benedict..."

"Lottie, who are you talking too?" A familiar voice filtered from the hallway as footsteps approached.

Neither of them could answer before Benedict rounded the corner, freezing as he took in the sight before him.

"Scarlett, what's wrong?" he asked, clearly able to tell something was amiss from her harried appearance.

The blonde opened her mouth in recognition before crinkling her eyes in a smile that made her look suddenly much younger. She couldn't be much more than a girl, despite her willowy height.

"Oh you're Scarlett! I've heard so much about you," she exclaimed, striding towards Scarlett purposefully, as if to embrace her, but pulling up short.

"This is my little sister, Charlotte," Benedict introduced, sounding hesitant.

"You can hardly call me little when I'm nearly as tall as you," Charlotte argued.

Scarlett blinked. She hadn't considered that Benedict's sister and mother would be home now, back to being a proper socialite family with their debt forgiven. And here she was tumbling through their window with blood still crusted on her knuckles from the night before.

She shrank back, feeling small.

"Come, I'll ring for tea," Charlotte announced as if this situation were completely normal.

Scarlett glanced between the siblings apprehensively.

"Actually, could you distract mother and father for me?" Benedict interjected. "Scarlett and I need to have a private word. I'll take her up to my room."

It was Charlotte's turn to look between them knowingly. "I knew it!"

"There's nothing to know," Benedict insisted with a cough, beginning to herd his sister from the room. "We just have some things to figure out."

"It's good to meet you!" Charlotte shot over her shoulder as Benedict shooed her from the room. "We should still have that tea sometime!"

"Come on, let's get you upstairs before my parents see you and start asking so many questions that we never get to what it is you're here to talk about." Benedict took a step towards Scarlett and took her hand before leading her into the hall. She almost protested that she knew where his bedroom was already, but the feel of his smooth palm against her calluses was too pleasant. They darted up the stairs to his bedroom, and Scarlett slumped as soon as the door shut behind them.

"Sorry about my sister. Her inquisitiveness is charming, but discretion isn't part of her vocabulary," he commented once they were alone.

"She's lovely," Scarlett said honestly. In the few moments she had met her, it was already apparent the girl could charm the lid off a teakettle.

Silence fell between them, Scarlett suddenly feeling awkward in his presence. When they had parted last night, he had stormed away with sadness in his eyes, the taste of him still lingering on her lips. It had felt so distant after a sleepless night and the shock of Granny's injuries, but now it came crashing back as she shifted her weight from foot to foot, back pressed against his bedroom door.

Benedict didn't look angry though, eyes roving over her with concern instead. "What's wrong?"

Scarlett shook her head, unsure where to begin. She came with a plan to ask for his help, but first she needed him to understand the reasons behind her actions. Even if it made him think the worst of her, she desperately wanted him to comprehend why she pushed him away.

"My last name is Forster," she blurted out.

He stared in confusion, clearly caught off guard. After opening and closing his mouth a few times, realization dawned on his face. "As in the former Viscount Forster?"

Scarlett nodded with a heavy swallow.

Benedict swore colorfully and collapsed in a chair situated at the foot of his bed. "I had forgotten he had a daughter. Everybody assumed she had died."

"I wanted it that way," Scarlett murmured.

"But why? Didn't you have any relatives to stay with?"

Scarlett shook her head, thinking back to the memories she had dredged up this morning, trying to find the words. "I didn't know them anyways, and I couldn't do that to them."

Benedict watched her intently, waiting for her to continue. She licked her lips.

"Everybody was already suspicious of me, knowing Talented parents normally have Talented children. At that age, I didn't have great control of my shadows. Whoever I lived with would inevitably know about them. Their choices would either be to turn me into the Royal Police to hang like my parents or cover for me and die alongside me when the truth came out. I didn't want to stick around to find out what they would choose.

"So I disappeared. I took my dowry and ran to the lower city. Eventually I took up with the Raptors, knowing a gang was the best way to be protected from the Inquiries. They had enough officers in their pockets to keep the Royal Police from looking at me too closely. With everybody eventually assuming me dead, they wouldn't hunt me down."

Benedict scrubbed his hand over his face, looking weary with realization. "Why didn't you claim your title when the Inquiries were ended?"

Scarlett blinked, knowing she had come to the hardest part, but the part Benedict deserved to know.

"I killed somebody."

The words came out quietly, barely above a whisper. Scarlett didn't think she had ever said it out loud before.

"Who?" Benedict asked.

Scarlett shook her head. "I don't even know. It was one of the first fights with the Raptors. I saw one of the Rattlesnakes stationed on a nearby building, aiming a gun down into the fray, and I panicked. I used a shadow to blind him, and he slipped and fell off the roof."

"It was an accident," Benedict murmured. The sympathy in his tone, as if she were the victim, shot like an arrow into Scarlett's heart. She squeezed her eyes shut.

"He's still dead. And the other Raptors saw it happen. If I ever tried to leave them, I knew they would turn me into the Royal Police. And with the bribes in their pockets, they wouldn't give me a chance to defend myself, not that I could have. It wasn't just the murder either. I've stolen, intimidated, cheated...all of it."

When Benedict didn't respond, she peeled her eyes open, finding him staring at her as if crestfallen. This was the moment, she knew. The moment he realized he was better off letting her slip into the lower city, never to be seen again. She needed one more thing from him first.

"I figured I'm already a criminal, and I would rather be doing it to keep my friends safe than just for my own survival. But the Wolves—no matter how much I sacrifice, it's never enough to keep everybody I care about safe."

The admission tugged at Scarlett's guts. Tears pricked at her eyes for the second time in as many days, and she squeezed them shut again. The air shifted as Benedict pushed to his feet and approached, and Scarlett knew he stood right before her. She let out a shuddering breath to brace herself.

Then arms wrapped around her, pulling her into a solid chest warm with the masculine scent of citrus and earth. Scarlett stiffened in Benedict's embrace, unprepared to be the one comforted after all she had confessed too. He held firm though, and after several long moments she melted, tears finally slipping from her eyes to leave salty tracks down her cheeks. She was glad her face was buried in Benedict's shirt, her pain hidden from his gaze.

"Do you know how I know you're not a murderer?" Benedict asked, his voice stirring the hair on the crown of Scarlett's head.

She responded with a noncommittal noise of question and protest, followed by a muffled sniffle.

"Every interaction I've had with you has revolved around you putting your life on the line to save somebody else. When you impersonated Georgette, taking Leon's place in the fight, jumping in to save me even when I had tried to kill you just the night before—"

"You wouldn't have done it," Scarlett mumbled into his shirt.

"I know that now, but I still had a gun pulled with violent intentions. Even the man you claim you killed, you did it defending others. You're so single-minded in your protection of those around you, that you'll sell your own soul to keep them safe."

Now Scarlett pulled back to look up at Benedict. He loosened his hold so she could, but his arms remained looped loosely around her waist.

"My soul wasn't enough this time," she confessed.

"Tell me," Benedict prompted, walking backwards towards the chair he sat in before, tugging Scarlett with him. He sat, pulling Scarlett into his lap. She stiffened again, not sure she had sat in anybody's lap since she was a child. Benedict remained patient, settling her comfortably across his thighs and holding her to his chest.

Once Scarlett got over the shock of their current position and relaxed, she told Benedict what happened with Granny. Not one to have thought herself a lap-sitter, she found herself grateful for the comfort the position offered when she envisioned the blistered brand on Granny's chest. Benedict's thumb rubbed small circles between her shoulder blades, keeping the worst of the bubbling anger at bay.

"The Wolves need to be stopped," Benedict said with a shake of his head.

"I'm not sure I could kill Fang, and even if I did, one of his lieutenants would just take his place." Scarlett kept her gaze downcast.

"I might have an idea," Benedict started.

Scarlett looked up and tilted her head in question.

"When I realized all you had sacrificed for us, I knew I couldn't just leave you to be killed or beaten in the fighting pits. In my time with you, I certainly proved that I wouldn't be able to get you out by force in any way. It occurred to me though, if I'm going to be labelled a high society scoundrel, I might as well use my charisma and my connections to my advantage. Maybe I could recruit the help of people that *could* stop the Wolves."

"What did you do?"

"I'm going to Mr. and Mrs. Woodrows for dinner tonight."

Scarlett blinked. "The Beast?"

"I wouldn't call him that to his face," Benedict said. "He's one of the king's bodyguards now after all, officially pardoned for his work with the Lions. And his wife is advisor to the king now, helping him dismantle the remnants of the Inquiries. They are the only openly Talented people in his inner circle. If anybody would care about what's happening to the Talented and have the power to do something, it's them."

"Do you know them?" Scarlett asked.

"We haven't been officially introduced, but I mentioned my father, and his name has a lot of sway," Benedict admitted. "Besides, I doubt they get many social invitations with everybody giving them a wide berth. They probably see this as a way to start integrating the Talented back into polite society."

"It seems like a stretch," Scarlett conceded, even as her mind whirled with possibilities. The Woodrows might very well want to leave the violence of the lower city in their past, given that their pardons had made it possible. Even so, Scarlett couldn't pin down her feelings towards the couple. Mrs. Woodrow, formerly Miss Cook, had stood at the front of the crowd next to her father, the Chief of Royal Police responsible for the executions of so many, as her parents hung. Still, she was credited with the end of the Inquiries and the conviction of Chief Cook for the murder of his wife a year ago.

"It would be less of a stretch if you came with."

"Me?" Scarlett's eyebrows shot up.

"You have an intimate awareness of the Wolves' operation that I don't. And your name...it would hold weight to have a member of a prominent family entangled in this asking for help."

Scarlett swallowed. Using her real name and presenting herself to prominent members of society in the open went against everything her instincts wanted. Her shadows tugged at her consciousness, wanting to cover her in darkness where she could survive safe and unseen. Hiding had only gotten the people she cared about hurt. Maybe it was time to try things Benedict's way.

She nodded. "Alright."

"We'll need to find you something a bit more befitting of your status to wear," Benedict mused, looking her up and down.

"Former status," Scarlett clarified, even as she cringed at the state of herself. She still wore the loose shirt and trousers she had fought in last night, crusted in sweat and grime.

"I'm sure my sister wouldn't mind lending you a dress, but you'd trip over her hem. She shot up a few years back and we had to get a whole new set of dresses or risk her exposing her entire calf every time she took a step."

"How scandalous," Scarlett remarked drily with a glance down at her trousers, fitted in a way that showed off a lot more than her ankles. "Georgette's dresses always fit me well, and I owe her a visit anyways."

Scarlett shifted her weight, but Benedict's arms tightened around her waist, as if he weren't entirely ready to let her go yet.

"Are you sure you don't want to stay for breakfast? I could scrounge up some kipper," he offered, resting his chin on her shoulder. Even if the way he kissed her last night lit a fire in her veins, the way he held her now made the softness in her chest melt like a pool of butter on warm toast, simultaneously soothing and uncomfortable in its intimacy.

"Then I might have to risk meeting your mother, and I think your sister and the Woodrows will be enough socialites to deal with in one day. My manners are still a bit rusty. Besides, I need at least a few hours' sleep if I'm going to be fit for company tonight." Scarlett slid from his grip to stand, acutely feeling the loss of his arms, even as she stepped away. His hands hung in the air for a moment before letting them drop to his lap. Scarlett was grateful for the distance, allowing her to think straight. Even if she itched to let him hold her in reassurance, there was still work to be done.

"Should I fetch you from the Wards' for dinner tonight?"

Scarlett nodded.

"Then I'll make sure my parents are distracted and you can slip out." Benedict pushed to his feet and walked to the bedroom door.

Scarlett stopped him with a shake of her head.

"I may have told you who I am, but you haven't yet convinced me that doors are superior to windows for entering and exiting unseen."

"As long as you don't throw me out with you, you're allowed to climb in and out of my window any time you like," Benedict responded with a crooked grin.

Despite herself, Scarlett smiled back.

"One more thing before you go." Benedict stopped her, stepping forward until he was mere inches away. "Don't disappear on me again."

He leaned forward and pressed his lips to hers in a whisper of a kiss, somehow still enough to send sparks skittering down to Scarlett's toes. It was a promise that he hadn't forgotten where they left things the night before. Neither had Scarlett, not when the feeling of his body trapping hers against the alley wall was burned indelibly into her brain.

"I'll try not to," she said, voice not rising above a whisper. Then she turned and hopped onto the windowsill, already open to let in the warm summer breeze, before swinging down to the trellis below.

As used to fragmented sleep as Scarlett had become over the past years, her body had been pushed to its limits. After checking on Granny and finding her sleeping soundly as she had left her, Scarlett pushed into her room to find that it hadn't escaped the destruction either. Her bedframe had been smashed against the wall, splinters of broken wood scattered across the floor. Her ripped mattress lay on the floor, stuffing strewn about, tiny bits floating in the air like snowflakes as they were stirred by the breeze blowing in through the open window. She didn't have the energy to deal with the carnage now, just making sure there were no sharp fragments of wood or her smashed basin in her way before collapsing onto the remains of her mattress and falling immediately into unconsciousness.

When she woke, bright afternoon sun high enough to peek over the surrounding rooftops told her she had only been asleep for a handful of hours, but even that amount of rest left her much more prepared to deal with the mess of her situation.

Rising from the thin cushion on the floor, she glanced around her. In the corner, she spotted her chest, tipped on its side as if somebody had thrown it against the wall. Crouching down, she was relieved to find it hadn't been opened despite the apparent efforts to smash it. The lock she invested a month's worth of rent in to protect her dowry held fast, despite the fact that it only protected a handful of coins and a change of clothes at this point.

Tipping it flat again with a dull thud, Scarlett fished into her pocket for the key, ready to put on clean clothes now that she was awake enough to feel the way her shirt clung to her skin, stiff and pungent. Clothes in hand, she hesitated before closing the lid once more. Her gaze snagged on the crimson shadowed in the bottom, where she rarely looked.

Her hand drifted into the chest, fingers stroking against the velvet fabric and finding it as plush as the day she hid it away. She didn't even know why she had brought her mother's cape with her when she fled her old home with nothing but a fat purse of coins and the clothes on her back.

It had been lying across the back of a chair in the entry, right where her mother had left it after coming in from a carriage ride the day she was arrested. It had been a cold day, snow on the ground. Wet spots dotted the hem of the velvet from splatters of snow when her father had playfully lobbed a snowball at her in the park. Despite mother being one of the most elegant ladies in London society, she had giggled like a young flirt at Father's antics, retaliating with her own snowball, which hit Father full in the face, knocking off his top hat and leaving him spluttering.

It was with that image in her head that Scarlett had tucked the velvet cape under her arm before dashing out the door and slipping down to the lower city. If she ever found the strength in her heart to remember her parents without melting into a nonfunctional heap of emotions, that day in the park was how she wished to remember them. It was the only piece of her parents she had left.

Now she pulled out the cloak, shaking it out. Creases marked the fabric where it had remained folded and untouched for years. It wasn't something Scarlett would have considered wearing herself, loath to wear anything but browns and greys. She preferred colors in which she could readily blend in and escape from unfriendly eyes. Tonight though, she was walking into a dinner with the intent of being seen just as she was. For so long, remaining invisible had been her best tool in keeping herself and her friends alive. Tonight, maybe she could use some of her parents' strength.

After changing into her clean clothes, she bundled the weighty velvet under her arm and headed down the stairs. Hopefully Georgette had a dress that went with red.

Scarlett swallowed a lump in her throat with difficulty and gazed up at the tall doors before her, painted emerald green to offset the intricate brass knocker. It seemed odd that she had been less nervous to participate in a fight to the death than she was to knock on her best friend's door. She considered circling back around to climb directly into Georgette's window but shook the idea out of her head.

Georgette wouldn't be expecting her at this time of the afternoon and likely wouldn't be in her room. Besides, today she was visiting as Scarlett Forster, not the shadow of the lower city. She wouldn't be able to enter dinner with the Woodrow's via the window, she might as well practice using the front door at Georgette's home.

The sharp rap of the knocker felt jarringly loud. Scarlett cringed as she looked up and down the street, but nobody seemed to be paying her any mind. After a few moments where Scarlett considered shrouding herself in shadows and darting away before anybody answered, the door swung open.

The Wards' butler looked down at Scarlett and blinked in surprise. The last time he had seen her, she had been leaving for a ball with Mr. Ward dressed as Georgette. Without the wig and dress, she doubted she was recognizable.

"I'm here to see Miss Ward," Scarlett said, suppressing the urge to shift her weight from foot to foot.

Recognition dawned on the butler's face. "Of course you are," he said as he stepped aside and beckoned Scarlett in. "She's in the parlor."

As he led her around the corner, Scarlett barely had time to take in the delicately appointed room before she was nearly tackled by a missile of chiffon and lace.

"You're alright!" Georgette exclaimed, voice so shrill in her excitement that Scarlett winced against the volume so close to her ear. Still, she embraced her friend. She couldn't remember the last time she had been hugged this much in one day.

"And so are you," Scarlett commented as they separated. She bent to pick up the embroidery that had been tossed aside when Georgette flew to her feet.

"Thanks to you." Georgette blinked watery eyes, tears clinging like crystals to her unfairly long lashes. "You left before I even knew what was happening. I wanted to find you, but then I realized that I didn't know where you lived. I couldn't even thank you for what you did to keep me and Leon safe, let alone tell you how much of an idiot you were."

"An idiot?" Scarlett asked.

Georgette shoved her in the middle of the chest with frustration but no force. "Yes, an absolute wooden spoon." She huffed and returned to the settee, collapsing on it in a rustle of fabric.

"I don't see how thinking on my feet to get everybody out of trouble makes me an idiot," Scarlett settled onto the cushion next to Georgette, moving her gunmetal skirt out of the way to make room.

"Because you had to have known that I wouldn't want you to do that for me." Georgette slumped back, her voice losing some of its enthusiasm.

"It wouldn't have changed my decision." Scarlett toyed with the silk tassels trimming the decorative cushions of the seat.

Georgette considered Scarlett for a moment, her normally expressive eyes unreadable.

"I don't think I've been a very good friend," she murmured eventually.

Scarlett stared. It wasn't what she expected from somebody who was the literal embodiment of goodness.

Georgette sighed and smoothed her hands down the front of her dress. "You just did what you've always done, sacrificing to protect me. It's what you did after your parents died. When you ran away and refused to let me be seen with you, it didn't take a genius to figure out that you were trying to protect my reputation.

"I couldn't begin to figure out how to help you, so I did the only thing I could think of. I tried to be positive. To be the best friend I knew how to be. You never told me about what you were doing, and I assumed it was because you didn't want to talk about it. I hoped I could make your life a bit brighter by giving you a place to escape. But now…Now I think I might have made a mistake by making you feel like I had to be protected from the realities of the world. I tried to focus on the good, and I made you think you had to shelter me from all the evil in this city."

Scarlett shook her head before Georgette even finished talking.

"No." Scarlett spat the word out with vehemence. "You were the best friend I ever could have asked for. Your light—the way you always had a smile for me, even when you must have guessed what I'd become—it was the reason I kept coming back to see you, even when I knew I should stay away. It was the reason I would give anything to protect you. Your optimism is what kept me going for so long."

Georgette tilted sideways to rest her head on Scarlett's shoulder. Her silky curls tickled the crook of Scarlett's neck.

"And now you've thrown your life to the Wolves for me. Leon told me what it was you agreed to." Georgette's tone brimmed with sorrow.

"How are things with you and Leon?"

The edge of a smile chased some of the sadness from Georgette's expression. "He's used the money from the Wolves to restart his art business, and we came clean to Father about our feelings for each other. He's decided to let Leon properly court me. It turns out that after having my life threatened, a less than advantageous marriage doesn't seem quite as much of a catastrophe."

"I'm glad," Scarlett said earnestly. If Georgette could get her happy ending, then perhaps what Scarlett had done wasn't completely in vain,

"And it's all because of you." Some of the sadness returned to Georgette's eyes.

"I'd happily sell my soul to keep yours bright," Scarlett murmured.

"I know, but I wish you wouldn't." Georgette paused, and they sat in silence for a moment. "You know, I had never seen your Talent before the other day. I had assumed you had one, but you never used it in front of me."

"I didn't want you to have to lie if the police ever asked you about it, or to implicate yourself by keeping my secret." Scarlett lifted one hand before them and let the thinnest of shadows weave between her fingers. "Keeping it secret is a hard habit to break."

"And now you're using it to entertain bloodthirsty crowds," Georgette said, a bitterness Scarlett had never heard from her before creeping into her tone.

"That's actually why I'm here." Scarlett quickly recounted the details of the past day. As she spoke, Georgette turned to face her. Even though Scarlett had never mentioned her living situation to her friend, Georgette seemed appropriately horrified that the Wolves would violate the neutral territory and brand an old woman who, while not helpless, definitely couldn't put up much of a fight.

"Benedict and I are going to tell the Woodrow's what the Wolves are doing, since they seem like the ones with the power to do something about it who might be the most sympathetic. I don't exactly have anything to wear to dinner with the king's bodyguard and advisor." Scarlett looked down at her threadbare clothes and the canvas bag now in her lap. "Well, I have one thing to wear, but it would hardly be decent to wear it alone."

"Lord Pearce might like it if you showed up indecent," Georgette commented.

Scarlett spluttered and Georgette politely covered a giggle with her hand.

"I'll find you something fitting to wear," Georgette assured. "I'm glad I can finally be the one helping you for once."

Scarlett blinked at her image in the mirror and was surprised to find her own face looking back. The only times she had been made up in past years, she had been trying to make herself look as much like Georgette as possible. Now though, no heavy powder obscured the freckles scattered across her nose, and the only hair on her head was her own cropped locks. Still, Georgette had made the few inches of hair she had look better than she had seen it, several sprigs of small white flowers pinned in as decoration. Something about it even made the color that Scarlett would usually describe as 'mousy' look richer.

Standing from the vanity, she fidgeted, trying to get her skirts to fall right. Georgette had found a forest green dress that had few enough ruffles to meet Scarlett's approval, even as she looked at the amount of fabric cascading around her and wondered if she could put her pants back on.

"We can't forget the finishing touch!" Georgette grabbed the canvas satchel where it sat on her bed and took out the red velvet cloak within. With a graceful movement, she swept it around Scarlett's shoulders, fastening it at the neck with the brooch in her parents' symbol—a crown made out of a combined *M* and *W* for their initials.

When Scarlett looked at herself in the mirror once more, her mother looked back at her for a moment. Then she blinked, and she was gone, replaced by her and Georgette, who looked proud of her handiwork.

Still, even though it was likely too warm out for a cloak to be strictly necessary, it felt like armor around her. In it, she could use her own name and be proud of it.

A knock snapped the pair out of their admiration of Scarlett's appearance.

"A Lord Pearce is here with a carriage for Ms. Scarlett," the Wards' butler announced through the door.

"If they aren't impressed with you, then they're blind," Georgette declared with an encouraging pat on her shoulder before Scarlett left the room and headed down to meet Benedict.

When she stepped out into the mild spring night, Scarlett couldn't tell if the rush of heat that ran over her skin was from the thick cloak around her or Benedict's gaze as he spotted her from where he leaned against his carriage.

She stopped just steps away from him, but he hadn't moved, just staring at her with his mouth slightly agape. Scarlett shifted awkwardly in the silence and Benedict shook himself from his stillness.

"You certainly are a sight in a dress," he complimented as he helped her up into the carriage. His hand on the small of her back as she made her way up the step made her insides twitch in a pleasant way.

"You've seen me in a dress before," she argued as she settled onto the velveteen seat.

"I've seen you as Georgette in a dress," Benedict corrected as he settled in across from her. "The effect is different when you aren't pretending to be anybody but yourself."

Scarlett looked down with a hot face, finding that her hands were already worrying at the lace on her skirt. Something about the compliment pierced the softness in her chest, and now it bled warmth into the rest of her body.

"So what's our strategy with the Woodrows tonight?" she asked to distract herself.

"The strategy is that I act like my charming self, and you tell them what you know about the Wolves' operation."

"You make it sound so simple," Scarlett worried out loud.

"I think simple is best here," Benedict commented. "We tell the truth and let the chips fall where they may. We're more likely to get their help if we show our hand."

"I'm not sure I'm comfortable with the amount of gambling analogies used in this plan." Scarlett bounced her leg.

"Unlike my father, I tend to be rather lucky," Benedict promised, giving her a smile that almost reassured her.

It didn't take long to reach the Woodrow's house, which sat central amongst the upper city. As Benedict helped Scarlett down from the carriage, she blinked at the sight that greeted them. Instead of an austere show of wealth that seemed to be the way of most houses in this area, the front of the Woodrows' house seemed almost quaint. A sky-blue front door made for a welcoming entranceway, surrounded by flower bushes blooming impressively for early spring. She pulled her cape around herself despite not being cold, the feeling of safety it provided combined with the hospitable entranceway almost enough to assuage Scarlett's apprehension.

Benedict used the knocker, wrought in the shape of a rearing lion, to rap sharply on the door. Silence greeted them, and they shared an uneasy glance. As the quiet stretched on, Benedict raised his hand to knock again, and Scarlett opened her mouth to advise him not to be rude when they were about to ask for aid.

The door swung open to reveal a sandy-haired man, his round face reddened as he panted lightly.

"Lord Pearce, I presume," he greeted, to which Benedict nodded. "I apologize for the delay. We're not accustomed to having guests who don't take the liberty of letting themselves in." His eyes landed on Scarlett. "And who might you be?"

Scarlett had to pry her suddenly dry tongue from the roof of her mouth to respond. "Ms. Forster," she murmured with a slight incline of her head. Her family's name still tasted odd on her lips, but it was becoming easier to admit every time she said it, like a stuck garden gate swinging open more smoothly with each use.

"Mr. Topps at your service, but you can call me Gregor." The young man stepped aside and gestured them into the hall. Once inside, Gregor took Benedict's coat and cane. He hesitated, as if to take Scarlett's cloak as well, but when she made no move to remove it, he didn't mention it.

"Why don't you meet Contessa and Nate in the parlor while I set an extra place at the dinner table?" He gestured them towards an open door before rushing off towards the back of the house. It struck Contessa as odd that Gregor had referred to his employers by their first names, but he also seemed to manage the entire house by himself.

Benedict took Scarlett's elbow and led her into the room Gregor had indicated. The petite blonde they had seen in the garden what seemed like years ago but had actually only been a just over a month stood before a hulking man, straightening his cravat while he wore what must have been an expression of great forbearance. It was hard to tell on his mangled face, a rope of scar tissue twisting his mouth into a snarl and narrowing one eye to a squint. The sight reminded Scarlett of the violence she had seen the Beast commit the one time she had been unlucky enough to encounter him in action, and shadows tickled at her fingertips as if ready to jump to her defense.

"Lord Pearce," Mrs. Woodrow greeted upon seeing them. She swept her voluminous gray skirts behind her and approached Benedict with a hand outstretched in greeting. The elegance of the movement made Scarlett feel more like an imposter in her dress. Even Contessa's gray eyes made her stomach turn. She could still see the same gray eyes of the police chief who had dragged her parents from her home to hang for something they couldn't control. Scarlett took a deep breath, reminding herself this woman was the reason the Inquiries were over. Still, Scarlett's feelings swirled as they tried and failed to decide their stance on Mrs. Woodrow.

A sharp exhale of breath from the Beast drew Scarlett's attention, and she looked up to find him staring at her with an intense, unreadable expression.

"I see you brought a companion," Mrs. Woodrow commented, turning her steely gaze to Scarlett. Despite the pale gray of her eyes, almost unnerving in their colorlessness, they held a warmth that Scarlett didn't recall in the former Royal Police chief's.

"I'm sorry I didn't think to ask if you would be bringing anybody," Mrs. Woodrow continued on. "I'm afraid we're rather unaccustomed to having company. Social calls are few and far between."

"Something tells me this isn't really a social call," Mr. Woodrow cut in, stepping up next to his wife and placing a proprietary hand on her lower back. His voice was not the harsh growl Scarlett had expected, but a smooth tenor that made him seem much younger than his grisly appearance suggested.

"Well now you've deprived me of the opportunity to soften our purpose with my substantial charisma. You've really done yourself a disservice there, I've been told I can be quite charming," Benedict cut in with a crooked smile, and Scarlett didn't know if she wanted to laugh or be swallowed by the carpet at her feet.

Mrs. Woodrow huffed a breath through her nose by way of laugh. "Nate here has a way with reading people," she said with a wry smile. Scarlett wondered if the rumors of the Beast's Talent being the ability to read minds were true.

"Now that we're not bothering with pretenses, allow me to introduce Ms. Scarlett Forster." Benedict gestured to Scarlett. Contessa's brow furrowed for a moment before her eyes widened in recognition. To her credit, she schooled her features quickly, shaking Scarlett's hand politely.

"And what business did you hope to discuss?" Mrs. Woodrow asked, seemingly wary now that she knew who Scarlett was.

Benedict hesitated for a moment, clearly seeking a place to begin.

"We need your help," Scarlett blurted out, shocking herself with her candor. Apparently now that she had come this far, admitting her family name and making herself vulnerable to those she had always hidden from, she was determined to plunge forth with abandon.

Everybody in the room stared, and she gripped the edge of her mother's cape, letting the soft texture of the velvet in her hands ground her.

"It's the Wolves. They have to be stopped," she plunged forwards.

"I know they've taken over our—the Lions'—old territory, but it's inevitable that one of the gangs would move in," Mr. Woodrow pointed out.

"It's not that." Scarlett shook her head. "They've started a fighting ring. Now that people in the lower city are no longer hiding their Talents, the Wolves are tracking them down and coercing them into fighting each other for entertainment." Scarlett swallowed heavily, forcing the last words from her throat, "Sometimes to the death."

Benedict's warm hand wrapped around her wrist, thumb rubbing circles while her pulse fluttered erratically with nerves.

It was Mrs. Woodrow who swore colorfully, surprising Scarlett "Are you sure?" she asked, oddly enough looking at her husband and not Scarlett.

Mr. Woodrow stared at her with piercing golden eyes, and Scarlett was struck once more with how accurately the name the Beast described him. He nodded sharply, not breaking eye contact.

"Come sit." Contessa gestured them towards a settee in the middle of the room. "Tell us what you know."

Scarlett settled onto the seat, maneuvering to spread her skirts around her and not managing it quite as elegantly as Mrs. Woodrow did across from her. Benedict sat next to her, hand coming back to rest on her forearm. Scarlett opened her mouth to start, but now that she had gotten over the first hurdle of stating her purpose, she didn't quite know where to go.

Benedict spoke first instead, giving her a chance to collect her thoughts.

"They've set up in one of the warehouses in the lower city, but many socialites come to bet on the fights," he explained, starting to describe everything he could tell from being in the audience.

Mr. and Mrs. Woodrow chimed in with questions as he went.

"Are all the fighters' members of the Wolves?" Mr. Woodrow eventually asked. This time Scarlett answered.

"No, although many are. They have managed to make agreements with other gangs, at least the Scorpions and the Raptors, to have more fighters if they get a cut of the house's earnings. And some of the fighters aren't even gang members," Scarlett explained, remaining deliberately vague about how she knew this. Still, Contessa pinned her with a discerning gaze. "They're making so much money on this that everybody wants in on the action."

"Which means getting rid of Fang wouldn't be enough to stop it." Mr. Woodrow ran a hand through his shaggy auburn hair, already tousled enough to show that this was a habit of his. For a moment, Scarlett was distracted by how odd it was to be familiar with such a human mannerism on a man that she had considered more a legend than anything else for so long.

"We'll need Joseph and the Royal Police's help to take down the whole operation," Mrs. Woodrow said as if thinking out loud.

Scarlett stiffened, heart skipping a beat in her chest. Benedict's hand on her arm tightened, but it was Mr. Woodrow whose gaze met hers.

"You needn't worry about the police chief. He works with us, after all," he commented with what might have been a wry smile, although it was hard to tell with one side of his face frozen by scar tissue.

"Easy for you to say when you've been personally pardoned by the king. We haven't all been so fortunate," Scarlett snapped before she could think better of it, surprising herself once more. Despite having spent her whole life trying to stay hidden and prioritize survival, she certainly wasn't shying away from antagonizing some of the most powerful people in London now that she had their attention.

The room was silent for a moment that stretched painfully, broken when Mrs. Woodrow cleared her throat. "Nate, why don't you go fetch

Joseph, and probably Kristoff too so we can strategize. Ms. Forster and I will take a moment to find Gregor to tell him about the change in dinner plans."

Mrs. Woodrow stood and shot Scarlett a pointed, but not unkind look. Scarlett hesitated, but Benedict subtly nudged her forward with the hand on her arm.

"My man should still be around. I'll have him help Mr. Woodrow here fetch his associates," he suggested. He offered Scarlett a hint of a smile.

With that she followed Mrs. Woodrow from the room. She led her towards the back of the house into a dining room that was cozier than the large halls fit for formal dinners Scarlett expected to see in the Upper City. Gregor bustled about the table, rearranging plates.

"There's some unforeseen business, Gregor," Mrs. Woodrow announced as she entered. "Nate and Lord Pearce have gone to fetch Kristoff and Joseph to join us. I hope we can stretch dinner to feed everyone and that you don't mind keeping it warm."

Instead of seeming disgruntled by the continuing changes, Gregor smiled at the mention of more guests.

"You know I always make enough for guests," he responded. "Let me go get more silverware."

As he bustled from the room, Scarlett hovered awkwardly in the doorway, at a loss for what to say after her brief outburst. Mrs. Woodrow didn't address her right away, instead walking to the sideboard and grabbing a decanter and two crystal glasses. After pouring a finger of amber liquid in each, she offered one to Scarlett.

"I'd offer you tea, but I have a feeling something stronger is warranted with the type of conversation we're having this evening," she explained.

Scarlett took the glass from her outstretched hand but didn't drink.

"Mrs. Woodrow, I—"

"Call me Contessa, and you can call my husband Nate," she cut in. "As much as I'm anxious for Nate and I to integrate into society more thoroughly, I find I don't have the stomach for too many formalities anymore."

"Contessa," Scarlett amended, "I didn't mean to imply anything about you and your husband."

"You did more than imply," Contessa pointed out as she took a sip of her drink, but her tone lacked venom. Still, the steely eyes that pinned Scarlett unnerved her with their cutting intelligence and their resemblance to the late Chief Cook's.

"I suppose it's fair for me to be an object of your ire though, considering my father hung your parents," Contessa continued on when Scarlett remained silent. "You are that Ms. Forster aren't you? The one everybody assumed dead or gone?"

Scarlett nodded, surprised by how openly Contessa discussed the tension between them, but unexpectedly glad to have her cards on the table. Contessa blew out a breath through pursed lips.

"I guess we both lost our parents to the Inquiries then, albeit in different ways. If it's taught me one thing, it's that forgiveness is a fickle thing," Contessa mused.

"I don't blame you," Scarlett responded, shocked to find that she meant it. Seeing Contessa and her husband had ignited some of the anger that still simmered inside her when she thought of the Inquiries, but Scarlett found she didn't have it in her to be angry at somebody who had been as much of a girl as she had at the time.

Contessa shook her head, the elegant blond curl that fell artfully from her twisted hair brushing against the skin of her neck.

"I've found the hardest person to forgive is myself, both for things I did do and for the times I failed to act when I should have. There are days I feel like I've moved on, and there are days when I can think of nothing but the times I should have intervened when innocents were dying for things they couldn't change. The most important thing I've found though, is that without forgiving myself I don't have the power to set things right again. And that atonement is the most important part of forgiveness after all."

Scarlett digested Contessa's words, remembering they came from a woman who put her own father behind bars. As different as Scarlett thought she might be from somebody who had become an invaluable advisor to the king, guilt was something she understood all too well. The damage dealt by the Inquiries echoed through both their lives, but Contessa had made it her work to undo the damage they had done. The growing softness behind Scarlett's ribcage yearned for a purpose beyond survival as well.

"I'm sure I have more to be forgiven for than you," Scarlett said, even as she wondered at their similarities.

"Don't judge a book by its cover," Contessa countered.

"That's silly. I always choose my books based on their covers," Scarlett shot back.

"Me too."

The women shared a tentative smile, and Scarlett found a spark of hope flickering within her. Meeting Contessa's steely gaze, Scarlett saw an ounce of recognition there, acknowledgment from another woman forced to live in the gray areas by the horrors of the Inquiries.

Boisterous laughter from the hall interrupted the moment. A dark-haired man rounded the corner with a winning smile on his face, similar to Benedict's flirtatious grin but overflowing with even more mischief. Upon spotting Contessa, he swept into the room and kissed her hand in a dramatic fashion with which she seemed familiar.

Mr. Woodrow trailed after him, his stomping gait in caricaturish contrast to the other's easy manner. Benedict followed with a tired-looking man in uniform bringing up the rear.

"Scarlett, this is Joseph Thorne, Chief of the Royal Police. And this is Kristoff Mainsworth, Nate's...associate."

A myriad of rings glittered on Kristoff's fingers as he sketched an elaborate bow. Joseph merely inclined his head in greeting. Before Contessa could introduce Scarlett, another figure tumbled through the door, almost running into Joseph in her haste.

"And Rhosyn, apparently," Contessa added on.

The young woman blew an unruly red curl out of her face and grinned.

"You know she's impossible to keep away when she knows a plan is afoot," Mr. Woodrow grumbled as he threw himself into a chair at the table, although Scarlett got the sense he wasn't really angry.

"Even when her Chief tells her that cadets aren't usually involved in important strategy meetings," Joseph added.

Rhosyn, for her part, seemed unapologetic, folding her lanky limbs into the seat beside Nate. Scarlett recognized the easy grace with which she moved as belonging to somebody accustomed to fighting.

"If you're asking for Kristoff's help, then I already know we aren't exactly doing things by the book," Rhosyn said, her voice heavily accented with a Northern brogue, as everybody else took their seats at the dinner table. Benedict maneuvered so they sat next to each other, for which

Scarlett was grateful. The dinner party had doubled in size, and Scarlett acutely felt every pair of eyes.

"I've never been one for playing by the rules anyways," Benedict agreed as he settled in.

"I knew I liked you already," Kristoff shot across the table, only to look away quickly as Gregor entered the room carrying a roast, blue eyes fixing intently on the manservant.

"And you need somebody to actually pay attention, since Kristoff tends to be distracted whenever Gregor is the one serving dinner." Rhosyn shifted, and Kristoff jerked as if kicked in the shin under the table. Redness creeped up from Gregor's collar to his cheeks, but he didn't comment as he set down the roast and moved a terrine of potatoes from the sideboard to the table.

Scarlett shrank down in her seat in response to the easy familiarity of the group. After years of constantly looking over her shoulder in the Raptors, it was the sort of thing she had liked to imagine didn't exist. It made it easier to live with the fact that she would never have this kind of camaraderie.

Now Benedict put his hand on her arm and pulled her in headfirst, joking, "I get the impression that Gregor distracting Kristoff is the only reason anything can get done around here."

Mr. Woodrow laughed, and Scarlett jumped, not having considered that the former Beast would ever make such a sound. "Then we should get everybody up to speed before Kristoff gets tired of staring at Gregor's backside, although that seems unlikely."

Contessa jumped in and caught the newcomers up on the fighting pits. Occasionally she glanced over at Scarlett to fill in some detail, which Scarlett supplied despite suppressing the urge to squirm in her seat and shooting glances out of the corner of her eye at Chief Thorne. If he had any significant thoughts about her comments, he didn't show any signs beyond a deepening crease between his brows.

"You're right that we need to pull this operation out by the roots," Chief Thorne commented when Contessa finished, rubbing a hand over his face. "It's not going to help the public's trust in the Royal Police or the relationship with the Talented when it gets out that we let this spring up right under our noses. Things are already contentious enough as it is. If we could bring down Fang and his operation in one fell swoop though, it might help prove that the Royal Police have turned over in a new leaf."

"Are you thinking a raid?" Kristoff asked. Despite all their joking, he had listened intently to Contessa and Scarlett, although Gregor had ended up perched on the arm of his chair while they talked, Kristoff's arm draped familiarly around his waist. "That way you could arrest Fang, his lieutenants, and even some patrons in one move."

"That location is terrible for a raid," Nate said. "They would see you coming from a mile away from the front, but having it backed up to the Thames limits your options for surrounding them."

"It could also limit their escapes," Contessa mused.

"People are more than willing to jump out of a window into the river in a pinch," Benedict chimed in, with a pointed look at Scarlett.

"If we got them to move their operation to a specific warehouse though, we might be able to get the drop on them. Use an entrance they don't even know exists," Nate mused. Despite Scarlett's confusion at his statement, Contessa and Joseph were already nodding.

"We'd need somebody on the inside to get them to move their location though."

Every set of eyes at the table swung in Scarlett's direction, and she tensed, shadows tugging at her mind, wisps dancing where she gripped the arms of her chair.

"I—" she hesitated, shooting a glance at Chief Thorne, who met her gaze calmly.

"Would be doing a service the Royal Police," he said.

Scarlett sucked on her teeth for a moment before speaking again. "I'm willing to do what I can, but I'm not sure Fang trusts me as it is right now."

"Why not? Do you think he knows you've come to us?" Mr. Woodrow asked.

With a shake of her head, she haltingly relayed the abridged story of her last fight. As she told them of Fang's suggestion that she kill her opponent, Nate's fingernails gouged into the edge of the table, and Contessa twisted her skirt into knots in her lap.

"So he doesn't think you're violent enough in the ring?" Rhosyn piped up.

"And I'm not sure what Fang will do if I don't do what he wants in my next fight tomorrow night." Despite her best efforts, a hint of desperation tinged with rage laced her voice.

In contrast, Rhosyn's eyes glittered with mischief, a slow smile spreading across her face. "I think I have an idea."

Chapter Sixteen

Scarlett took a deep breath of the night air, more comfortable outside than she had been in the crowded dining room, considering she still wore her heavy cape. The sun had set as she and Benedict sat in the Woodrow's house, planning the Wolves' downfall, and now she glanced up, unable to see the stars beyond the low hanging clouds.

The still of the night was broken by the trundle of wheels as Benedict's carriage pulled up in front of the house.

"I can walk back to Granny's," Scarlett offered. "I know the Lower City is in the completely opposite direction." As uncomfortable as the fashionable shoes she wore were, she could stop by Georgette's to get her own clothes and boots.

Benedict cleared his throat, stance filled with an uncharacteristic awkwardness. "Why don't you come back to my house?"

"I wouldn't want you to have to choose between sneaking me past your parents again or having to try to explain to them who I am," Scarlett said, even as her heart fluttered faster. Benedict had been a grounding presence next to her all evening, but now his proximity had a different effect. Standing in the empty street beside his carriage reminded her of the look on his face when she first emerged from Georgette's house this afternoon.

"My family won't be home," he said with a shake of his head. "They took my sister to a ball this evening. Trying to make up for the fact that she missed the first half of her first season hiding out in the country."

Scarlett should say no. She should tell Benedict that just because he had helped her get the Woodrow's aid in shutting down the fighting rings, nothing had changed when it came to them. He was still the son of a duke, needing to marry for a large dowry. Even if Scarlett was free of the Wolves, she'd still be a criminal.

When Scarlett looked into his hopeful brown eyes though, she thought about how she was about to double-cross one of the most dangerous men in the lower city, and recklessness surged through her. Before the rational, cautious part of her mind took over, she nodded.

Silently, Benedict helped her up into the carriage. As he banged on the roof to signal the driver, Scarlett's stomach did a flip, unsure of the sudden thrill running through her. They rode in silence for a moment before Benedict sighed heavily.

"That didn't go quite as I planned it," he admitted.

Some of the blood pounding in Scarlett's ears calmed as she processed his statement and frowned. "What are you talking about? We have a plan to stop the Wolves now."

Benedict shook his head with a rueful smile. "This is just another time where I tried to help you, to do what I could to save you from a bad situation. Instead, you're going to be the one putting yourself in danger. If Fang suspects you or the raid goes wrong... You're the one who pays the price, while I do nothing once again."

Now it was Scarlett's turn to shake her head. "No, it's more than that. You've done something more important than save me." She swallowed, feeling like she was peeling back her own skin to show herself raw and exposed to Benedict. Uncomfortable as it was to reveal her feelings to Benedict after so long, keeping everything closely guarded in a cage in her chest, she forced herself to say the words. "You convinced me to save myself. You showed me that there are things worth fighting for besides just survival. As much that I hate that you made me want things I have no right to, it's given me a reason to push back. To hope against hope that I can claw my way back from this life I've fallen into." Scarlett's voice threatened to shake, but she tamped down.

"And what do I make you want?" Benedict's eyes glimmered in the light of a passing streetlamp.

"You." This time her voice did break.

"You have me. Everything that I am." Benedict's voice was low but didn't hesitate.

Scarlett let out a shuddering breath that had remained caught in her chest, hope igniting in its wake, although a new and fragile thing.

"Why me?" she asked, barely above a whisper.

Now Benedict smiled. "Because I saw your anger, snarling and savage, but you still cared for and protected those around you. You held all that rage inside you for so long, but never let it harden your heart. Those contradictions are what poetry are made of."

Scarlett could hear her ribs cracking as Benedict pried open her chest to clutch at her beating heart. Still, he continued.

"And the first time I made you laugh, you looked like you were surprised that you still knew how. But I knew nobody with a laugh that beautiful was meant to live a life of pain. Even if I can't save you all the time, if I can pry out some of that light you've held within yourself for so long, I'll feel lucky."

Before Scarlett could fling herself across the small space at him, unable to listen to any more of his speech without bursting into flames, the carriage jerked to a stop. Scarlett blinked in surprise, nearly having forgotten where they were.

Benedict wasted no time throwing open the carriage door and jumping out, pulling her after him. With his words still swirling in her head, he tugged her up the few steps to the front door. By the time the latch clicked shut behind them, Scarlett had regained her senses enough to execute her original plan.

She tugged Benedict back to her and he came willingly. His lips crashed against hers with the force of a thunderclap, and the electricity of a lightning strike surged through her body as she rose on her toes to meet him. This time, Scarlett wasted no time opening her mouth to him, pouring herself into him as he hoisted her up, letting her wrap her legs around his waist despite the hindrance of her dress. If she was going to risk everything to fight back against the Wolves and the situation she had backed herself into, she was going to let herself have this first.

Benedict carried her over to the stairs, breaking the kiss to navigate up them. While she was in a more convenient position than she had been the last time he carried her up these stairs, he now had to contend with the distraction of her tongue and teeth against the soft skin behind his ear.

He swore lightly and chuckled breathlessly at her antics as he kicked open the door to his now-familiar room. Benedict sat down on the foot of his bed, and Scarlett found herself straddling his lap, a position she took to with great enthusiasm. She busied her hands untying his cravat to expose his throat to her ministrations. He helped her by shrugging out of his overcoat and ripping his shirt off over his head. Feeling drunk on the sight of him, Scarlett ran her tongue hungrily over his Adam's apple. Her fingers wound into his hair even as she attempted to grind against him through the many layers of her dress.

Benedict halted her with a firm hand in her hair, pulling her back to meet his eyes. Even as Scarlett nearly panted, she was gratified to see the color high in his cheeks as his own breaths came rapidly.

"As much as I love you in this dress, I need to get you out of it, little bird," he said, dark eyes alight.

Scarlett nodded emphatically, unhooking the brooch at her neck and carefully laying the cloak across the corner of the bed. Benedict stood, setting her on her feet and switching their places so her back was to him. As he unlaced her dress, he leaned down to whisper in her ear.

"If I've convinced you to fight for yourself, now I'm going to convince you to be careful. I'm going to leave no inch of you untouched, ruin you so thoroughly that I know you'll keep fighting to get back to this—back to me." His voice was velvet against her skin as he pressed his lips behind her ear. Even as her bodice loosened, Scarlett found it hard to breath.

She wanted to tell him she would return to him, that she would fight to get back here in his arms. But she couldn't promise that, not when this was likely all they would have even if they did stop the Wolves. Instead, she responded with a soft moan, letting him know how good his fingers dancing across the bared skin of her back felt.

As the dress fell to a puddle at her feet, Benedict's fingertips grazed over her shoulder blade where an osprey was inked into her skin.

"You really are my little bird," he murmured, pressing a kiss to the nape of her neck. Scarlett leaned back into him, sighing with relief that Benedict saw the mark as her own and not a sign of her shadowed past. His hands snaked around to her front, tracing up her now-bare stomach before cupping her breasts. He sucked a mark into the juncture of her neck and shoulder as his thumbs stroked over her nipples, torturing her with waves of pleasure. She retaliated by grinding against the hardness she felt behind her, and Benedict let out a sound between a growl and a groan. He pushed forward to bend Scarlett over the bed. She went willingly.

He walked his fingers down her spine, and Scarlett sighed at how exposed she felt, although he had seen it all before. By the time his hand reached its destination between her legs, her nipples were so hard they rubbed against the coverlet beneath her, flirting with the border between pain and pleasure.

"You're incredible." Benedict's tone was hushed as he ran his fingers through Scarlett's wetness before wandering down to play with the bundle of nerves that throbbed for attention. She let out a choked sound as he rolled it between his fingers, her back bowing into the sensation.

Then his fingers disappeared, and a whine escaped her. She would have been embarrassed at the noise if she hadn't been so busy reaching tendrils of shadows back towards Benedict. Tracing them over his hands, she found that he was untying his pants.

"I like you like this, finally letting yourself want." Benedict's voice was accompanied by the sound of fabric as he slid his pants off. Scarlett crawled onto the bed the rest of the way to give him room to climb up behind her.

"I've wanted you for so long," she admitted, eyes fluttering shut against the admission and the heat of Benedict coming to kneel behind her.

"Open your eyes," he said, voice gentle but persuasive.

She did as he asked, wondering how he had known she had shut them in the first place. Looking up from where she had let her head hang between her forearms planted on the bed, she found that she faced a large mirror against one wall. Her gaze instantly found Benedict's burning into her. She might have shied away from the sensation if his hands smoothing over her ass to rest on her hips hadn't soothed her.

"I want you to see what I see when I look at you."

Scarlett nearly choked with desire as she felt him slide his member back and forth, slicking them both up with her wetness. Then he slotted into her entrance and pushed in achingly slowly, making Scarlett feel every inch. Her eyelids fluttered, but she managed to keep them open, pinned by the intensity of Benedict's gaze on her in the mirror.

"I want you to see how beautiful you are. How strong. How incredible." Benedict punctuated each sentence with a small thrust, pushing deeper until he was fully seated within her.

"Benedict," Scarlett breathed, other words failing her where they always came easily to Benedict. Still, she knew he could feel the tremor running through her body and see the slack-jawed expression of pleasure on her face that spoke volumes.

Then he began to move, and it was all Scarlett could do to keep her eyes on his in the mirror. She didn't want to miss a single expression that passed over his beautiful face, from his eyes half-lidded with pleasure to the clench of his jaw as he pounded into her harder. She pushed back against him, wanting more, greedy for all of him she could have in this moment and knowing it would still never be enough.

Seeming to feel her desperation, Benedict pulled her up so her back was flush with his chest, thighs spread obscenely over his as he continued to drive up into her. His hand at her throat, not tight but possessive, kept her face towards the mirror.

"I want this image burned into your brain, the way you look when you take me." Benedict's voice was broken with pleasure. "Because I'm never going to forget how good you feel, and I'll never stop wanting you."

Scarlett whimpered as his hand that wasn't on her neck trailed down her body to where they were joined, tracing the point where he entered her.

"And I want you to feel me here for a week, so every time you move, you're reminded that you have somebody who will fight for you, who wants you."

All rational thought flew from her brain at his words. The part of Scarlett that knew there were still so many reasons she couldn't have Benedict the way she wanted to dissolved into the bliss his words pulled out of her. She pushed back into him, wanting everything he could give her. He responded by rubbing fast circles over her most sensitive point with the fingers that danced between their legs.

The sensations threatened to overwhelm her, and she was eager to let them. Her head fell back against him, lolling against his shoulder as her pleasure built.

"Look at me," he urged hoarsely, squeezing the fingers on her throat gently.

Scarlett pulled her head forward and met his gaze in the mirror again the moment before she shattered, the adoring, hungry look in his eyes pushing her over the edge as much as the friction of his fingers. She tensed and shuddered on top of him, mouth open in a silent scream as he drank in her release. He pounded into her, extending her pleasure until he too tensed beneath her, shattering bliss written all over his face.

Only once both of their breathing returned to normal did Scarlett lean her head back against Benedict's shoulder again. Now she let her eyes flutter closed and drank in the citrus and earth scent of Benedict's skin that clung to her as well. As she went pliant in Benedict's arms, he tipped them sideways, laying them down while keeping her firmly pressed against the lines of his body.

Slick sweat coated both their skin, but Scarlett couldn't be bothered by the stickiness, not when the beast in her chest that so often prowled behind her ribcage with raised hackles now crowed in satisfaction. It would not get to rest long, but for now, Scarlett let herself drift.

Footsteps in the hall jerked Scarlett from her half-asleep haze. As she started, the back of her head slammed into Benedict, who had nuzzled into the back of her neck. He let out a soft *oof* and rubbed at his bleary eyes.

She could barely see in in the room, the thin moonlight coming in through the window indicating they hadn't dozed for that long. Even the intimacy of a short rest, bare legs tangled together, was a far cry from Scarlett's past experiences, which rarely even occurred in a bed.

She blushed as she detangled herself from Benedict, her heart squeezing at the sweet domesticity of falling asleep together. It made it even more difficult to tear herself away from Benedict's warm embrace, knowing what faced her as she entered the Wolves' den once more. This one night, the memory of it would have to be enough to carry her through the tests to come. Even if the Woodrows' plan to bring down the Wolves did work, and Scarlett was free of them, this stolen moment would likely be all she and Benedict would ever have.

Knowing how it felt to really be with Benedict—how all-consuming it felt to let herself feel and want—Scarlett knew that intermittent tastes would only be torture. She could endure a pummeling in the fighting ring, but stealing moments with Benedict when he would eventually marry somebody else would break her.

Benedict himself seemed unaware of Scarlett's turmoil as she rose from the bed, clutching a sheet to her chest.

"Lottie and my parents must have just gotten home from the ball," he whispered, sitting up. Scarlett's mouth went dry at the way the blanket he had draped over them pooled low around his hips, and she tore her gaze away.

Looking around, she cringed at the sight of Georgette's dress crumpled on the floor at the foot of the bed. She would prefer to exit through the window to escape the Pearces' notice, but she didn't look forward to climbing down in a gown.

"Do you have to leave right now?" Benedict asked, crawling to the edge of the bed and pressing a kiss to her bare shoulder. She shivered at the combination of casual intimacy and warm breath on her skin.

"I need to check on Granny and be back in my routine before the Wolves suspect anything," she explained, only slightly exaggerating how quickly she needed to depart. She picked up the dress and held it up, dreading lacing herself back into a corset.

"You could borrow some of my clothes, although I know they're too big," Benedict offered. "I can have my man bring Miss Ward's dress back to her."

When she nodded, Benedict stood and rifled around in his dresser, producing a gray shirt and basic trousers, probably the most plain clothes he owned. Scarlett tugged them on, making do with rolling up the sleeves and cinching in the waistband. Fully dressed, she looked down at the cape draped across the foot of the bed, a splash of crimson in a room leached of color by the darkness.

"You could leave it here for safekeeping," Benedict said, gaze tracking where she was looking. "Then I would be sure that you would come back to me."

Despite her better judgement, Scarlett nodded. "Alright."

She stepped towards the window and Benedict followed, catching her by the wrist and pressing a brief kiss to her lips. She closed her eyes, savoring the fleeting contact as she thought it might be a kiss goodbye, even when the new-but-stubborn hope flickering within her whispered that maybe it wouldn't.

"Keep my cape safe," she murmured. Even if she didn't manage to come back for it, Scarlett could think of no place she would rather it stay. It seemed fitting to leave the strongest link to her identity with the person she had let see all the hidden pieces of herself.

"I will," Benedict promised.

Scarlett launched herself out the window, plunging back into the night and her waiting shadows.

Chapter Seventeen

Scarlett kept her eyes on the boots she was currently lacing up as the door to the backroom at the fighting pits swung open.

"No funny business until you're out in the rings where the audience can appreciate it, alright?" Zed said as he ushered the newcomer into to room.

"Of course. A show is what I promised and a show is what you'll get," came the answer in a familiar Northern brogue.

An odd mixture of relief and dread churned in Scarlett's gut, turgid as the water of the Thames, as the door swung shut behind Rhosyn. Other fighters lingered in the room, preparing and posturing for their own brawls, and Scarlett only made the briefest eye contact with the young woman as she strode across the room to a bench on the opposite wall. Rhosyn responded with an infinitesimal nod before taking her seat in the corner and pulling out a strip of fabric to wrap methodically around her knuckles.

As always, Scarlett ground her teeth until she was surprised they were more than useless nubs as pairs of fighters filed out of the room to be pummeled to a bloody pulp before a riotous crowd. The numbers in the room dwindled until only Rhosyn and Scarlett were left. Alone, they finally looked at each other.

"I'm honestly surprised that Fang let you enter the headliner fight at such short notice," Scarlett observed. Even as she didn't relish brutalizing the girl, Scarlett knew she would have to display a penchant for violence with whoever she fought tonight to get back in the Wolves' good graces. At least Rhosyn had volunteered for the thrashing.

"It wasn't hard to convince him of how lucrative two pretty women fighting might be once I put the idea in his head," Rhosyn admitted with a shrug.

"And you were even able to convince him you have a Talent?" Scarlett asked, keeping her voice low in case of unfriendly ears outside the door.

"Not everybody's Talent is as flashy as yours. I just told him I have Nate's Talent, so I can read people's intentions to know what moves they will make in advance," Rhosyn said. "It shouldn't be difficult to fake if you telegraph your moves like we discussed."

Scarlett nodded before wincing as the sound of a thud and a crunch filtered through the door, followed by a large cheer.

"You sure about this?" Scarlett asked, even though it was likely too late for Rhosyn to back out. "Even with us making it look worse than it is, I'm going to have to rough you up pretty badly."

Rhosyn smiled ruefully. "I've been done down for less noble causes. Besides, police training doesn't get your blood pumping like a good old-fashioned brawl."

Scarlett winced at the reminder that she was about to thrash a new member of the Royal Police, even if the cadet did volunteer for it. Then again, Rhosyn had a very different background than most officers.

Before they could say anything else, the door banged open to reveal Zed, wearing an impatient expression.

"Last fight was way too quick. Hope you ladies are ready to put on more of a show," he barked, shooting a pointed look at Scarlett as he waved them out of the room. They approached the ring just in time to see a limp form pulled from the raised platform and into the crowd. The spectators obscured the figure before Scarlett could discern if he was breathing or not.

True to Rhosyn's estimation, the hall shook with stamping feet and enthusiastic hollers as Zed announced the matchup. The redhead took the part of the showman, using her long legs to step over the ropes of the ring as she grinned and waved.

"She might not be very showy, but something tells me our resident shadow is going to have a hard time landing a punch on this one here!" Zed riled up the spectators.

As Rhosyn didn't have a visible Talent to show off, she settled for flexing her slim arms, leading to cheers and laughter from the crowd. Scarlett didn't bother with seeming enthusiastic as she stepped in behind Rhosyn, opting for her normal angry demeanor. Still, she let shadows drip from her fingers more than strictly necessary as she squared up, putting on the show the Wolves desired in her own way.

As they faced off, Scarlett met Rhosyn's eyes one more time. The redhead's eyelid twitched in the barest of winks as the bell clanged, and then she leaped.

As Rhosyn moved first, Scarlett danced out of the way, a fist just brushing across her shoulder as she spun clear. As she did, she swung out a leg to trip Rhosyn, making the movement a touch larger and slower than she might with another opponent. Seeing it coming, although with her eyes instead of a Talent, Rhosyn neatly leaped over the limb with her crooked grin still in place.

They continued like that for a few minutes, Scarlett lashing out with fists and shadows, albeit relatively slowly, and Rhosyn dodging out of the way. Scarlett's fists missed her by a hairbreadth several times, close enough to brush the wild red curls coming free of their tie. The crowd gasped at Rhosyn's seemingly uncanny ability to dodge, as Scarlett mentally patted herself on the back for purposefully missing so narrowly. A few times Scarlett's shadows connected with Rhosyn, and if they weren't completely solid when they snapped her head to the side, only Rhosyn and the lack of ringing in Scarlett's ears were any the wiser.

As the fight dragged on and both women were coated in a sheen of sweat, Rhosyn shot Scarlett a meaningful look. This time, when Scarlett swung for her, Rhosyn didn't dodge as quickly, allowing the punch to hit her in the flank. While Scarlett used only half her strength, Rhosyn let out a dramatic *oof,* sounding convincingly like the wind had been knocked out of her. Doubling over with an arm across her abdomen, she looked up at Scarlett and cocked her head in challenge.

Scarlett lashed out, kicking Rhosyn in the shin, although purposefully avoiding her knee joint and trying to hit to the side of the bone so as not to break it. The redhead stumbled but didn't fall, instead stepping forward. With a movement so fast it was lost to Scarlett's eyes, Rhosyn lashed out, elbow catching her square in the windpipe.

Scarlett sputtered and coughed, tears in her eyes blurring the lamplight to white smudges as the crowd roared. Somehow, the shock of pain and breathlessness spurred Scarlett into action. Before she could think on what she did, shadows sprang forward, attacking Rhosyn from every angle. This time the woman didn't, or couldn't, dodge, letting out several pained grunts that Scarlett had the wherewithal to hope were exaggerated as the darkness pummeled her.

Taking advantage of Rhosyn's distraction, Scarlett dove forward, taking the woman to the ground with the weight of an elbow to her gut, even as she surreptitiously caught most of her momentum on her knees. Rhosyn flailed like a feral animal, spurring on some of Scarlett's more violent instincts. Rhosyn managed to flip them over, pinning Scarlett for a split second before she lifted her feet and drove them into her abdomen, driving the redhead back once more.

Scarlett fell on her with a detached ferocity, feeling as if she gave her anger more slack on its leash while still watching it from a distance. This time, her fist connected with Rhosyn's jaw with a solid thud, loud enough to be audible over the now-uproarious noise of the crowd. The snap of Rhosyn's head to the side was no longer completely exaggerated. Still, she fought back, squirming and wrestling until they were both short a few chunks of hair and the familiar tang of blood coated Scarlett's tongue.

Only then did she land a blow solid enough for Rhosyn to cease fighting back. Thinking this was the end of their fight, Scarlett pushed back to her feet. To her horror, Rhosyn turned her head and spat out a gob of blood containing a few teeth. Scarlett took a step back, thinking Rhosyn was tapping out, but the woman struggled as if to get to her feet again. Even as she pushed to sitting, she used her other hand to beckon to Scarlett in a universal taunt.

The spectators shouted and hollered with renewed fervor, and Scarlett took a moment to wonder, not for the first time, if Rhosyn was actually insane. Before she could think better of it, she took a kick aimed at Rhosyn's side, sending her falling back and rolling away again.

Still, Rhosyn pushed to try and stand. This time, Scarlett's foot connected with her shoulder, then her thigh. Rhosyn refused to tap out though, and Scarlett decided to take the matter into her own hands. She fell on the woman, grappling her into a choke hold, straddling her back to pin her down. As Rhosyn squirmed against her, Scarlett watched her hands like a hawk, but the woman only used them to weakly try and dislodge Scarlett until she slumped to the floor.

Scarlett lowered her down and stood up, trying to not let her horror at knocking the redhead out show on her face even as she raised an arm in triumph. A wave a nausea crashed over Scarlett as stamping and clapping deafened her, but she forced a victorious smile onto her face.

"An incredible showing by our reigning champion!" Zed leaped into the ring and lifted her other arm in the air, shaking it enthusiastically. As spectators excitedly moved to cash out their bets, he leaned down to murmur in Scarlett's ear so only she could hear, "I see you learned Fang's lesson. You'd be making a killing fighting like this if you weren't taking such a small cut of the purse."

Scarlett shoved down the urge to punch Zed that overwhelmed her as violence worked its way out of her blood stream, instead plastering on a grin that was more a baring of teeth than a smile. "I guess I'll just have to draw in enough people to make five percent of the earnings more than enough."

"That's more like it." Zed clapped her on the shoulder before meandering off into the crowd.

As they spoke, Scarlett watched out of the corner of her eye as a familiar sandy-haired figure darted into the ring to kneel by Rhosyn. She desperately wanted to join Gregor and make sure she hadn't seriously injured the other woman, but she didn't dare give herself away now. With some difficulty given Rhosyn's height, Gregor hoisted her onto his shoulder and made to carry her from the ring.

For a split second, as Rhosyn's face lolled towards Scarlett, her eye cracked open. She raised her eyebrow so slightly Scarlett might have imagined it before her eye slipped closed again and Gregor bore her out of sight.

With a heavy sigh, Scarlett made her way to the edge of the ring on the far side, ready to collect her winnings and collapse onto her under stuffed mattress at Granny's to catch a few hours of rest before starting on the next part of their plan. As she ducked under the ropes, she caught sight of Fang in the corner of the room. Seeing her looking, he tipped his hat at her with a slight nod. At least she hadn't knocked Rhosyn's teeth out for nothing.

Georgette giggled so hard, she snorted as Scarlett shied away from the crates on the stable floor.

"Ladylike," Scarlett teased, even as she avoided thinking about what inside the crate was making the persistent scratching and squeaking noises.

"I think in this situation, you're the one acting like the fainting lady while I'm just being reasonable." Georgette continued to laugh, hiding her smile behind her palm.

"I'm being reasonable! Rats bite, and they carry diseases." Scarlett took another step away from the crates on the ground.

"Don't you have to deal with rats in the lower city all the time?"

"There are a lot of them, but usually not in such high concentrations. And I don't voluntarily make contact with them because of the biting."

"These ones don't bite," Georgette proclaimed confidently. "I caught them all myself."

"If they don't bite, then how will they be enough to drive off all the Wolves' gamblers?" Scarlett worried out loud.

"They are quite large," Georgette explained, cracking the lid on one of the crates to peek inside. Scarlett chanced a glance in at the writhing mass of brown fur and tails and recoiled instantly when she found that Georgette was telling the truth.

"Those are easily three times the size of any rats I see in the lower city," Scarlett admitted with a cringe. She had certainly run into her fair amount of vermin running in the gutters and scavenging for discarded food, but normally they ran from her footsteps and had thin patchy fur. The four large crates before her now were filled to bursting with rats nearly the size of a housecat.

"That's because they're well fed. It's also how I was able to catch them so quickly. They're used to me feeding them when I come to ride my horse, so they let me approach them and pick them up," Georgette explained lightly.

Scarlett gaped. "Your groomsmen have to hate that." Georgette shrugged, a blush coloring her pale cheeks. "They think it's sweet, if a bit silly."

Scarlett had to agree, but she found herself smiling, despite the fact that she was about to take possession of several large crates of vermin. It was so incredibly unexpected, yet in character for Georgette to have tamed a veritable army of rodents through kindheartedness and general goodness.

"You do have a way with strays," Scarlett admitted.

"I just like to think I see creatures for what they are, and not just how other people perceive them," Georgette argued with a pointed look in Scarlett's direction. Scarlett tore her gaze away from the earnestness in Georgette's eyes.

"It's going to be a job and a half to get these all into the fighting hall without being seen," Scarlett admitted, thinking that perhaps Kristoff's cheery suggestion that they force the Wolves to move their operation by burning the current location down hadn't been that bad of an idea after all. Arson seemed like a good option compared to the writhing mass of rodents she currently faced down.

Still, it was true that Scarlett was likely to burn down the whole block if she tried to light the building on fire, with how densely packed the structures were in the lower city. The goal was to protect as many innocents as possible, so she had to resort to more subtle means.

With a sigh she began loading the crates onto the cart behind her, pointedly ignoring the scrabbling of tiny claws against wood and the way that the weight inside them shifted as small creatures crawled their way over one another.

"Thank you so much for this Georgette," Scarlett said as she placed the last crate on the top of the stack.

Georgette smiled softly. "I just wish I could help you more. What I've done...I know it's not nearly enough with all you've risked."

Scarlett smiled wryly. "It's more than you know."

It wasn't just about the rats either. Georgette was in no small part what had helped Scarlett protect that softness in her heart that Benedict saw when he looked at her. Even if what Scarlett had shared with him couldn't last, she owed Georgette's unwavering friendship for the endurance of the girl she had once been.

"I suppose it's too much to ask that you don't let them hurt the rats, but do try to keep yourself safe at least." Georgette stepped back to allow Scarlett to maneuver the overloaded cart through the door.

"Oh wait!" Georgette fished into the pockets of her skirts. "I forgot that the Woodrows' man came by and left this for you this morning."

Scarlett took the folded paper from her outstretched hand, unfolding it easily, as it hadn't been sealed. As she read the writing scrawled across it in messy script, the warmth of hope that was growing stronger by the day blossomed even further.

Scarlett,

Thanks for the best fight I've had in a while.

Rhosyn

P.S. The teeth were fake.

Scarlett looked down to keep her cap low on her face, even thickening the shadows there to keep herself guarded as she pushed her cart down the street. She carefully maneuvered around the myriad divots and bumps in the cobbles, not wanting to jostle her cargo. She could easily pass herself off as a delivery boy bringing wares to one of the businesses in the area, as long as the rodents didn't give themselves away with too much squeaking and scratching. Luckily in the light of day, the street was busy enough that the occasional scuffling in her cargo was drowned out by voices and wagon wheels.

Stopping beneath an overhang, Scarlett leaned against the door as if resting for a moment. It wasn't truly an act, as her breath came in quick spurts from pushing her burden such a long way. Still, as she folded her arms and bent her head, her gaze darted up and down the street appraisingly. As it wasn't business hours, bouncers didn't stand outside the door to the fighting hall, but it still wouldn't do to have her seen entering. Besides, there were still probably a handful of Wolves inside to avoid.

Scarlett had only waited a minute when a carriage far nicer than any of the other carts trundling around rounded the corner. It made it halfway down the block, just a few doors away from the entrance to the fighting hall, when a loud crack spilt the air, making everybody on the street jump.

Wood splintered onto the street as one of the large wheels broke, the carriage listing to the side dangerously before the driver pulled the spooked horses to a stop. Benedict sprang from the coach in fighting form, door swinging open to display him in opulent dress. Scarlett nearly smiled at the visible gold chain and pocket watch, even as he wore entirely too much velvet for her taste.

"Goodness me, I could have died!" He looked over the damage with his hands on his hips. "How will we get this home?"

Others on the street began inching towards him as if they could smell his wealth and an opportunity. Benedict encouraged them, looking at one of the young men approaching him.

"You wouldn't know how to fix this would you? I promise to reward you handsomely if you help me get my coach home in one piece," Benedict offered magnanimously.

A few more onlookers jumped into the fray, offering their expertise or to drive Benedict home in their own cart. Scarlett didn't miss the handful of street urchins creeping up, eyes on Benedict's purse and pocket watch.

A few of the bolder ones inched towards the carriage instead, obviously curious what valuables they could find inside such a lavish vehicle.

As the racket in the street grew, the door to the fighting hall banged open, and Scarlett ducked her head more determinedly. A handful of the Wolves' enforcers barged into the street to see what all the fuss was about. Catching sight of Benedict, gesticulating and waving madly at his broken carriage, the eyes of the lead thug twinkled at the sight of such a rich mark dropped directly in his lap.

They took a few steps into the street, ready to rob Benedict blind under the guise of helping him with his broken wheel, but Scarlett didn't stick around to watch. As they cleared the doorway, Scarlett pushed her cart over to the entrance. With a quick glance behind her she made sure nobody was looking before ducking inside.

Once inside, she worked quickly, prying the lids off the crates. Scarlett recoiled as the rats scurried out through the shadowy room, finding plenty of nooks to hide in and chair legs to chew on. As she turned to leave, the sounds of scuffling and squeaking were audible even over the commotion on the street.

She just hoped the rodent infestation would bother the other patrons as much as it bothered her.

Scarlett hugged her legs to her chest on the little stool where she perched, setting her chin on her knees as she tried to avoid touching the floor at all costs. She wasn't the only fighter in the backroom to take such a posture, although some tried to show their toughness by continuing to stand around. Their efforts to seem unphased were undermined when they would let out a undignified squeal as a large rat darted across the room and over their boots.

They scurried across the room every few seconds, and even when they weren't visible, the quiet *scritch* of their tiny claws against the wooden walls was ubiquitous. Georgette had been right about their size being truly intimidating, especially for lower city dwellers used to malnourished vermin. What was more, they weren't nearly as afraid of people as normal pests, Georgette's kind handling of them emboldening them to dart over feet and even attempt to crawl up pant legs.

A bang caused Scarlett to jerk, almost losing her balance on her stool and tumbling to the rat-infested floor. The door slammed open on its hinges so hard, Scarlett was surprised the shoddy thing didn't fall right off.

"We have no spectators," Fang snarled as he burst into the room. "These vermin have driven them all off."

Zed trailed behind him, looking nervous. "Should I call the rat catcher?"

"Do you think the rat catcher will be able to get rid of an infestation of this size? Besides, I already heard some gentlemen saying this building is clearly full of disease. How else could the pests get so big?" As if to punctuate Fang's question, a rat sidled up to the base of his cane, sniffing around it curiously. He smacked it away in annoyance, and Scarlett winced at its squeal of distress, remembering how much Georgette liked the creatures.

"What should we do then?" Zed wiped his hands on his pants, visibly perspiring.

When Fang paused in thought, Scarlett seized her opportunity.

"We could always move the fights to another building," she offered with what she hoped was a nonchalant shrug. Benedict was better at persuasion than she was, and she hoped for a bit of his way with people right now.

"Where would we go?" Fang spat.

"There has to be some vacant buildings here in the Lion's old territory, so you could stick to the same area." Scarlett cocked her head in thought. "Has anybody taken over the Lion's old Den?"

Fang's eyes narrowed, and Scarlett hoped it was in thought and not suspicion.

"It is a few blocks from here," he admitted. "Everybody has stayed away though."

Scarlett shrugged again. "It was just a thought. It certainly does make a statement about who's the new boss in town to take over the Beast's old lair."

Fang's eyes flared, and she knew she caught him. Greed and pride were his twin downfalls, and Scarlett had learned that playing into them could get her what she needed.

"Zed," Fang snapped over his shoulder, "grab the boys and see how fast you can get a new ring built. Everybody else, your fights have been rescheduled for tomorrow night."

Scarlett's stomach performed a somersault of victory and nerves as she thought about what tomorrow might bring.

Scarlett was so distracted staring at the riot of blooms in the Woodrow's garden that she didn't hear Nate until the tip of a knife touched her throat.

"It's just me, Scarlett." She put up her hands in surrender, showing she held no weapon.

With a soft *shink*, the lethal blade disappeared back under his sleeve. Some of the hardness in his golden eyes softened in relief. Still, Scarlett's heart pounded from the moment of adrenaline. Thanks to her shadows, she was used to being the one sneaking up on people and not the other way around. Despite cloaking herself in darkness as she snuck into the Woodrow's garden to deliver her message, Nate had been able to sense her. No wonder he had earned a reputation as the deadliest man in London.

"It's done?" Nate asked, as if greeting somebody with a knife to their throat was common practice despite his perfectly polished clothes and immaculate garden. Something in his attitude made Scarlett want to smile despite the desperateness of the situation. Nate was a man who straddled the lines between lower city gangster and prominent socialite more thoroughly than most, giving Scarlett evidence that it was possible.

Scarlett nodded. "They'll be at the Lion's old Den tonight." She passed off all the details she had on the coming fights, anything that might give the Royal Police an edge during the raid.

Nate nodded. "We'll get this information to Joseph. You just need to make sure that the secret entrance is clear."

It was Scarlett's turn to nod, nerves about tomorrow night's operation returning in full force. Nate tilted his head as he considered her, scarred face unreadable.

"Do you want to stay for tea?" Nate offered. "It might calm your nerves, and I know Benedict would be happy to see you, as well as Contessa."

Scarlett blinked in confusion. "Benedict?"

"He's been over for tea most evenings, and to get updates on our plan." Nate shrugged. "He wants to help however he can."

Scarlett swallowed thickly but shook her head. "I need to get some sleep before tonight."

Nate continued to consider her with piercing eyes, and the full force of how disconcerting it was to have somebody know what she felt hit her.

"He would go with you tonight if you asked." Nate's voice was low. "Against my better judgement I probably would too. I shouldn't be seen near anything like this, but I still wish I could do more to help too. Sometimes things like this were easier when it was just me and the Lions."

"That's why I won't," Scarlett admitted. Truly, she itched to see Benedict, but Scarlett feared what she would say if she did. She couldn't let Benedict risk himself by joining the raid tonight, and so she wouldn't even give herself the chance to ask. "Tell him—tell Benedict I'll come get my cloak tomorrow."

"I will." Nate paused. In the quiet, a breeze ruffled through the leaves of the beautiful garden, and the sound of a trickling fountain drifted through the air. Scarlett turned to go.

"I noticed you on the garden path that afternoon," Nate started.

Scarlett turned back to him, puzzled.

"I was walking with Contessa, and I felt how angry you were. Out of all the people in the park, your emotions grabbed my attention immediately."

Scarlett recalled the way his eyes had snapped to her that day with Benedict, freezing her in place. She opened her mouth to defend herself, to say that she hadn't been angry at him, but Nate cut her off.

"I myself met an angry woman not all that long ago, and she also tends to want to carry the weight of the world on her shoulders. I don't mind sharing it with her sometimes." Nate's perpetual scowl softened a little as he spoke of his wife.

Scarlett's chest squeezed and she looked away. "Tell Contessa and Benedict I say hello." With that, she vaulted herself over the back fence to head back to Granny's. Tonight, Scarlett would face the Wolves, and she would be damned if anybody besides her got hurt.

Chapter Eighteen

The Wolves hadn't set up a back room for the competitors yet at the new fighting hall, making Scarlett's job increasingly difficult. Nothing blocked her pacing along the back wall from the view of the spectators, and worst of all, the other Wolves. She tried to play her walking back and forth off as nervous energy, which wasn't too hard considering what the night had in store.

When not glancing up to see if anybody was watching, Scarlett kept her eyes on the lower edge of the back wall, searching for the crack indicating the entrance to Nate and the Lions' secret tunnel. He had been reluctant to let the Royal Police know of the tunnels in an official capacity, as now they were no longer his secret, but just this once it would give the Royal Police the edge they needed to pin down and surround the Wolves.

Scarlett paused under the pretense of tying her boot as she saw a promising-looking seam in the panels of wood. She chanced a run of her fingers along the gap, shoving her fingernails into the groove and finding it to be the opening she was looking for. Luckily, nobody seemed to notice her odd behavior, as the first fight of the night was starting and everybody was busy finalizing their bets and vying for the best view.

Turning back to her task, Scarlett frowned as she saw a crate and a large sack partially blocking the other side of the door. She would have to move them to give the police a clear path when they came charging in.

Standing from her crouch, she leaned her back against the panel of wall holding the hidden door and crossed her arms. Scowling at the fight getting going before her, she leaned to the side slightly, using her thigh to push the barriers out of the way. The racket of the nearby fighters offering their own opinions on the current match drowned out the scraping of wood against the floor. Satisfied that the tunnel entrance was clear of obstacles, Scarlett pushed her weight off the wall but didn't go far.

She took the opportunity to scan the crowd, mentally cataloguing where all the Wolves stationed themselves. Many mixed with the spectators, collecting bets and jangling their bags of coins. That would cause difficulties for the police trying to arrest them without hurting civilians. Then again, many of the spectators would find themselves arrested for participating in such illicit activities, but their well-stocked coffers would have them walking free in the morning.

Scarlett's gaze strayed to where the most important cogs in the machine of the Wolves lingered. Fang himself sat in a heavy chair, one leg thrown over the other casually while a hand caressed the head of his cane, his posture holding all the arrogance of a king holding court while waving his scepter. Scarlett fought to keep her facial expression blank as her lip threatened to curl in distaste.

Stationed around Fang were several lieutenants and enforcers, some lounging comfortably as well while others stood with beefy arms folded, making sure nobody approached Fang uninvited. Zed flitted back and forth between Fang's corner and the ring, alternating between riling the crowd up for the coming matchups and whispering gossip in his boss's ear.

Scarlett was mapping out the quickest path to Fang's corner, so she could engage his protection immediately when the Royal Police arrived, when her gaze snagged on a familiar head of dark hair, pulled into a low tail. Her stomach plummeted to the splintered floorboards when the figure turned, displaying Benedict's familiar face.

Scarlett opened her mouth before she tamped down the urge to scream in frustration, or perhaps march up to him and shake him as she demanded to know what he thought we was doing. Benedict saw her staring and met her eyes calmly, which did little to reassure her. He did maintain eye contact as he patted absently at his coat though, where a slight bulge might be concealing a weapon. Hopefully it wasn't just a letter opener.

Scarlett's eyes narrowed in irritation laced with fear. He wasn't supposed to be here. She had told Nate as much in the garden earlier. Only the Royal Police would be doing the raid, and Scarlett was here as the inside agent, especially as her absence would arouse suspicion. Even Contessa and Nate, who had been instrumental at coming up with the plan, were sitting this one out as they tried to stay out of visible trouble to boost the reputation of the Talented in polite society. Not to mention, the Royal Police needed a victory to patch up their own image as well.

Her feet were taking steps before she decided to move, taking her towards Benedict. Even if she gave herself away, she needed to make sure he got out before the raid started. She couldn't let him get caught in the crossfire.

She didn't make it two steps before a flash of light in the window stopped her in her tracks. It was too late. If she didn't give the officers at the back entrance the signal, the whole raid would be botched. They had already given too much to back down now. With another cry of frustration clawing at the back of her throat, Scarlett darted back to the wall with the hidden panel. She rapped on it sharply three times and then jumped aside just in time for the panel to swing open to admit a swarm of officers. At the same moment, the front door crashed open, revealing Chief Joseph himself armed with a baton and determination.

Chaos erupted immediately, tables and chairs knocked to the floor as people scattered. Wolves and patrons alike ran for windows, but the Royal Police would have the place surrounded already. Seemingly realizing their predicaments, gangsters started jumping into the fray, hoping to fight their way out.

Scarlett didn't spend any time watching to see who had the upper hand, leaping back towards where Fang and his crew were stationed. Already, the enforcers were pushing a path towards the back where there might be another exit. Scarlett couldn't let them escape. Still, as she dodged fists and batons to get to Fang, her gaze darted away from her target to find Benedict.

To her dismay, he was pushing through the crowd to intercept her instead of away from the danger. Scarlett would just have to make the fight quick so he didn't get hurt. Using her smaller size and years of stealth, Scarlett slipped through the chaos quickly, jumping free to leap onto one of the enforcers. Catching him by surprise, she dropped him quickly with a knee to the gut and a grip that left the bones of his wrist cracking beneath her fingers.

Seeing her attack, several lieutenants pulled guns, aiming them into the crowd. Scarlett dropped and rolled as the gunfire split the air, the Wolves seemingly not caring if the bullets embedded themselves in friend or foe. None of them hit her as she sprang to her feet and tried not to think about the agonized scream somewhere behind her. She leaped forward once more, taking on two Wolves. She managed to kick the gun out of one hand and punch another in the flank before a third joined the fray and grabbed her around the neck from behind.

The feral beast inside Scarlett ripped free from its leash as she kicked out and bit down hard enough on the forearm before her to draw blood. It loosened just enough for Scarlett to squirm out of the grasp, stomping on her assailant's foot as she did.

Her shadows began dripping from her hands with abandon, blinding some attackers while shielding her movements from others. The ringing in her ears grew so loud that she almost didn't hear the bloodcurdling shout from her left, but Benedict's voice was enough to draw her attention. She looked over just in time to see Benedict launch himself onto Fang's back, yanking up the arm holding the gun pointed directly at her. Fang fired just as Benedict landed, the bullet whizzing by Scarlett's side so closely she felt the heat of it. Her opponent collapsed to the ground as the shot hit him in the shoulder instead.

Before she could recover from the shock of her brush with death, she was shouting again. Fang grappled Benedict easily, hitting him in the shin with his cane before twisting around to get the gun to his temple. Scarlett screeched in fury, leaping towards Fang wearing shadows like talons, letting them ripple in her wake like wings, but the few remaining Wolves stopped her. She forced herself to look away to deal with her opponents quickly, even as Fang marched Benedict out the door, the officers unwilling to stop him with a civilian in his grasp.

Scarlett barely thought about how she dealt with the next few opponents, feeling nothing but the insistent tug in her chest dragging her towards the exit where Benedict had just disappeared. Still, it took too long for her to extricate herself from the fight, dashing out into the night. By the time her boots hit the cobblestones of the street, Benedict and Fang were nowhere to be seen. She looked around frantically, searching her surroundings for any inkling of where they might have gone, when she heard receding hoofbeats at the end of the street.

Scarlett ran faster than she ever had, wind whipping against her face and tugging at her clothes. As the carriage turned a corner, she vaulted over a fruit stand onto an awning before pulling herself up onto a roof where she could track their progress better.

Sprinting across the roofs, shadows trailing behind her in angry wisps, Scarlett momentarily imagined she could fly. She could be that little bird, that fierce osprey, just to get to Benedict. The horses pulled the carriage faster than Scarlett could run, but she managed to keep sight of them from her higher vantage point.

The carriage stopped in front of a rundown chapel near the town square. From this distance, through watering eyes, Scarlett could barely make out two shapes heading into the building, the one in front holding his arms up as if a gun were pressed between his shoulder blades. At least Benedict appeared uninjured.

Instead of bursting through the front doors after them, when Scarlett approached the building she let a flying leap carry her to the roof. Looking up, the clock tower sported several broken windows she could use to enter. Fang might not expect an attack from above.

Scrabbling up the uneven stones, Scarlett tried to stay as silent as possible, hoping to maintain the element of surprise. As she edged through a broken window, the lingering shards of sharp glass scraped across her arm, cutting her shirt and the skin underneath. She bit her lips to avoid grunting in pain, but when she turned her intention to the inside of the clock tower, she saw she shouldn't have bothered.

Fang stood in the opposite window, gun aimed directly at Scarlett's head. What caused her squeak of distress though, was his grip on Benedict's throat, keeping him balanced just at the edge of the window, cantilevered out over the sill just enough that if he were to loosen his grip, Benedict would go plummeting to the ground below. Up several stories as they were, with unforgiving cobbles lining the street, Benedict would be lucky to survive.

Scarlett put her hands up and stepped around the large bell in the middle of the room.

"Let him go, Fang," she said, trying to keep her voice calm but unable to avoid the slight quaver in her tone.

"Funny, I thought you would be begging me to hold on tighter." To illustrate his point, Fang tightened the fingers at Benedict's throat, who let out a slight choking noise, toes scrabbling at the stone windowsill. Scarlett's gaze darted to him briefly before focusing on Fang once again. She had to stay calm, and she had to stay focused, but the panicked look on Benedict's face threatened her grip on the remaining threads of her composure.

"A hostage like him, the younger son of a duke, he's definitely worth more to you alive than dead," Scarlett reasoned. "You could use him to bargain your way into an escape."

"I came to this safehouse with the plans of using him to negotiate my escape, but now that you're here, I'm tempted to drop him. The look on your face would be priceless," Fang snarled. "And you would deserve it, you traitor. It was you who sold us out to the Royal Police wasn't it?

And why? Just to impress your little lover here even though you're still lower city garbage."

A more insistent choking sound from Benedict distracted Scarlett from the sting of Fang's words. She glanced at him to find him looking at her and then down several times in quick succession. The moment she saw his fingers inching towards the bulge in his jacket, her eyes snapped back to Fang. If she stared, she might give him away, although if he attacked Fang, he would surely fall. Still, it's not like they hadn't gone out a window before. She would just have to buy him enough time to get the shot off. She knew he wouldn't miss.

"Traitor?" Scarlett shot back. "That's bold coming from somebody who forces the Talented to kill each other when the Inquiries were supposed to be the end of our deaths serving as the public's entertainment."

At the edge of her vision, Benedict edged a familiar pistol out of his waistcoat and leveled it at Fang, holding it low. The safety clicked softly, and Fang frowned, making to look at Benedict.

Scarlett leaped into action as time warped around her. With an exaggerated cry, she launched herself at Fang, drawing his attention back to her. She drew thin shadows around herself, making it harder for him to aim. Two gunshots echoed in quick succession, followed by the deafening ring as one of them hit the bell behind her. Or maybe that noise was just the ringing in her ears as her momentum carried her into Fang and the trio all tumbled out the window. Screwing her eyes shut, Scarlett summoned a soft cushion of shadows to break their fall, the effort causing searing pain to shoot across her skull as the screaming in her head became deafening.

The shadows were solid enough to slow their fall, but not as pillowy as Scarlett hoped, and they hit the ground hard enough to knock the wind out of her. She felt, more than heard something crunch beneath her.

She lay there, stunned, unable to form any thoughts around the unwieldy pounding in her head. The tangle of limbs around her had other ideas, pushing her off and rolling her over.

"Scarlett!" Benedict's warped voice echoed in her head, distant and strange as if he were speaking underwater.

She lay on her back now, and he appeared over her, face haloed by the backlighting of a flickering streetlamp. She was drowning, staring up at an angel leaning down to save her. Even in her oddly dazed state, she was happy to see him well, although he held one arm to his chest with his wrist bent at an odd angle. What concerned her more was the look of abject terror on his face.

"Fang," she mumbled, knowing that she couldn't let Benedict be threatened again. She flopped her head to the side to see a crumpled form beside her.

"Is he…"

"He isn't going to hurt anybody else," Benedict assured, even as he cupped her face and turned to look at her once more. She yelped as the touch felt like a hot wire pressed against the side of her head. The sound was somehow lopsided.

"Oh god, what happened," Benedict pleaded, looking panicked. He took his hand away and Scarlett was shocked to see it covered in blood as he dug a handkerchief out of his pocket. He pressed the lacy cloth to the side of her head once more, and Scarlett hissed in pain, although it was feeling oddly distant.

"I think you were shot," he murmured.

"In the head?" Scarlett mumbled, thinking she would definitely not be talking if that were the case. Still, she remembered two gunshots and a searing pain before she tumbled out the window. Benedict said some more words, but Scarlett couldn't make them out. Sound didn't seem to process right on the side of her head with the injury.

"Why did you come?" Scarlett asked instead, feeling that she urgently needed to know before she lost consciousness. She already felt the familiar fuzziness creeping up in the back of her mind.

"Because you were definitely going to do something like this," Benedict admitted. "I knew you'd jump in front of a bullet to save us all, and I wanted to make sure there was somebody there who would do the same for you."

Scarlett blinked, and she wasn't sure if her vision was hazy from blood loss or emotion. With her one good ear, she just made out the last words Benedict uttered before her eyes fluttered shut.

"I couldn't live without you."

Chapter Nineteen

The idea of Hell as a fiery pit had never really resonated with Scarlett, but as she peeled her eyes open to burning crimson light, she was forced to re-evaluate her conception of the afterlife. As her blurry vision focused more, she saw that the fiery color above her was ostentatious red velvet drapes on a four-poster bed. That didn't explain why everything seemed to be glowing crimson though.

Turning her head to the right, she snapped it forward again with a hiss. The pillow, soft as it was, felt like a dagger against that side of her head. Raising her hand to investigate, she found bandages wrapped around her forehead and coating the entirety of the right side of her scalp and some of her face. Still, it was shocking to wake up at all considering she was pretty sure she had been shot in the head.

"Little bird," came a relieved voice from her side, muffled through the bandages.

Benedict appeared in her line of vision, the bed dipping with his weight as he sat by her side.

"Where are we?" Scarlett asked, her voice scratchy.

"We're in the Woodrows' house, in one of their spare rooms. Their sense of style leaves something to be desired."

Scarlett lifted her head to look around, this time more careful of her sore side. Indeed, the wallpaper sported gaudy splotches she could just make out to be roses, while the red light came from the sun filtering through the sheer crimson drapes on the windows. The effect was generally hideous.

"Still, it was generous of them to let you stay here while Gregor patched us up," Benedict said.

Scarlett noticed Benedict's own wrist in a splint, and the concern on his face as he knelt over her in the street came back to her. She worked to sit up, and even though her head pounded slightly, she was able to do so easily with Benedict's helping hand on her shoulder

"What happened?" She gestured to her own bandages.

Benedict grimaced. "The bullet barely missed your head, but it managed to take off most of your ear and burned a bit of the side of your face. An inch over and you'd be dead." Benedict's voice was very quiet.

"Good thing I gave up on vanity long ago," Scarlett murmured.

"I'm so sorry." Benedict's voice was mournful. He reached out to trail his fingers over her unbandaged cheek.

"For what? We made it out alive."

Benedict nodded as his fingers worried at the blankets over Scarlett's legs. She reached out and interlaced her hand with his. He squeezed it in thanks.

"Fang?" she murmured quietly.

"Dead."

Scarlett opened and closed her mouth, not knowing how to ask the question that weighed on her.

"I don't know if the fall killed him or the bullet, and I didn't check," Benedict offered, voice above a whisper.

Scarlett nodded, lump in her throat. Somehow, Benedict volunteering to share in the weight of a man's death, even a man so horrible as Fang, meant more to her than words could express. She squeezed his hand, eyes stinging.

Benedict smiled sadly. "But you shouldn't have had to take a bullet for me."

Scarlett swallowed, remembering Benedict's last words before she lost consciousness.

I couldn't live without you.

She wouldn't want to live in a world without Benedict either.

"I would jump in front of it for you again, even if the bullet got me properly in the head next time," she murmured truthfully. "And besides, you saved me from Fang first. You're the reason any of this was able to happen."

Benedict shook his head. "You need to stop keeping score. Whether you saved my life a million times or not at all, or even if you spent the rest of your life flinging me out of windows, which at this rate seems likely, I would still love you the same."

Scarlett blinked, sure that she must have understood Benedict wrong, given that she didn't seem to have any hearing in her right ear.

"You love me?"

"You've stolen my heart, little bird."

Scarlett harbored no doubts that the heart hammering away in her chest right now belonged to him in return.

"You have to know I love you too, but—"

"There are no 'buts' to the way I feel about you," Benedict declared determinedly. "It's not something that will be stopped by logic. I know firsthand now what it's like to look at a life without you, and it's not something I'm willing to do again. If I have to sing for coins on the streetcorner or become a pickpocket to stay at your side, I will."

Scarlett's mouth hung open. There was nothing she could think to say to a declaration like that. Only two words came to mind.

"Kiss me."

Benedict obliged, using his uninjured hand to pull her close by the waist. Her head may have been aching earlier, but all of that dissolved into the feeling of floating. Kissing Benedict before had been over-whelming, but mixed with the incandescent joy of knowing this might be the first of many embraces, his touch was intoxicating.

Soon she was gasping into his kiss, tugging at his waistcoat with grasping fists. Benedict pulled back slightly with a chuckle.

"I don't think it would be very gentlemanly to take advantage of a lady with a headwound, in somebody else's bed no less," he teased, nose still nuzzled against hers.

Scarlett grinned back. "Who said I was a lady?"

"You are a lady to me," he explained with a nip to her lower lip that drew a very unladylike noise from Scarlett.

He drew back, much to Scarlett's dismay, even as she knew he was right. Even their kissing had made her woozy in her current state.

"I should let the others know you're awake. They'll be pleased," he said with a pat to her shin.

He left for a few moments and returned with Gregor, who smiled upon seeing her sitting up. He proceeded to check her bandages and ask her how she was feeling, to which she responded honestly that she felt surprisingly well.

Gregor nodded understandingly. "Honestly, the bullet mostly took off cartilage, which people poke holes in for jewelry anyways. You probably passed out from pain and blood loss, more than anything, combined with your use of your Talent. It should heal quickly as long as you keep it clear of infection, although I'm sad to admit that there is nothing I can do about the appearance. Your ear is pretty much gone."

"I guess I'm in good company when it comes to scars," she mused, thinking of Gregor's employer. "If I grow my hair out, I can probably come up with some styles that cover it well."

"Mrs. Woodrow's lady's maid would have fun helping you. She's obsessed with trying out new hairstyles on anybody she can get her hands on," Gregor commented.

As if summoned, Contessa herself peaked her head around the doorframe.

"Scarlett! So glad you are alright." She smiled, and Scarlett found herself happy to see the other woman, despite their brief acquaintance. "Joseph is downstairs to collect official statements for the police reports."

Benedict glanced at Scarlett, who glanced down at herself in turn, dressed only in what she assumed was one of Contessa's nightdresses and still feeling rather discombobulated.

"I'll go down and tell him my perspective first while you take a moment," Benedict suggested. He leaned in and pressed a kiss to her cheek, making Scarlett's heart stutter that he would show such affection in front of others. Contessa and Gregor seemed unphased as Benedict stepped from the room.

"I'll get you some tea and some breakfast as well," Gregor offered.

"I'll keep her company," Contessa offered as Gregor exited and left them alone.

Contessa perched herself in the chair at the bedside Scarlett assumed Benedict had been stationed in before she woke. Scarlett awkwardly fiddled with the blankets over her lap, feeling odd about entertaining a proper lady in a borrowed nightdress, looking like...well she wasn't sure what she looked like at the moment, but she was sure it wasn't good.

"This used to be my room," Contessa mused, breaking the silence.

"Oh." Scarlett hedged, finding it unusual that Contessa had once slept anywhere besides her shared room with her husband. "It's lovely."

Contessa huffed in a ladylike version of a snort. "No, it's not. I always hated it, but I forgot that I wanted to redecorate it after I moved down the hall. I've just been so busy."

"I'm sure being an advisor to the king keeps you occupied," Scarlett agreed.

"It does." Contessa sighed. "And dealing with the aftermath of the Inquiries... The damage they did runs deeper than even I imagined, and I despised them to begin with. What happened with the Wolves, it really emphasized to me how far my work is from over, and how much I need more help from people who understand."

Scarlett cocked her head but stayed quiet, unsure what Contessa was getting at.

"You know, it would do wonders to have more people helping the Lions with our work."

"I thought the Lions were gone?" Scarlett asked, eyebrows shooting up in question before she winced at the pull they caused in her scalp.

"The gang may be gone, but Kristoff, Rhosyn, and Nate will always see themselves as the Lions. So will I, in all honesty," Contessa explained. "They fought the Inquiries from the beginning, and now that they're over, our purpose has shifted. Rhosyn is becoming a police officer, and Nate and I work with the king, while Kristoff works odd jobs that are better off the record. We could use somebody like you though, familiar with the ins and outs of the lower city as well as society."

Scarlett swallowed thickly. This morning seemed determined to dangle in front of her everything she wanted most but had been sure she could never have, making it seem so close in the light of dawn. She had brought down the Wolves, maybe she could have Benedict and a purpose beyond survival too.

"I'd love that," Scarlett admitted. "But I would have to work some things out first."

"I'm sure you'll be able to make arrangements," Contessa nodded, smoothing her elegant silver skirts as she stood. "I've already asked the king to approve my starting an official task force for helping Talented after the Inquiries, and I mentioned that I want you on it. After hearing about your involvement with our latest activities, he requests an audience with you next week."

Scarlett tugged at the clasp at the throat of her crimson cape. She had insisted on wearing it to her audience with the King, but the bright color combined with the bandages still wound around her head drew many eyes. After years in the habit of staying invisible, it was an odd sensation. Benedict held her hand as they walked through the palace though, not caring about the heavy gazes on them. Scarlett found she didn't mind their weight as much either when she focused on his fingers intertwined with hers.

Her nerves returned anew as a footman ushered her into a room with a long table, announcing her presence.

"Lord Benedict Pearce and Ms. Scarlett Forster, Your Majesty."

King Byron sat behind a large desk while Contessa sat at one corner, papers strewn before them. Nate stood at alert a few feet away, hands clasped behind his back.

"Lord Pearce, Ms. Forster, thank you for joining me," the king said kindly, gesturing for them to come closer.

Scarlett fought not to slump her shoulders in an attempt to take up less space as she approached the desk,. She wasn't sure what she had expected of the King, especially one whose father had been partially responsible for the Inquiries, but his easy manner took her off guard. As she drew closer, lines around his eyes and a stray silver hair around his temple became visible, which Scarlett wouldn't have expected from his age.

Stopping before his desk, Scarlett offered a wobbly curtsy while Benedict executed a more elegant bow.

"Mr. and Mrs. Woodrow here have filled me in on your...situation," the king started. Scarlett stiffened, but he continued lightly, "They also told me of your significant role in bringing the Talented fighting rings to the law's attention and subsequently helping with their dismantling. You have done the Crown tremendous service."

Scarlett nodded dumbly, unsure what to say. Her tongue seemed glued to the roof of her mouth.

"What's more, you have done this despite the monarchy having wronged your family in the past. This being said, I would like to officially honor you for services to the Crown. Of course, this comes with a full pardon for any gang involvement you may have had, as it was part of an undercover mission to aid the Royal Police."

Scarlett looked back and forth between the king and Contessa, who was smiling knowingly, although she didn't meet her eyes.

"Thank you, Your Majesty," Scarlett managed to squeeze out of vocal cords that were frozen in shock and relief.

"You should know that this honor comes with a significant sum of money as well. It would make a sizeable dowry," the king mused. "Certainly enough to make a good match with the younger son of a duke."

Benedict coughed beside Scarlett.

"Of course, this does all come with one stipulation," the king continued.

Scarlett froze, not that she had been doing much but staring with wide eyes as her life was irrevocably changed.

"Mrs. Woodrow here insists you join her new task force, or I can't give you this recognition."

Scarlett almost laughed. "Nothing would make me happier."

It was partially a lie. Being able to marry Benedict would make her the happiest of all.

Scarlett elbowed Benedict in the side to prompt him to flip the page on the sheet music before her. He tore his eyes away from her face to do as she requested, allowing her to continue the song she had been playing on their piano. It was the first thing they moved into their new home, a few blocks down from the Woodrows'. The Duke of Pearce had let them take theirs from the parlor as a wedding gift, even though Scarlett nearly choked every time he mentioned it. These keys had seen a lot.

Now she picked out a new melody she had learned as their dinner guests relaxed in their sitting room. Contessa and Nate sat in one corner, heads bent over a chess board, while Leon and Georgette shared the settee, inching closer to each other by the second. Though their wedding in a few weeks was sure to be the celebration of the season, they didn't seem inclined to keep their hands off each other until then.

Despite the relative modesty of their new home compared to Benedict's former residence, he insisted on having guests over often. Scarlett found she loved the life and laughter it gave the house after years in a stark bedroom at Granny's. Of course, that was part of why they had chosen to buy a cozier home. Scarlett insisted on sending money to Granny every month to make up for the loss of rent. Benedict had offered to buy her a new home closer to theirs, but Granny had waved them off, stating that she would stay right where she was as long as there were hungry urchins on the streets of the lower city.

Benedict leaned in closer as Scarlett continued to play, and she missed a few notes as he pressed his lips lightly to the juncture of her neck and shoulder.

"You play so lovely, little bird," he murmured.

"I would play even better if I didn't have somebody distracting me with their breath on my neck," she countered.

"Maybe you just need more practice," he whispered into her good ear. Gregor had been right that most of her right ear was now gone. A hint of Scarlett's vanity had reared its head as she looked at the patch of scar tissue on the side of her head for the first time. Rhosyn had stopped by to visit that day though and promptly declared that she and Nate now matched. Just like him, nobody would cross her if they could avoid it.

Benedict certainly didn't mind, if how often he distracted her with hands up her skirts and lips on her jaw were any indication. He only ever joked that he could spoil her with jewelry twice as much, as he would only ever need to purchase one earring. Now as she finished the song, she turned to look at him in mock reproachment.

"Whatever am I going to do with you?" she scolded.

"Whatever you want," Benedict teased with a lopsided grin. "But I do have several suggestions."

Scarlett tipped her head back and laughed, heart soaring like a bird.

Don't miss more of the Talented Fairy Tales with book three, THE HOOD AND HIS THIEF

She picked his pocket. He stole her heart. A Robin Hood retelling where the most dangerous crime is falling for your enemy.

Also by S.C. Grayson

THE TALENTED FAIRY TALES

Beauty and the Blade

Little Red Shadow

The Hood and his Thief

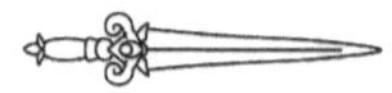

THE BALLAN DESERT TRILOGY

Blood of the Sands

Crown of the Dunes

Heart of the Desert

Acknowledgements

It's always a Herculean task to thank everybody responsible for making this book possible in a few short paragraphs, but as always, I will do my best.

First and foremost, I'd like to thank my family. Rhys, you're my rock and my wings and everything in between. Mom and Dad, thank you for taking me to the library so much as a kid, even if it took me in a direction you maybe didn't expect at first. Amanda, you fanned the spark of my love of reading into the flame that got me where I am today.

Of course, the team of people who made this possible deserve a round of applause. This current version would not be possible without the incredible book of some amazing authors, who have had my back at every turn. Lily, you're the most amazing author bestie a girl could want. Alexis, Megan, Charissa, Erin, Stacy and so many others, you are all absolute treasures.

Last but not least, thank you so much to my readers. You're my cheerleaders and my motivation. None of this would happen without you.

About the author

S.C. Grayson writes fantasy and paranormal romance filled with dangerous magic, slow-burn tension, and heroines who refuse to stay in their place. She is the author of several gaslamp fairytale retellings, as well as *The Ballan Desert*, an epic fantasy romance series set among nomadic clans in a brutal magical desert. Across her worlds, she delights in complicated loyalties, immersive world building, and romances built on emotional connections that still bring the heat.

When she is not sitting in a local coffee shop writing and drinking an iced americano, Grayson is a professor and nurse researcher, focusing her efforts on breast cancer genetics. She lives in Chicago with her loving husband and their two cats, who enjoy contributing to her work by walking across her keyboard at inopportune moments (the cats, not the husband).